As she tried to pull away,

he held her the more strongly, staring down into her blue eyes. Then he said something, and pulled, yanked her to himself.

She was caught off balance. She fell against him, felt the hard warmth of his body against her whole length. He had her hand in one arm, his other hand went up to her head, his fingers thrust through her hair, mussing it, tearing the neat arrangement into loose curls. He held her head so her face was just under his. Then he bent his face closer, closer. She saw his dark stormy gray eyes changing, changing, like the sea under a hard fierce wind. Then his mouth was on hers . . . .

Published by POCKET BOOKS

THE SIGN OF THE GOLDEN GOOSE

Janet Louise Roberts

PUBLISHED BY POCKET BOOKS NEW YORK

POCKET BOOKS, a Simon & Schuster division of
GULF & WESTERN CORPORATION
1230 Avenue of the Americas, New York, N.Y. 10020

ISBN: 0-671-83017-1

First Pocket Books printing April, 1980

10 9 8 7 6 5 4 3 2 1

POCKET and colophon are trademarks of Simon & Schuster.

Printed in the U.S.A.

To Jay Garon
Because this book is one of
his many ideas.

Chapter 1

As the stagecoach rattled along the cobblestones of the small town, and the horses were drawn up, Sarah Overmiller leaned forward to ask eagerly, "Are we there? Is this Paintsville, ma'am?"

The farm woman opposite her shifted her immense basket on her equally immense lap and said heartily, "Bless your soul, dear, no, it isn't. Or if it is, we've missed my stop at Rose of Sharon. No, dear, this is Rose of Sharon. There's my man waiting for me, and cross he does look, to be sure! He hates waiting five minutes, and it be five hours late we are."

Sarah leaned back with a little sigh. She was cold and weary. She had never realized the trip of seventy-five miles from the railroad station could have taken such a dreary long time. Of course, the heavy rains must have held them up.

The man opposite her said quietly, "I regret this, Miss Overmiller. You are unaccustomed to the delays which we have been forced to take for granted out in this rather primitive country! More settlers are coming all the time, however, we are not yet powerful enough to demand railroads in this area!"

She smiled at the young handsome lawyer, who had done his unobtrusive best to see to her comfort on this two-day journey. "I am very foolish, sir. I had thought the longest part of my journey would be the trip from eastern Pennsylvania to Ohio, and indeed the train seemed slow enough. But the coach—of course, the rains held us up," she ended hastily, not wanting to sound so ungracious.

"They always do, spring and autumn," said the farm woman, preparing to descend from the coach as the horses were halted. "Rainy and bad, lucky if the bridges don't go out! And in the winter, it's the ice and snow, even worse," she added with a chuckle, as though hardships amused her. "Here I am, dearie!" she called out, waving to "her man," who was proceeding across the muddy slough of the street toward the coach.

The coach driver, Billy Dexter, came around to help the woman out. "You'll want to go in and get a bite to eat while the horses are changed, ma'am," he said to Sarah and the lawyer. "We'll go on in about thirty minutes. But take your time!" He was big, tanned, hearty. Sarah had liked him from the first, he seemed so immensely competent, with such a way of looking after his passengers."

Mr. Hugo Forrester escorted her into the small shabby inn. "Not elaborate, but the food is good, Miss Overmiller," he told her. "If I may suggest, you may wish to go upstairs to wash up before dinner. Then you may eat at your leisure." He beckoned to a shy serving girl, who led Sarah upstairs.

She had found unexpected help and courtesy everywhere she went, she thought gratefully, as the girl found her a fresh towel, soap, and hot water. It was refreshing to wash, and she lingered over it until the thought of the passing minutes drove her downstairs to the crowded tavern again.

She found Mr. Forrester holding a table for them in the corner, not far from the huge fireplace which held cranes and steaming pots of hot food. He rose at her entrance, held her chair for her with the graces of an Eastern gentleman. She sank down wearily, aware of the mussed condition of her dark blue wool dress. At least she had brushed back her light golden-brown hair, and washed the dusty streaks from her face and hands.

"Everyone has been so kind to me," she said, following the train of her thoughts. "Indeed, it has amazed me, how courteous and friendly everyone is. In the East, they are much more formal, and reserved. They mean well, but everyone goes his own way."

Mr. Forrester smiled with pleasure, and nodded thoughtfully. "Yes, ma'am, I think you are correct. It is one of the reasons I determined to seek my own fortunes out in Ohio, after my graduation from law school. My father and his firm think I have taken leave of my senses, however!" And he laughed heartily.

Billy Dexter came up to them as they were eating and chatting. "Ma'am and Mr. Forrester, we got us a problem," he said.

"Pray, sit with us, Mr. Dexter," said Sarah quickly, indicating a nearby chair. "Have you had time to eat?"

"Yes, ma'am, did grab me a bite or two. Thank you kindly, I will sit a mite. You see, the problem is this. It be coming on to rain harder, and folks tell me the bridge is still in, but it could go out anytime. That's the bridge between here and Paintsville."

Sarah stared at the blunt words of the driver. "You mean—the bridge may go out?" she echoed, rather in a daze. "How soon would it be repaired?"

He shrugged. "Known it to take a month or more, even when old Adam—I mean, Mr. Overmiller, your grandfather, prodded them along. Now that he's dead and gone, rest his soul, don't know what will happen."

"What do you mean to do, Billy?" asked Mr. Forrester, cutting his meat carefully as though it absorbed all his attention.

"I got to go on. I be due at the end of my run tomorrow night, come hell—excuse me, ma'am—come high water," he said, and chuckled heartily. "So I'll go on tonight. Reckon I can reach Paintsville in a couple or three hours, and get a sleep at the inn there, that your grandfather did have, Miss Overmiller. Then I'll go on in the morning. Got to finish my run, and start back."

Sarah felt deeply puzzled. She did not want to wait, she was impatient now for the end of her journey. Yet she knew she was so weary that her judgment was impaired. That was always the way of it, when she was too tired, she could not think sensibly. She turned to the lawyer.

"What do you advise, Mr. Forrester? Do you mean to go on?"

"I shall do whatever you wish," he said, with a slight smile. "I have constituted myself your unofficial guardian, if you will permit me! If you go on, I shall go on. If you stay, I shall stay."

She found she was blushing and warm at his kindly interest. "Thank you, sir, you are indeed helpful. I am grateful," she said, a little stiff with shyness. It had been a long time since she had heard gallantries, she thought. Men to her had been patients, to be cared for, helped, assisted to return to battle, or turned over to their relatives for burial. She had not thought of romantic notions for more than three years, indeed, she had felt too old and weary to have any more.

Perhaps this trip would be good for her exhausted soul in more ways than one, she thought.

"If—if you intend to go on, Mr. Dexter, then I believe I shall also," she decided impulsively. "I am anxious to reach Paintsville, and the thought of a delay of a month or more is very unwelcome!"

The driver beamed his approval. "There, I said you were an all right one," he said. "You finish up your dinner, then, and come out to the coach when you be ready. We'll go on tonight, and by golly we'll get to Paintsville!"

The decision was relatively easy to make in the cosy warmth of the tavern. Out on the road again, with the rain pouring down and the chill striking to her bones through her wool cloak and wool dress, she wondered if she were an idiot. She and Mr. Forrester spoke little, both were weary. They had thick blankets to cover them, but still the cold was penetrating. The sound of rain had changed, she thought. She looked questioningly at Mr. Forrester through the dimness of the dark interior of the coach.

"Is that—it can't be ice, can it?" she asked.

"I'm afraid so. It is a trifle unusual for this time of the year, but I have known October to turn icy and freezing. We shall be in for a time of it. I do hope Billy can make Paintsville in a decent time, as he suggested."

"I hope so," she said, and must have sounded forlorn, for he went on more cheerfully.

"Tell me about yourself, if you will be so kind, Miss Overmiller. You said Mr. Overmiller, your grandfather, had left you the Inn at the Sign of the Golden Goose. Had you met your grandfather prior to this time?"

"No, sir. I have not met him—at least not since I was such a small child that I do not recall him. My father married against his wishes. Indeed, he must have been hard to please," she added, with a little chuckle. "My father was similar in disposition, a trifle obstinate!"

"If he was like old Adam, he was very obstinate," said Mr. Forrester. "No disrespect to the dead but old Adam—I beg your pardon, I keep calling him that, everyone did, except to his face!"

"I do not mind," she said. "My father told me that his father came after I was born. He met my brother, Adam the third, and approved of him. They were somewhat reconciled, though he never liked my mother. I don't know why—she was so pretty and sweet," and Sarah gave a sigh. Her mother had been tiny, dainty, pretty, adored. Not like her tall sturdy daughter, who was strong enough to turn an injured man in bed, carry huge pots of steaming food in an Army camp, assist at surgical operations that would have turned her mother into a fainting hysteric.

"So old Adam left the inn to your father," said the

lawyer. They had been over that earlier in their journey, but she did not mind. The conversation took her mind off the icy rain pelting the roof, and the possibility of the next bridge being out and their being stranded somewhere in the desolate countryside.

She had peered out the steaming windows again and again, only to see mile after mile of straight land, a few farms, forests stretching for endless lengths, then another farm, so desolate it seemed thrown carelessly on the landscape. Rain filled the ruts in the fields with muddy waters. A few small creeks were overflowing their banks. She shuddered to think of the river they must cross before entering Paintsville. What if it had overflowed its banks and broken away the bridge?

"Yes, sir. A lawyer sent me the notice, that is, he notified my father, but the letter was given to me, because father—" She paused, swallowed, got control of her voice, and went on. "He died early in the war. My brother came home, made out his will, and returned to the battle. He was fortunate in surviving some two years further, then he—he was wounded—"

"Yes," said the lawyer, gently, as she was unable to complete the sentence. "And so you are alone. Do you think to run the inn, or sell it? I understand it is a good investment, I should imagine you will receive good offers for the inn."

"I have not yet decided," she said, but already the gloomy landscape and the endless rains were making up her mind. She liked the friendly people here, but oh, the weather! She longed to be back home in her own cozy house, empty though it was of her family. She would be warm and snug, perhaps receiving some callers in the afternoon, being invited out to dinner in an evening, beginning to resume some normalcy. She had left her hospital position upon her departure, and had told them not to expect her return. Many of the soldiers had been sent home, many had gone into permanent hospitals and homes as incurable. Her heart ached and her body ached, and she wanted rest and quiet.

They lapsed into silence again, Sarah deeply occupied with her thoughts. She was only twenty-two, but she felt at least fifty. Would she ever be young again? Not the happy thoughtless laughing young she had once been, before the war, the pet of her father and brother, their housekeeper—needed, wanted, turned to. Entertaining young suitors, not serious about anyone, but giddy enough to want to wear pretty ribbons in her hair, and flirt at a party. Her father had said, with pretended gloom, "You will marry one of those wild young men and leave us here to fend for ourselves, Sarah!"

She had passionately denied this; she would make a home for him forever, she had declared. Now her young suitors were all dead and gone, her father and brother dead. Her youth gone before she had tasted of it more than a sip. Shall I ever laugh again, she thought, leaning her head back against the hard coach and trying to adjust to the jolting she was getting.

"The bridge," said Mr. Forrester, suddenly. "I do believe we are crossing the bridge to Paintsville. We are almost there, Miss Overmiller!"

"Oh, indeed?" she asked, eagerly, and leaned forward to peer out the window for the hundredth time. She looked right down into an ugly swirling mass of brown waters and uprooted tree trunks. "Oh, dear! Oh, it is overflowing—isn't it?"

"No, I don't believe so," he said in his calm thoughtful manner. "Not yet, at any rate. No, we are quite safe. You see, we are almost across."

She held her breath, as though that would assist the horses in pulling the coach across the bridge, and they did make it. The horses broke into a little tired run as they came to the cobblestoned streets of a town, and Sarah looked out again eagerly for her first glimpse of the inn.

Mr. Forrester leaned across her to point. "There it is, the Sign of the Golden Goose! Your property, I believe!"

"Oh, my goodness," she said, in wonder and alarm. It was both more and less than she had expected. The inn was completely dark. It looked shuttered. A huge goose and its golden egg dominated the front of the building, hanging from a signboard outside the windows of the second floor. They were streaked with dark marks of tarnish.

The place was immense, she thought. It was about twice as big as she had expected, and four times the size of the tavern at Rose of Sharon. A long porch with white columns stretched comfortably across the front of the inn. She could imagine rocking chairs sitting there, with hotel guests sitting and rocking—

Guests? Why were there no lights? No candles flickered, nothing gave out any light from the darkened inn.

Billy Dexter was pulling up in front of the stagecoach office, just beyond the inn. He let out a bellow, "Ho, the stage! Ho, there!"

"It is dark!" said Sarah, blankly. "The inn is dark. Is it closed for the season?"

"Your grandfather never closed it," said Mr. Forrester. "Sometimes the winter saw few guests, but we could always count on a welcome, fresh sheets, hot food, no matter what the day of the year." He too was peering out curiously. "I wonder what could have—" he said, half to himself.

"Ho, there, ho, Joel Walden!" bellowed Billy Dexter, climbing down from the box, and opening the stage door. "Got to raise somebody," he said. "Reckon they thought we wouldn't make it tonight, it being such a bad night. Ho, Joel!" he bellowed again, so close to Sarah's ear that she jumped.

Next door, at the inn, a shutter banged, and she jerked with nervousness as Billy helped her out to the comparative shelter of the porch outside the coach office. She stood staring at the dark—ominously dark—inn, as Billy clattered up to the door and banged on it. "Ho, someone. Anyone at the inn? Anyone at the stage? Come on, it's Billy Dexter and I have a lady here, and you open up right now!" he yelled cheerfully.

This was not at all what she had expected, thought Sarah. She had pictured a warm welcome, her grandfather's servants coming out to welcome and look at her curiously. People from the town greeting her, telling her about her grandfather, wondering if she would keep on running the inn. She had heard tales of its hospitality. But this ominous silence, this darkness—

The inn was completely dark. There was not a single light in any window. Some of the shutters seemed nailed closed. She peered in the window at a parlor, and saw with something like shock and horror that it was a tattered mess! Chairs had been knocked down, stuffing pulled from a sofa, a table lay on the floor with its plants spilled from it, dirt left to lie about.

"What could have happened—a bar fight? No, of course not—" she murmured. The men were paying no attention.

"Ho, there, Joel, was you dead?" called Billy jovially.

"Just about. Didn't think you would make it, Billy. What's this about a lady?" A young man limped out, holding a candle, wrapping an overcoat about him. His bare feet were thrust into shoes. She could just make out a dark face, black straight hair, non-colored eyes, a funny twisted grin, as he stared at their small party.

"Thought that would bring you out. Yep, got a lady. Old Adam's girl—his granddaughter—last of the tribe," proclaimed Billy, as though he had himself produced her out of a hat.

The candle was held impudently close to Sarah's face, as the young man stared at her. "She sure is! Pretty too. You must be Miss Sarah," he said. "Welcome to Paintsville! The inn is closed," he added.

"Why?" she asked bluntly.

"Let us get in out of the rain," said Mr. Forrester, rather wearily. "If you don't mind, Mr. Walden! We are wet and cold and extremely tired."

"Sure, sure, come in the office. The inn is all locked up. We can go through from the stage office," and he led the way inside that way. The stage office was a small bare room, with a wooden rail to keep the workers from the customers, a bare wooden bench to sit on, few other facilities.

He went to the wall, got down some keys, and proceeded to unlock a door toward the inn side. "We built this so I can look after the inn while old Adam is away—was away," he corrected himself hastily. "Hard to think he's gone," he said, and opened the door. The smell of musk came out strongly. He sniffed. "Won't look very good, but I don't know where else you can sleep. After Adam died, the cook quit. The people left because they couldn't get good food, and the laundress got a job in Rose of Sharon," he added, as cheerily as though he told them good news of the town.

"They was still open last week when I come through," said Billy, as indignantly as if it were a personal affront. "I thought old Justina would do the cooking. She said she would. She isn't bad."

"Not as good as the previous cook. Then when the laundress quit, the folks walked out. Didn't get paid either, the servants didn't," added Joel, thoughtfully. "The bank in Columbia held the money, and wouldn't pay out anything until the heir came. So everyone left, except Justina. I'm afraid there aren't any fresh sheets," he added, dolefully, as though this fact had suddenly hit him, and was more important than the others.

Sarah shuddered. The inn was stone-cold, and worse—there was a feeling here, a strange feeling. She knew somehow in her bones that the inn was not empty. Someone was here, in the shadows. Someone was here, waiting, evil, listening, waiting—for her?

She shivered again and again. Mr. Forrester said,

impatiently, "Miss Overmiller must have a room! She is extremely weary! Can't you find something for her, Mr. Walden? I wish you would stop chattering, and do something practical!"

"At your service," said Joel Walden ironically. Sarah thought he was impudent, he was at no one's service, really. "We'll ramble upstairs, and look at the rooms. You shall have the pick of the house. There are about twenty rooms, and the choice is wide-open!"

Only Billy chuckled, and it was a hollow chuckle. "Hope there's still some blankets about," he said, hope rather dim in his voice. "The guests didn't walk off with stuff, did they? Place looks torn up."

"I'll tell you about that tomorrow," said Joel, more soberly. "There is a story about that, Miss Overmiller, but it will keep." He led the way to the lovely white winding staircase, and lighted their way up.

Now she had a distinct clear feeling, an eerie certain feeling they were being watched. She looked about herself uneasily as she followed the strange limping young man up the staircase. In daylight this might be a beautiful place. At night, it was shadowy, musty, cold, ominous somehow.

At the top of the stairs, Joel paused at a closet. "Should be piles of blanket here," he said, opening the door. "Yep, here they are. Help yourselves, folks. Grab a pile, the rooms are stone cold. We didn't light fires, for fear of setting the inn ablaze. The wind is something fierce."

Sarah took several blankets thankfully. They were thick and woolly, and she would at least be warm tonight. She followed Joel more happily as he paused at room after room, and finally chose the front bedroom for her. "There, you are here, Miss Sarah, the pick of the house, for your very own room, number one, the most expensive place," he said cheerfully.

He lit the tall white candles on the dresser and chest, and the lovely room sprang into pretty light. It was a beautiful blue and white room, as fresh and spring-like as though it had been painted yesterday. She exclaimed in pleasure.

"Oh, this is lovely. Thank you."

He made her a jerky bow, laughing again. "It is your very own, Miss Overmiller! All your own property—for how long, nobody knows!"

She heard Billy Dexter and Mr. Forrester talking in the hallway, evidently choosing other rooms. Then suddenly she gasped, and stifled a scream. Her jumpy nerves—or did she see someone beyond Joel Walden—She stared at the hallway, a shadowy figure moved—

Joel turned around quickly, in spite of his game leg. "Roscoe, is that you? Roscoe, come out, you old fool!" he called. "It's old Adam's granddaughter, come to stay. Come and pay your respects, and stop sneaking about like a ghost!"

At first, she thought he called in vain. But finally a dark bent figure appeared in the doorway. The old man stared at her in the light of the candles, and she stared at him. He was so old his face was seamed with a multitude of wrinkles. He was a very dark Negro, with a shock of thickly-curled white hair. He shook his head in an odd way, as though he had palsy.

"Miss Overmiller, this is Roscoe. Roscoe, Miss Sarah Overmiller, old Adam's grandaughter," Joel introduced them. "Roscoe came up on the railroad—the underground railroad—about thirty years ago. They almost caught him, but Adam paid for him, bought him and him free. That right, Roscoe?" He raised his voice, and Sarah realized the old man was deaf.

"Yes, sir, sir, that's right, sir," said the old man in the dull monotone of the deaf. "Old Adam, he been good to me. You his daughter?"

"His granddaughter," said Sarah in a loud clear voice.

He nodded his woolly white head again and again, staring at her. "Yes, yes, ma'am, you look like your pitture," he said.

Joel explained. "Your grandfather has a—had a picture of you. It is in his bedroom. But you are prettier. Or would be if you put some beef on you," he said, with amazing gall, she thought. "You look like you been starving. Don't they have any food in the East?"

Mr. Forrester had returned in time to hear this latest slam. "Miss Overmiller has been working terribly hard as a nurse in the army hospitals," he said, austerely. "May I remind you again that she is very weary? She came West for a rest and a change from her extremely hard labors, helping out gallant men! Must you keep chatting?"

Joel had the grace to look a little ashamed and surprised. "A nurse? Didn't know—sorry, ma'am. Well, we'll soon put some weight on you! Can't beat Ohio food," he added cheerfully. "Did you choose a room, sir? Billy, how about you?" He went off down the hall with his candle bobbing as he limped.

Roscoe lingered in the room as though he had forgotten he was there. Mr. Forrester remained briefly to speak to Sarah.

"Please forgive the young man, he is always like that, but he is indeed a fine man usually. He would not insult you, really. It is his way of being friendly. He was a gallant soldier, I believe," he added, as though he must be fair.

"I am sure of it, pray, do not worry about me, Mr. Forrester," she said, with a faint smile. She was so weary, she thought if she could not curl up soon on the mattress and pull blankets about her, she would fall down on the floor. "In the morning, things will look better. Do you proceed with Billy Dexter, then?"

He hesitated. "I think I shall await the morning for my decision," he said, frowning, with some reserve. "I don't like the looks of this place. It isn't at all the way I remembered it. The mess in the parlor, the locked state—yes, I shall wait until morning to decide. I shall see you then, Miss Overmiller! Sleep well!"

She held out her hand to him. "Thank you, sir," she said, "for your many courtesies. I do not mind at all having you as my—temporary—guardian!"

He looked quite pleased, and bowed over her hand seriously. "You are very kind, Miss Overmiller. I should be remiss to your grandfather and his many kindnesses to me, if I did not make certain of your welfare and comfort before I take my departure. Good night, then."

He went off down the hall, and she heard Joel speak to him, evidently that he had lighted his room. She looked at Roscoe. If the old man would leave, she would go to bed, she thought.

The old man hesitated. She wondered if he were feeble-minded, he did not look well.

He muttered something, leaning toward her, looking at her with anxious earnestness. "Miss—I tell you, miss—"

"What is it, Roscoe?" she said, loudly, clearly.

He seemed to shake, putting his finger to his lips. He leaned closer, as though to tell her a secret. "The horse—it don't never shy, miss! It don't never shy. Don't tell—" he whispered.

"I won't tell," she said, kindly. She thought he was a little mad. Poor old soul. She smiled at him, and escorted him to the door.

The hallway had too many dark shadows. Did something move near the stairs? Was there a darker shadow waiting there? She shivered suddenly, the sense of evil lurking. She shut and locked the door firmly, and went thankfully to the cloth bag where her night things were packed.

She had just stripped off her wet cold dress, and reached for a robe, when someone banged on the door of her room. She stiffened, shocked.

"Who—who is it?" she cried, alarmed.

"Just me, Joel Walden. You are all right?"

"Yes—fine! All I want is some sleep!" she cried back, almost hysterical with fatigue.

"Fine. See you in the morning! It'll look better then," he yelled encouragingly, and she heard his limping step as he walked down the hallway.

The shadows and silence seemed to close in on her. The shutter banged outside her window, and she jumped nervously. She was going to have to do something about her nerves, she thought.

Maybe the arrogant young man was right, she needed more beef on her frame! She smiled a little at the thought. He was certainly cheerful, getting up in the middle of a rainy night, showing them about, handing out advice freely, limping about—

Limping. He had been a soldier in the war. Union or Southern? She paused, wondering. She had not thought to ask. Her father had said that this area was a hotbed of Copperheads. She grimaced. That was all she needed, a war on the soil of Paintsville! But the war was over—wasn't it?

More soberly, she washed herself, dressed in a warm woolen robe for bed. She lay down, wrapped blankets about her, then realized she had left the candles burning. She contemplated getting up, then decided to let them burn. They would drive away the ugly unpleasant shadows.

The mattress was comfortable enough. If the bed had had soft linen sheets, smelling of lavender—Tomorrow she must do some laundry, she thought sleepily. And get a cook if she intended to stay. Or she might sell the inn—Where had all the guests' gone? Would they return—

Copperheads. Her grandfather had been an agent in the underground railroad. She jerked awake. Was that important? Was the town bitterly divided? Perhaps the war wasn't over after all, though it was October of 1865, and peace had been declared, and papers signed.

There were many things she must find out, she decided, punching the bare pillow under her cheek. Tomorrow—so much to do tomorrow.

She finally fell into a deep sleep, troubled only by the recurring nightmares of her nursing service, the usual dreams of blood and amputations and soldiers crying out—She wakened, found herself in a strange place, but the candles were burning brightly, and she was able to sleep again.

Chapter 2

〰〰〰〰〰〰〰〰〰〰〰〰〰〰〰〰〰〰〰〰

Sarah slept very late. When she wakened, she found herself quite stiff, and reluctant to rise. The sun was shining brightly in the windows, and the pretty blue-colored room was quite cheerful. It made her feel much better.

She yawned, stretched, then groaned again as her bones seemed to creak in her body. She was hungry. Was it very late? She tried cautiously to sit up, and made it on the third try.

"Um, oh, ummmm," she yawned, throwing back one blanket after another. At least she had been warm and dry last night. What a ride she had had! And how kind everyone had been!

She opened the door cautiously to see if anyone was about. Outside the door was a copper kettle and a basin. She touched the kettle tentatively. Hot water!

She thought, "Someone was thoughtful and kind." Were the servants about? Perhaps it had been Justina, the woman who was the cook. Gratefully she pulled the kettle and basin inside the room, locked the door again, and proceeded to wash.

She found a fresh wool dress, a light blue with a pretty white lace collar, and put it on. Somehow she wanted to make a better impression on the men today than she had yesterday, looking so weary and worn.

When she was dressed, and her golden-brown hair freshly brushed and shining, she started out. The inn seemed even larger than it had last night. She peered down the front stairs. All was dark and quiet and closed up. She would try the back steps, she thought. She might find Justina, and some breakfast.

She walked down the long hallway, glancing curiously at the many white-painted doors. Everything seemed trim and neat, as though her grandfather had taken pride in keeping order and cleanliness. It gave her a good impression of him.

She came to the back stairs, and they were white-painted, trimly wooden, with darkly glowing rails—to a landing, and another small door. How curious, she thought, a little room on the landing.

The door was just open. She stared down, and something chill and ominous began to flow through her, making her cold.

She had seen that stain before—on a wooden floor. Blood stain.

She swallowed, frozen, waited. There was no sound.

Gently she pushed back the door. She gasped, her eyes widening. "No, no, no," she whispered.

She had seen blood before, gushing out the veins of a wounded soldier, spurting from an artery on an amputation. Blood on the operating floor. But not like this.

There were no neatly garbed surgeons about to help. No nurses, trim and efficient in their uniforms. No men ready to help with rough and ready strength.

Just the old dark man, lying on his back, his open eyes staring up sightlessly. Blood had spurted from his torn throat, gushed about on the carpet, seeped to the floor and the doorsill. His white woolly hair was stained with it, his dark shirt was light red.

Involuntarily, she thought of the lines in Shakespeare, "Yet who would have thought the old man to have had so much blood in him?"

What was it from? Macbeth, she thought. Murder.

She reprimanded herself sharply. She stepped forward, trying not to see the horror of it, knelt over the old ex-slave, then touched his hand gently. It was cold, stone-cold. He had been dead for some hours.

Poor soul. Poor old soul. No harm to anyone. Yet—someone had feared or hated enough to kill.

She forced herself to stand, her knees wanted to give way. She closed her eyes tightly, opened them, and went out to the stairway. She clung to the railing as she went down to a large open kitchen.

Hugo Forrester was sitting at a long table, eating breakfast. He looked up and smiled when she entered. "Then I'm not the only late one! What a pleasure to see you—Miss Overmiller! What is wrong?" His tone changed sharply.

A middle-aged colored woman stood at the huge old stove, and she had turned about to gaze at Sarah Overmiller. Her face was dark, anxious, her eyes shuttered.

Sarah paid no attention to her. "It is—Roscoe," she said faintly. "I think—he is—dead."

Hugo Forrester got up at once and came to her. He took her hands in his. "This is too bad," he said gently. "But remember, he was an old man. Perhaps the shock—"

She shook her head violently. "Come with me," she said. "Please—come—"

He said to the woman, "Get Billy Dexter, and Joel Walden. Tell them to come."

She nodded, dropping the soup ladle with a clatter. Hugo followed Sarah up the winding stairs to the little landing. He looked in the room, then he too turned pale and swallowed. He seemed to hesitate a long moment before he forced himself to enter.

"He is cold," she said. "He—is very cold. He must have—died—last night. Sometime in the night."

The lawyer bent, touched the hand, touched the face, gently closed the eyes. Then he straightened and looked about the room. It was a plain room, but a pleasant one. A narrow bed was covered with a quilt of many colors. There was a neat white washstand, a tall dresser, a rocking chair covered with a pretty knit cushion. A plaited rug on the floor, now half covered with Roscoe's body.

"There are no signs of a struggle. Of course, he was old, and deaf," said the lawyer, half to himself. The lamp stood neatly on the dresser. A vase of straggly flowers was set on the windowsill.

A clatter of footsteps on the stairs. Sarah turned around, and saw Billy Dexter coming up, closely followed by Joel Walden. The colored woman waited at the bottom of the stairs, looking up at them. Her hands were clasped at her waist, over her apron.

The two men stared. Even Joel seemed dashed and horror-struck. "Cold?" asked Billy. Hugo nodded.

"Last night, then. What did he say to you, Miss Overmiller?" asked Joel, seriously. "Did he say anything particular?"

"No, nothing special. He just spoke—then left. I went to bed." She said this, then shuddered. She had gone to bed, and to sleep. He had gone to his room—and death.

"Best take her down," said Billy quietly. He nodded to Joel. "We'll take the details, then call the law. Get her out of here."

"Right," said Joel, and tucked her efficiently under his arm, or seemed to, to take her out of there. He turned her about, guiding her down the stairs to the kitchen, helped her sit down in a rocking chair near the fireplace.

"What is it?" asked the woman finally.

"Roscoe—dead. His thoat cut." Joel was blunt.

The woman shivered. "God have mercy on us," she said faintly.

"Amen," said Joel, and grinned a little, a tight fighting grin. Sarah stared at him in anger. How could he be flippant at such a time? An old man, frail, feeble, hurting no one—callously murdered.

Someone knocked at the back door. Sarah jumped visibly. Joel shook his head at her. "I'll go," he said. He opened the back door. "Come on in. Hi, Leonard. Hello, Maxine. Come to meet the new owner of the Golden Goose? Here she is—Miss Sarah Overmiller."

The couple came in, stared at her, smiled in friendly fashion. Justina had turned back to her cooking, and seemed to be working in a sort of daze. Sarah gazed up at the newcomers.

"She has had a shock," said Joel quickly. "Old Roscoe—he's up in his room, dead."

"Really? He was getting up in years, I'm not surprised. Seemed more frail all the time," said the man called Leonard. "Well, we all come to it some day. The end of the road for every man."

Joel flung up his hands in mock horror. "Spare me this morning, Leonard! I hope we don't all come to what Roscoe came to. He got his throat cut."

The pretty woman screamed out. "No! Joel, what are you saying!"

Leonard got her a chair, and scolded Joel all at the same time. "You fool! Getting her all faint! Here, Maxine—a glass of water—come on, now, don't faint. Brace up!"

The blonde-haired woman opened her eyes again. They were large, beautiful, an unusual violet shade. Her face was of a perfect oval, her cheeks and complexion some heavenly kind that made Sarah feel drab and ordinary. The thick black dress she wore was of a shiny fabric, with a white lace collar that set off her blonde fairness. "Roscoe—throat cut? Oh, my dear God!"

"God have mercy on us," said Justina again, dully, from the stove.

"Was it theft? What did they get?" asked Leonard, seriously. He seemed a dark gloomy sort of man, rather an odd companion for Maxine, whoever she was.

"We haven't searched yet. Just found the body."

Sarah jerked impatiently. Joel seemed to take delight in jabbing them, watching their reactions with his cool gray eyes. What kind of man was he? He had gotten over his shock quickly enough. Was everything humorous to him? Perhaps his wounds had turned his brain.

They discussed it for a few minutes. The woman seemed to recover slowly, her color returning. Sarah still felt the shock of it keenly, but of course she had seen the body with the blood spilled from it.

Billy and Hugo Forrester came downstairs, and greeted the others. "How are you, Mrs. Gibson," said Hugo. "Mr. Ensley, do you know where the sheriff might be found at this hour?"

"In another state," said Leonard, with gloomy satisfaction. "Went to bury a cousin. Won't be back for a week, he thought."

The men frowned and went into consultation. It was finally decided that as Mr. Forrester was a lawyer, he should write down their statements, and they should proceed to bury the old man.

"But wasn't something stolen?" Maxine Gibson finally insisted. She was sitting up, alertly interested in the proceedings. "Surely no one would just kill poor old Roscoe. They must have been after something!"

"The gold," said a suave voice, and they turned as a man came in from the front part of the inn. He was an extremely handsome older man, perhaps fifty, thought Sarah. His graying hair had been blond, and was still springing in curly waves. His blue eyes were dark and vividly handsome. He was as trim and slender as the younger men, well-dressed in a gray suit.

"Hello, dad," said Maxine, getting up to kiss his cheek lightly. He accepted the salute as his due, nodded to the other men, looked curiously at Sarah. "You haven't met her," said the blonde girl. "This is old Adam's granddaughter, Sarah Overmiller, come to claim the inn."

The man smiled, clasped her hand, then said with great coolness, "I was one of old Adam's worst enemies. They will tell you that, I expect! I'm Clarence Gibson, run the store next door to your inn."

She could not help showing her shock. He grinned, a twisted mirthless grin, his dark blue eyes darker.

"Dad, you should not talk like that," Maxine reproached him. She turned kindly to Sarah, "Dad likes to shock people sometimes. He and old Adam quarreled, but they never really—"

"Yes, we did," the man interrupted her. "We fought, bitterly. I'm a Copperhead," he told her proudly.

The word dropped into the silence like a cuss word. There was a very awkward pause until Sarah finally said, "When you came in, you said gold. What do you mean?"

"Haven't they told you?" He leaned easily on the back of a straight chair, frankly examining her. "Your grandfather had it stacked up somewhere. Ever since he passed on, people have been getting into the inn and trying to find old Adam's gold. Making a mess of the parlors and everywhere they could think to look. Wouldn't mind finding it myself, except now you are here. Do you mean to run the inn?"

Sarah hesitated, trying to take in everything he had thrown at her all at once.

"I wouldn't," said Maxine, who seemed to like to interrupt. Her violet eyes flashed. "I wouldn't stay in Paintsville another minute if I could leave! Miss Overmiller, I seriously warn you not to stay! It will only mean trouble. Isn't that right, Leonard? We came over to warn you."

"That's right," said Leonard, leaning on the back of Maxine's chair. "Came to warn you. And we were right. Old Roscoe got it first. Paintsville just isn't safe. Old Adam kept making enemies. That underground railroad thing isn't forgotten. This town is still bitterly divided."

"The war is over," said Sarah.

"It won't ever be over," said Clarence, losing his grin. He spoke passionately. "Injustice has won temporarily! But the people who fought truly for what they believed will not be stopped! There are other ways to fight!"

"Dad, please don't! Hasn't there been enough blood shed, do more have to die?" Maxine cried out passionately, and put her hand over her eyes.

Joel interrupted quickly. "Don't fight the war now, please. Not in the kitchen. Maxine, be a good girl, and take Sarah away, and get her some breakfast in your kitchen. We have some cleaning up to do. You'll want to get acquainted with Sarah, too."

Maxine seemed to fight with herself. Her hand dropped, her face was pale. "Forgive me, my dear. My husband—Dad's son—he was killed in the war. I cannot forget—everything reminds me—of him—"

"Yes, come on over to the house," said Mr. Gibson, more humanly, kindly. "This has been a terrible shock. You ought to get out of the house—come on, Miss Overmiller. Come on to the house, and get acquainted."

Sarah allowed herself to be persuaded, more to get out of the inn while the grisly proceedings of taking care of Roscoe were managed. She found herself liking the Gibsons, father and daughter-in-law, and even gloomy Leonard, whom she found out was a clerk in Gibson's dry goods store. She wondered if Leonard was courting the widowed Maxine, he seemed quite fond of her.

They insisted on her having some breakfast, though she thought she could not force down any food. When Clarence Gibson went over to the front—to the store—Maxine said, eagerly, "Don't mind Dad, he doesn't mean everything he says. He exaggerates. And we adored your grandfather, really we did. He had the strongest influence on my husband! If only Tim had lived—" Then her violet eyes filled with tears again.

Clarence came back. "It's Mrs. Meyer, she wants some yardgoods, Maxine, and she wants a certain blue, not a greeny blue or a yellow blue but a certain blue, my God! Will you go out?"

"Sure, Dad." Maxine patted his hand, went out of the kitchen to the front of the large house where the dry goods store was contained. Leonard followed her, as though by long habit.

"She has been a big help to me, and it helps get her mind off her troubles," said Clarence, sitting down at the huge kitchen table, that was the twin of the one in Adam's kitchen. "Well, what do you think of Paintsville? No, that's the wrong question, the way you started out. Do you mean to stay and run the inn?"

"I don't know, probably not," she said slowly, fingering the silver on the table. The cup from which she had drunk her coffee was a pretty white china with a flower pattern. How luxurious to have fine china and silver. Perhaps if she sold the inn—

"I'll buy it from you," said Mr. Gibson. "Might seem too early, but I believe in getting my bid in early. I'll make you a good offer. Leonard and Maxine help me in the store, I can run the inn also. I've lived here all my life, I know Adam has built up a fairly good business."

She smiled faintly. "Fairly good? I heard it was excellent," and she looked at him with her eyebrows raised.

"Doesn't hurt to bargain," said Mr. Gibson, his mouth twisting. "You think about it, young lady. Running an inn is a man's job. You probably want to go back East. But mind you—" And his voice dropped. "You find that gold first. You're Adam's granddaughter, maybe you got a mind like his, sharp as a tack. You think about it, where he would have hid it, then you'll find it. Don't go 'til you find his gold."

"You said," she remarked slowly, thinking, "that the house, the inn, was torn up by people getting in and trying to find the gold. Was there much? Is it that much temptation?"

Clarence Gibson shrugged. "Probably was. Adam

was a tight man, and he spent only on food and help for the inn. Never for himself. Only time he spent money foolishly was buying runaway slaves so they couldn't be sent back South." At the ring in his tone, Sarah looked at him again. He was frowning heavily.

"He bought Roscoe, I understand, and set him free."

"Yes, that was years ago," said Clarence. "Seems like we've been fighting for a long time. Can't believe me and Adam have stopped fighting, we've done it so long."

Sarah thanked him for the breakfast and slipped back to the inn, just a few feet separating the back doors of the two buildings. As she went in, she heard low voices. Curious, she turned to look at the side door of the kitchen, and discovered two rooms there, with the doors open.

Inside was Justina—and two other persons. As they saw her staring at them, they went silent.

Justina came out of the room. "Miss Sarah," she said, with dignity. "I ain't had a chance to interduce myself. I am Justina. Your grandpa, he helped me escape years ago. I was sent back South later, and got away again. So he took me in and hid me 'til it was safe. I brought back my daughter and my son. This here is my Pearl, and this is my Zeke. She helps with the maiding, and he is mighty good with horses." There was pride in her voice.

"Happy to meet you," Zeke muttered. Pearl stared at her with large frightened eyes. She seemed too small and slim to be a maid, she was but a child.

Sarah smiled at them, trying to put them at ease. "Thank you for staying, Justina. I understand you have been most helpful since my grandfather passed away. I hope you three will stay on, whether I decide to run the inn or sell it. I am sure you will be useful and needed here."

Justina's face cleared. Zeke grinned a big white flashing grin, and bobbed his head. Pearl just stared, her eyes two big dark question marks.

THE SIGN OF THE GOLDEN GOOSE   33

"We will shorely stay on, Miss Sarah, and I do hopes you keep the inn. I 'spect you're just like old Adam, and he was shorely a good soul, and a fine man to work for," said Justina. "Maybe Pearl and me could do the laundry today, and get ready in case we gets company? Joel Walden, he didn't know whether we should go ahead and do the sheets. He thought you-all might be mighty particular and want the laundress to do them."

Sarah hesitated. "No, you go ahead," she said finally. "We won't have much cooking to do. And we should be ready for guests. Do you know where the tubs are, and the soap? Can Pearl iron?"

"Oh, yes, ma'am, yes, ma'am! We'll get right to it," said Justina happily. "You, Pearl, get the sheets out, about ten sheets for the first loads. We'll get right to it, have everything spick-span. When we put them away, ma'am, shall we sprinkle in the lavender? Old Adam, he always wanted the lavender in."

Pearl scurried upstairs. Sarah agreed to the lavender, as Justina seemed to know just what to do. Pearl came down again, almost hidden by the immense load of sheets she carried. Sarah saw them started, saw that big sturdy Zeke was prepared to help them with the heavy wet sheets.

She was tired and concerned. She thought she would go up to her room and just sit and think for a while. There were so many puzzles. She looked out the windows. It was coming on to rain again, she thought. The sunshine had disappeared, and black clouds raced across the sky, driven by angry winds.

More rain, and the streams were already flooded. She sighed. There would be no guests for a while at the inn.

Slowly she started up the back steps, then halted. She winced as she thought of her earlier discovery. She almost turned and went back through the darkened first floor to the front staircase, then she scolded herself. They had taken Roscoe away, and washed the room.

She went on up the staircase, paused a moment. The

door at Roscoe's room was wide-open, and someone had scrubbed busily at the floor. Only dark stains remained. The plaited rug had been removed.

Thoughtfully she started on. Just then, she was caught by someone from behind, caught and held. She started to scream, startled. And that someone, with strong hands, clutched at her throat and choked her.

She twisted, fought. He was too strong. Mercilessly, the hands twisted her throat, strangling her. She choked, gasped for air.

She could not scream. She could only thump against the wall, fight, clasp at the hands at her throat from the man behind her. It was a man, she smelled the strong smell of sweat, felt the rough texture of male garments behind her.

A man cried out above her. "Miss Sarah—Miss Sarah—" Hugo Forrester dashed down the stairs.

The man let go, ran, down the stairs, through the kitchen, out the door. Hugo ran after him. Sarah leaned against the wall, gasping, choking, as Billy Dexter followed Hugo down the stairs. He caught her as she slumped.

The big man carried her down to the kitchen with gentle strength. He put her on a chair. It was minutes before Justina came up from below stairs, thumping on the basement stairs.

"Good dear God, what will happen now?" cried Justina, as she saw Sarah's throat. Billy Dexter was massaging Sarah's throat, trying to get her to drink some water. "Let me fix some herb tea, Miss Sarah— my God, God have mercy on us! This is a black day, to be sure! Pearl, Pearl, come up here!"

Hugo came back in, panting, his face flushed and angry. "He got away, not a sign of him. Who was he, Miss Sarah?"

She whispered, unable to speak. "Don't—know. From behind—grabbed me—"

"Poor child," said Hugo Forrester. "This is a terrible place for you! We shall have to arrange for you to leave at once! An attorney can sell the place for you. Someone means to frighten you—"

"To—kill—me—" whispered Sarah, hoarsely.

Joel Walden came into the kitchen, followed by Leonard and Maxine. "What's going on? I heard shouting—my God, Sarah!" said Joel, staring at her, losing his grin. "What happened, Billy?"

"Man tried to choke her. Caught her on the stairs outside Roscoe's room," said Billy Dexter. He was handling a delicate cup very awkwardly as he tried to help Sarah drink Justina's herb tea.

"Let me," said Joel, and took the cup from him. He got a spoon, and gently fed her some hot liquid. "There—swallow that slowly. Easy now, Sarah. Someone is damn serious about that damn gold," he added, forcefully.

"Oh, you poor darling," said Maxine. "Who could do such a thing? Oh, this is dreadful!"

Sarah looked into Joel's dark face as he knelt before her, spooning the liquid into her lips. Who had done it? Not Hugo or Billy Dexter, they had been coming down the steps. Who else would do it? Clarence? Leonard? Joel? Or even Zeke, with his big happy grin? Who had killed Roscoe, and wanted to kill her?

"You should leave town at once," said Maxine excitedly. "You could return home, and handle the sale of the inn from there. If we find the gold, we can tell you—"

"Nobody's leaving town," said Joel, shortly.

Sarah stared at him. He sounded so ominous, he was frowning so. "What—do—you—mean?" she whispered, forcing the words from her aching throat.

"The bridges are out. Both sides of town," he said briefly. "The rains swept them out, the river rose too high. We're hemmed in, unless someone feels like trying to get a boat out of town in a raging torrent!"

There was a long quiet as they absorbed his words. "It's usual, this time of year," offered Billy Dexter.

"But—this means—that we are trapped," cried

Maxine, shrill fear in her voice. "We are—all trapped! We have to stay here, in town! And Roscoe has been murdered, and Sarah was choked—and there must be a killer loose! We are trapped!"

In the room full of strangers, Sarah felt very small and lost. She had not met any of these people until two days before. And now, she was the next intended victim of a killer, a madman, who had struck once, who had tried, and would try again.

She wanted to cry out, to tell the killer he could have the gold, all he wanted, if only he would let her go free! She didn't need the gold, she could make a living as a school teacher. She could go back East, open her house again, live quietly and elegantly, without the gold.

But it was more than that, said a quiet voice inside her. Roscoe didn't have gold—but he was murdered, brutally, his throat slit. He had not even struggled, but a killer had put a period to the quiet life of a deaf old ex-slave. Why?

She remembered suddenly the words he had whispered to her, something about a horse that did not shy. And she had had the feeling that someone was nearby, listening, waiting, someone in the darkened inn had been waiting. And soon Roscoe had been killed.

Not for gold, thought Sarah. But why—why—why?

Chapter 3

~~~~~~

Sarah did not feel like going to her room to be alone now. She sat in a comfortable rocker in the warm kitchen, where people were coming and going so often she felt safe. Justina, Pearl and Zeke worked on the laundry most of the day, getting the sheets white and smooth again, folding them away in the closets in lavender.

"There, we are ready for guests again," said Justina, in great satisfaction. "When you feel good again, ma'am, I'll show you about the pantry and cold house, and all the meats and stuff. Your grandfather kept many things by. He has a good cellar of wines too, for those that want such."

"Perhaps tomorrow," said Sarah. Her throat was bound up with salves and a white bandage, which looked incongruous over the white lace of her blue wool dress. But it felt better now, though she felt stiff and sore from the bruising she had taken.

"And we'll get at the front parlor, what was all knocked about," said Zeke, taking quite an interest in the proceedings. "Should I take a broom and get up the dirt from the plants?"

Sarah got up at that. She had been wanting to see the remainder of the inn, but had no desire to be alone.

"Yes, Zeke, and I'll come with you. I'll be all right with him," she assured Justina, who was looking worried. "Zeke is so big and strong, no one will dare attack."

Her face relaxed into a broad pleased grin, and Zeke grinned his big happy grin. Only Pearl kept looking down at her ironing, and looking scared and depressed. Zeke took a broom and pail, and led the way into the front parlor.

It was worse than she had realized from the brief glimpse the night before, thought Sarah. Chairs and sofas were overturned, tables spilled over, even the wall had felt knife blades, as though someone had stuck a knife in at random, searching, searching.

"Why the plants?" she asked, in her hoarse voice.

"Looking for the gold inside, I guess, ma'am," said Zeke. "But old Adam, he was too smart for them. Reckon he done hid it where no one will think to look. That was old Adam, he was right smart."

There was deep admiration in his tone. Sarah looked about, picked up a chair, watched Zeke as he set to work briskly. He was a strong young man, and willing, she thought. He would work in the stables with the horses, which he obviously loved best, or work in the house with a deft neatness like his mother's.

He had set up the tables again, placed the pots of green plants on them, and scooped up some dirt to fill them again. She watched his big hands gently setting the dirt about the leaves and roots. Would he—could he have attacked her? Oh, no, not Zeke, she thought. He was gentle, kind. She swallowed.

Sarah went over to the sofa near her, and examined it. She poked at it, found the rent in the middle cushion. "Oh, Zeke, look at this," she exclaimed. "Someone—ripped—"

"Sure enough, they did. Ain't that a cussed shame!" he said, coming over to see. "One of the purtiest sofas here. Maybe Miss Maxine would mend it. She be good at sewing, ma'am. You just ask her, she do it. Maybe

Pearl could, but she's not so good at sewing. She was a field hand down in Georgia."

"A field hand!" Sarah stared at him. "That tiny—girl—"

He had lost his grin, and looked grim and hard, as though memories were not good. "Yes, ma'am. Reckon so. Old massa wanted her, Justina said she be good in the fields, she be quick with her fingers for picking. Justina got her outta massa sight, but the overseer, he want her. Finally Justina pack us up, and take us north, and old Adam, he take us in. He's a mighty good man—he was, ma'am."

Tiny frail little Pearl, a field hand. Desired by "massa" and by the overseer. Sarah shuddered. This was what the war had been about, she thought. The inhuman cruelty of people to other people—man's inhumanity to man. Slavery, in its worst moments. No wonder Pearl had such large frightened eyes.

It was getting on toward evening. Before the inn was too dark, Sarah wanted to see about her. She went back to the kitchen with Zeke, and told Justina of her intentions.

"I'll take—Zeke—with me—to explore," she said. It didn't hurt her throat so much when she spoke very slowly, and swallowed often. She took another sip of the herb tea which Justina kept ready on the stove for her.

"Yes, ma'am. Now, Zeke, don't let her out of your sight, mind, now!" Justina said sharply to her son. "Not for a moment. You follow her about like a watch dog. Don't want nothing to happen to ol' Adam's girl."

"I watch her good, mama," he said. "Won't nobody get by me."

The two of them wandered about the inn. There were several front parlors, once cheerful and pretty, now sadly ripped up. Sarah got a pad and pencil from the registry desk, and made note of the sofa cushions to be mended, the chairs to be fixed, the plants to be replaced, some scratched furniture to be painted or fixed up.

Zeke said, "Reckon Mr. Joel, he'll know where to get stuff for fixing. And he's a right handy man. He help me, I'll do it for you, ma'am. Old Adam, he don't trust people to come in and do things right. He always fixing up things hisself. Even did the regilding of the golden goose last summer."

"But the goose is tarnished already," said a familiar voice behind them. Joel Walden came in, grinning cheerfully, his dark face showing a flash of white teeth in the gathering dusk of the front parlors. "Reckon old Adam was cheap as usual, and got the poorer quality of gilding."

"I noticed it was—tarnished," said Sarah, with an effort. "Is the rain—letting up?"

"Not so it's noticeable," he said. "Bridges are out bad. Reckon they can't be fixed soon. We'll have to take boats out if the rains don't let up soon. Looks like a bad winter coming. Plenty of snow and cold."

"We are—looking about—seeing about repairs," said Sarah, as he looked questioningly at her pad.

"You seen the dining room yet? Not bad, and the china is all right." And he led the way to a long beautiful room filled with tables and chairs. There was a beautiful hardwood table along the windows, with chairs about. "That's where the singles sit, the single people, mostly men, who come in," Joel explained. "Then the others sit at small tables. There's the china."

He pointed with pride at the two huge dish cupboards filled with shining china and glassware. Sarah went over to stare.

"Oh—Joel—how beautiful," she gasped. "Did—grandfather—use this—for everyday?"

"Yep, everyday. You ought to see it on a day the inn is full," he said, as proudly as though the inn were his own. "All the tables taken, the chairs set about, people in their best clothes. Linen tablecloths on the tables, the glass so shining it sparkles in the candlelight, and this white china with the pretty blue flowers on it at every place. And the silver, shining, boy, it is beautiful!"

She opened the cupboard and took out a delicate fragile porcelain cup. She turned it over, looked at the mark, gasped. "Limoges!" she said. "I thought you said grandfather was cheap! This is expensive!"

"He was smart too," said Joel. "He said that when he put ordinary china on the table, folks got careless and he got breakage. He puts good stuff on, and they treat it like it was going to fall apart. You should see a rough farmer or a soldier touch this! Like they was living in heaven. Faces shining for pleasure in touching the stuff." He took out a plate, caressed it with his long slim fingers, and his own face shone. Zeke behind him was looking at the china affectionately.

"Pearl washes up," said Zeke. "Justina won't let me wash it yet, not 'till gentles, she says."

Joel took her about, with Zeke following her patiently, like the watch dog he had promised to be. They went upstairs, looked in the unoccupied bedrooms. Joel told her about some of them.

"Clement Vallandigham was here a week one time, had this room. Your grandfather argued with him night and day, and Clarence Gibson defending him, boy did they have some hot talks! But old Adam, he got out the best foods and wines for the company they had, never mind the politics. Everyone could meet here, there wasn't no war on in the Golden Goose, he always said."

Joel told her other stories about her grandfather, whom he evidently had held in great affection. Her grandfather must have practically adopted Joel, Sarah thought. He had gotten him the position at the stagecoach office, which he now ran by himself. He let him come to the inn whenever he chose, slept here if there wasn't much company, even took care of the register when her grandfather was busy.

"Reckon I've worked the inn about as much as

anybody but old Adam," said Joel. "Look at this room. I told him to fix it up in gold and green, because it's a back room and don't get much light. See how pretty it is? Almost as pretty as your blue room. Which reminds me—when you get settled, you may want to have your grandfather's suite. You seen that yet?"

When I get settled, thought Sarah. She still hadn't quite made up her mind to sell and get out. She should, she thought, after all the attacks, after that horrible murder. She hesitated as she saw that Joel Walden was leading her toward the back stairs. He saw her pause.

"Come on, we won't let anybody get you," he said gruffly. "Zeke, you bring up the rear. Anybody attacks, you jump on their back!"

Zeke chuckled, and the sound was oddly comforting. Joel might be a mindless, thoughtless human being, with a quirky sense of humor, and always laughing at nothing, but he was fun to be with. He could almost make her forget the horror of the inn, she said to herself.

And he had been through the war, and returned with the limp which would never be better, Justina had told her that. He had fought for four years, and only returned last spring when peace was declared.

"He a brave man," said Justina. "Good as they come, and a comfort to old Adam."

Joel opened the door at the back of the inn and promptly swore. "Damn it to hell, by God, if they haven't gone and ripped up this!"

Justina called up the back stairs. "Joel? Mr. Joel, that you cussing so bad?"

"It's me," he yelled back. "Justina, they've tore up old Adam's rooms! I thought you kept them locked, but they are open!"

"God have mercy on us," said the woman, and toiled up the stairs to have a look. "Lord God, they have shorely ripped it up for good!"

"They shorely have," said Joel, grimly, frowning

about. "Oh, Lord, isn't it enough to try the patience of a saint! They've been looking for gold here too."

Sarah looked about the room, a strong feeling of desolation filling her. These had once been attractive rooms, she felt, reflecting the interests of her grandfather. Her own portrait hung over a white-painted mantel, as she had been four years ago, before the war, pretty and smiling, with a blue ribbon in her hair. The portrait hung askew, as though someone had thrust it aside to explore behind it at the wall. Books had been pulled from the cases, attractive cherry wood cases, with glass paneling and scrollwork.

Zeke began picking up plants again, as though that was the first order of business. Perhaps it was, decided Sarah, because the dirt from them had spilled into the lovely rug. She bent closer to examine the rug—"A French one," she decided aloud. "My land, he did have pretty things from Europe."

"That's pretty, and it's not from Europe," said Joel, laughter in his voice. She looked where he was pointing, and blushed to see he was gesturing toward her portrait.

"That's Miss Sarah," said Zeke, in a pleased voice, staring at the picture. "Looks just like her—"

"Except she is peaked now, needs beef on her frame," said Joel, in a provocative tone. "All right, don't glare at me! Justina will soon beef you up, won't you, Justina? You can't help being thin, you've been working too hard, and besides, the food back East isn't good like it is here."

He went on before she could reply indignantly.

"Wonder what the bedroom looks like?" He went on into the next room, and cussed again, and Justina covered her eyes in resignation.

"Lord God," said Justina, "it do be a bad mess. Zeke, I guess you better get at the rooms tomorrow. If Miss Sarah is going to use them, they better be all fixed up again."

Sarah opened her mouth to say she was not going to use them, but her attention was caught by the sturdy locks on the doors. She examined them thoughtfully. Perhaps it would be safer here, in the back, near the kitchens, even though she had been attacked here. And with the locks on the doors, she would be safe. Someone had unlocked the doors with a key, but there were bolts on the inside. She could lock herself in.

"Yes, I would like—to use them—" she said, her voice hoarse and almost giving out. "I could lock—myself in—"

"Right. And I'll change the locks tomorrow," said Joel. He came back to her and examined the locks in a business-like manner. "I'll bring up some fresh locks and keys in the morning. Zeke, can you sweep out this mess? Throw those plants away, they are dying anyway. We'll get you fresh ones from the gardens. Plants ought to be dug up anyway for the winter. Everything has been neglected since Old Adam went."

"Is anyone there?" Maxine's voice echoed up from the kitchen. Justina went to the hallway to call back.

Sarah took a last look at the bedroom. It did look so cosy and lovely. The bed was a huge cherry wood one, handcarved, with beautiful acorn posts on the four corners, and a scroll on the headboard and footboard. She felt the mattress, it was sturdy and firm. A huge afghan covered the bed, in gay colors of reds, blues, greens, yellows. In spite of the chaos caused by someone searching, the room gave an impression of cheeriness and warmth. A large fireplace matched the one in the living room of the suite. Over this mantel was a winter scene, probably the country about here, with flat fields, some trees, a dash of a red barn and a beautiful black horse in the foreground.

She went over to the bathroom, and exclaimed. It was lovely, in blue tiles and white paint. Huge tub, large washstand, and a commode in the latest fashion from the East.

Maxine's voice came from behind her. "Isn't it nice? Quite the nicest bathroom in town! Shall you move in, Sarah? It is such a lovely suite."

Sarah turned around to smile at her. "I think I shall," she said, with composure, "as soon as it gets fixed up. Perhaps tomorrow. Can you—stay for dinner—Joel, you will stay?"

Both accepted so promptly that she got a good impression of Justina's cooking. Justina wanted to serve them in the dining room, Sarah refused. "No, the kitchen is so warm and cosy. We'll eat at the table here."

Far from being displeased, Justina beamed. "You are just like old Adam, he liked to eat in the kitchen here, with more life about, he always said. Pearl, you get some of the pretty china. Zeke, you bring the silver and glasses, mind, be careful!"

They scurried to set places about, and Maxine, Joel and Sarah sat down to a feast.

"I don't know how you did this, Justina," sighed Sarah, as she finished her soup of some delicious fish, vegetables, and herbs. "After all your work on the laundry today, how did you manage?"

"Lord, child, I can cook with both hands behind me," she chuckled in pleasure. "This here I called fish soup, but old Adam, he was always calling it fish gumbo to the guests. And I got chicken and corn for the main course. And a bit of raspberry custard for dessert."

"Well, that should put beef on my frame," said Sarah, without a smile.

Joel gave a shout of laughter, and Justina chuckled again. Maxine shook her head.

"I would get fat it I ate here all the time," she said, frankly. "Adam used to ask me all the time, and how I dearly loved to come. He was such a marvelous man, dear Sarah. You didn't know him well, did you?"

"No, I only met him once, when I was a small child. I wish you would tell me about him." Sarah sighed over the lovely crisp chicken, the corn on the cob, the greens. "Oh, my, I don't care if I do get fat! Justina, this looks and smells so good—"

"And tastes so good," said Joel, attacking his piece of chicken with vigor. "Lord, when I remember the nights on the battlefields, and no fire to be set, and eating cold rations, Lord, I do get hungry all over again." But the memory didn't seem to make him as sad as it made Maxine.

Sarah hurriedly changed the subject back to her grandfather, and got Maxine to reminiscing.

"He was a gruff man," said Maxine, with a smile, presently. "I was a bit scared of him when I was little. He seemed to—bark—! Tim and I would play in the back yard, and he would come out, and bark at us. Do you want some ice? he would yell. We would run at first. Then finally we came over to the kitchen, and he would have some ice and cold drink, my it was good!"

"Oh, all you had to do was bat your eyes at a man," said Joel, munching on the chicken. "Nobody would bark at you. You are exaggerating."

She laughed, pleased, and shook her finger at him, the violet eyes glowing. Her blonde hair shone in the light from the fireplace. She was a beautiful woman, thought Sarah. Why did she have to wear black all the time? She must be a real beauty in blue, or violet, or pink. But she was still mourning her husband.

She spoke of him, often. "Tim and I—Tim said—we went to—Tim thought—Tim—"

"Tim said your grandfather was a real character. Oh, he meant it nicely," said Maxine, in a rush, her face a little alarmed. "No one loved him as much as Tim. Tim would do anything he said. And Tim was hard to manage, Dad always said that. I was from down the street," she added. "My family lived in the house on the second corner to the west. After I married, they moved farther out west, to some new land. Dad wanted to farm again. I never wanted to live on a farm."

"So you came to live with the Gibsons," said Sarah. "Your Dad seems to value your help in the store."

Maxine smiled, pleased. "Yes, I can help with the yardgoods, and colors, and such. The ladies seem to value my advice on clothing, I am happy to say. And bonnets—Dad had such old-fashioned bonnets! I advised him to buy the new styles, and they have done well."

"Are your quarters connected with the inn here?" Sarah asked casually. The food and hot tea seemed to have helped her throat. "The stage coach office next door is."

Maxine's face shadowed. "No. They were going to connect, but—well, Dad and Adam disagreed violently. You see, Adam, he was against slavery, and he had agreed to take in slaves, and help them get North. He ran an underground railroad station, I guess you heard about that. In the basement, I think he hid some slaves. And other places, I don't know where all."

"Paintsville was divided bitterly," added Joel, leaning back with a sigh of deep satisfaction and patting his stomach. "Half were abolitionists, half were Copperheads. We all knew who was who, though, and that helped. Always knew who not to talk to about matters. Right, Maxine?" His half-closed eyes seemed to glitter at Maxine.

She looked down at her plate. "That is right," she said, with some reserve. "Of course, Dad made no secret of his feelings. My own Dad, I mean. He was against helping the slaves. I talked to him, and to Tim's dad, it did no good whatsoever. They were firmly convinced that people had a right to do what they wished."

"Except slaves," said Joel, with a little grin.

She sighed. "I do wish you wouldn't keep bringing it up! The war is over, and slavery is abolished, that is finished!"

"Praise God," said Justina, bringing custard cups to

the table. "God had mercy on us, finally, praise God. We is free."

Joel patted her hand as she leaned to place the cup before him. "Yes, finally free," he said. "No more worries, eh, Justina?"

Just then, Sarah caught the gaze of small Pearl. Her dark frightened eyes were fixed on Joel, she did not join in the talk. In fact, Sarah could not remember her speaking at all. Was the child frightened for life? Poor thing, thought Sarah.

"Some people loved Adam," mused Maxine. "But some hated him. I guess they were as divided in their feelings about him, as their feelings about the war. They took such definite sides. The people in Paintsville—they don't have half-way feelings, Sarah!" She sounded proud. "They have strong emotions. And old Adam roused their feelings just as the war did. He would talk and roar about slavery, and the war, and how it was every man's duty to serve his country and free the slaves—"

She fell into a sort of wistful sad musing, and Sarah did not have the heart to interrupt her. She soon left after the meal, saying she did not want to leave her Dad alone. He had eaten his supper with Leonard Ensley and Leonard's mother, she added surprisingly.

"Didn't they invite you, Maxine?" Joel teased her.

She grinned a little, impishly. "I said I had a previous invitation, with Sarah! I hope you don't mind, Sarah. They are always throwing me at Leonard, and his mother is especially bad! I am still in mourning for Tim, and I don't want to be too emotionally involved as yet. You know how that is."

Sarah thought she did, and said so, kindly. "Anytime you want to come over, you feel free to come. I shall enjoy your company, and I'm afraid I shall always ask you to tell me more about grandfather. It helps me come to know him, through other people'e eyes."

Maxine thanked her prettily. Joel left with her, to

escort her next door, then returned to talk to Sarah. They lingered long at the table, while Pearl carefully washed up, and Justina put some things on to soak for morning. Sarah noticed a huge kettle of beans to soak, and thought they would be having a big pot of beans and bacon, or maybe pork. She would surely get beef on her frame now, she thought, in amusement.

"How long did grandfather have the underground railroad station, Joel?" she asked.

"Oh—it was before your father left, I think. That was before my day. Maybe thirty years or more." That seemed to set Joel remembering, and he told her some stories about the slaves who had been hidden.

Justina and Zeke and Pearl frankly listened to the stories, and he knew it. He raised his voice so they could hear him talking to Sarah about the old days.

"I remember one time, I was just a kid in my first long pants. Your grandfather came to me, and said he wanted a message taken to a farm. He didn't ask if he could trust me, and that made me proud. I rode his horse out on a farm, and gave the message, and how they went scurrying about! It seems the law was going to try to take back some slaves. The owners had come up, and somehow had word the slaves were hidden in the meat house. Well, they got away that time," he said, with satisfaction.

"And other times—did they always get away?" Sarah asked quietly.

She was watching his changing animated face in the firelight. He leaned on his elbows, looking at her, talking, his eyes quite clear now. She saw they were a dark gray which seemed to change like the surface of a river with his changing moods. As light moved over the waters, so his ideas seemed to flicker over his eyes, and make them sparkle, or darken, or half-close with a moodiness, then like lightning flash to humor.

She sipped her tea, looking down at it. She was interested in Joel. He might have a whimsical humor, but she had decided he had more of a mind than she had first thought. He quoted the Bible once, another time said something from Shakespeare, and if she had not known her Shakespeare so well she would have missed it, he said it so casually. He must have had a good education, or read much.

"Not always," said Joel, his eyes darkening as though in pain. "Once—I remember—there were some slaves hidden in the basement here, back in a room your grandfather had built with his own hands. It was behind a cupboard where the wines were kept. No one would think to move it. He had a special spring adjustment, so he could move out the cupboard—I'll show it to you tomorrow if you want. Well—some slave owners came, and demanded to go down to the basement. They went right to that spring and touched it, and got the slaves. My, I never saw old Adam so mad. He knew someone had betrayed him."

Justina was listening intently, her dark face so sad. Sarah decided to change the subject. It was bringing back some bad old memories.

"How did you come to know grandfather so closely? Were your parents acquainted?" she asked.

"No, well, they knew him a little. Everybody in town knew Adam Overmiller. He had run the inn for so many years. No, my parents died of a fever when I was thirteen. My sister died with them. No other folks around. He took me in a while, then got me the job at the stage office. I slept up there, except when the winters came cold, and there weren't many guests. Then he put me up in one of the guest rooms here, and I lived like a king, with great cooking. He always had me over for Sunday dinners, too, besides meals through the week—spoiled me rotten," said Joel, affectionately.

"And your schooling—was there a good school here?" asked Sarah.

"Yes, ma'am! It was one room, but it was good. Old

maid teacher, strict as they come, made us memorize our Latin. Lord, how Maxine did get mad at her, and cry! Her violet eyes couldn't move Miss Wiggins!" And Joel laughed at the memory. "She did like her Shakespeare too, made us give plays, and take all the parts. Handy when I went to college. Your grandfather staked me to two years of college, the winters I could go. I still owe him that," said Joel, more quietly.

They talked long, near the fireplace, and she did not know when she had enjoyed an evening more. Justina chimed in freely when she wished, with the freedom of a woman treated well in this house. Joel spoke often of old Adam, and Sarah thought he was more the son of Adam, than she was the granddaughter.

When she was ready to go to bed, Joel and Zeke escorted her upstairs, examined her room thoroughly, advised her about the lock, and saw her inside. Zeke would come up in the morning and take her down, said Joel, and Zeke nodded seriously.

She felt well protected when she finally crawled into her bed, fresh now with newly ironed sheets, smelling of lavender. She put her head down on the fresh pillowcase, snuggling down with a sigh of great relief.

Perhaps she would remain here after all, she thought as she lay in the haziness of almost-sleep. It was so—nice—so warm—so pretty. And the inn would be a good investment. Perhaps Joel would assist her in running it.

It might work out—it might—

Then, with a jolt, she remembered that only that morning, she had been attacked and practically choked to death, before her rescue. If Hugo Forrester had not been nearby, he would have killed her—that man who wanted her dead.

Who wanted her dead?

She shivered, and drew up another blanket over her. The evil was still there, and hovering about her. It was not safe here, not for Sarah.

Tomorrow, she would talk to Hugo Forrester. He had been busy today, going about with Billy Dexter, trying to discover a way to leave town, and keep his appointment to the South. But tomorrow, she would consult with him. He was wise, he could advise her what to do.

Chapter 4

〜〜〜〜〜〜〜〜〜〜〜〜〜〜〜〜〜〜〜〜〜〜〜

The next morning, a watery sun glistened in the windows of Sarah's bedroom. She leaned from the bed to peer hopefully out the window nearest her. The sky was still dark with clouds, rain filled the gutters with muddy waters, but at least the downpours had paused for a time. She felt better at once.

She got out of her comfortable bed and padded to the door. Cautiously, she opened it. At once, Zeke, sitting on the floor opposite her door, grinned up at her and began to rise.

"You awake, Miss Sarah! I get you hot water! You lock your door again till I come back." And he was off down the hall with a cheerful clatter.

She locked her door again, with a good feeling of being protected. Now, who had set him to watch her door? Joel? or Justina? Whoever it was had been kind.

Zeke soon returned with a boiling hot kettle. She had a wash, dressed herself in a gray practical dress of warm wool, added a cameo of her mother's to dress it up a bit, and was ready for breakfast. Zeke escorted her proudly down to the kitchen, following closely behind her.

Justina greeted her with a happy smile. Pearl looked

up from chopping vegetables, the dark reserved look still in her big childish eyes. Sarah thought to herself that before many days had passed Pearl *would* speak to her! She would find a way to unlock that tongue somehow! But the poor child, she added to herself. What a wretched frightening life she had led until she had come to old Adam's house.

She smiled to herself as she realized she too was calling her grandfather "old Adam." It seemed to suit him, her memories of him, the stories that Joel and Maxine had told her. A lusty strong man, full of humor and pranks and obstinacy and pride and courage. She liked to think he was her grandfather, that she might be something like him.

Joel came in as she was finishing a large breakfast of bacon and eggs, bread and coffee. He sat down without asking, and Justina brought him some coffee. He seemed quite at home here, she decided, and she did not resent it.

"Good morning, Miss Sarah," he said, with his crooked grin, His gray eyes were shining as he took in her gray dress, the cameo. She wondered if her golden-brown hair was smoothly brushed into neat waves, or if a curl had escaped and was sticking out willfully. He seemed to like to look at her, that was sure. "Pretty as your picture. Only you need—"

"I know! More beef on my bones!" she said, and finally laughed. He grinned at her, as though he knew what she was thinking.

"You must have slept well. How about a walk this morning?" he suggested, taking a sip of the hot steaming coffee.

"A walk? Isn't it wet out?"

He peered around the table, and stared frankly down at her thick practical black shoes. "You won't get wet, not with those. Come on. I want you to start meeting some folks in town. You need to get acquainted. Everybody is curious about you," he added, meanly, a new glimmer of fun in his eyes.

She made a face, quickly, before smoothing out her features. He didn't miss the look, he didn't miss much at all, she decided.

"Sure, you go out, get some fresh air, Miss Sarah," Justina chimed in. "You need to get out more. I have Zeke and Pearl clean your grandfather's rooms while you gone. They be all fresh for you by tonight."

They seemed eager to arrange matters so that she would be encouraged to stay, Sarah thought. It was nice to be wanted! Joel, Justina and the others, Maxine and Clarence—they all wanted her to stay in Paintsville, and not go back East. She had a warm feeling in her heart, when Zeke brought her cloak down from her room and Joel put it about her. They liked her already. It was very nice. She felt at home with them.

She hesitated as they went out the front door of the inn, and looked at the street. It was mud from one end to the other, with thick rivers of muddy water in the gutters. She could see toward the river, how it had overflowed its banks, and uprooted trees and bushes in a tangled mass along the riverside. The muddy waters were so high she could see them clearly from the veranda of the Golden Goose Inn.

She looked up involuntarily toward the tarnished golden goose and its egg above her, swinging from a pole at the second story. "I must have that repainted, or regilded, whatever it needs," she said.

"Sure. I can do it for you," said Joel, quickly. "Come on, don't keep looking at the mud, or you'll never start out, Sarah!" He grabbed her hand and pulled her firmly down to the sidewalk with him. She winced as she set foot in the thick ooze, and thought with resignation that Zeke would clean her shoes for her. He would do anything for her, because she was the granddaughter of old Adam. She hoped she would not disappoint them.

For the first time, she thought consciously of what would happen to Justina and her brood, should Sarah sell the inn. What if the next owner was a Copperhead, like Mr. Clarence Gibson? Would he get rid of them? Or worse, work them meanly?

She walked with Joel along the muddy sidewalks, looking curiously at the houses and shops before them. They were all built about the same period, she thought. Most of them were painted white, or gray, mostly of wood or part wood and part stone. One solid red brick house stood out, and another huge building which Joel said was the home of a man who had left town. "He was a Copperhead, got in trouble with authorities, and old Adam told him he might as well leave town. He did. Never came back. The house just stands there, nobody claiming it. We were afraid the inn would be the same," he added, quickly, and swung her hand boyishly.

They paused at a shop, and the owner came out, apron over his ample girth. He looked at their hands, clasped and swinging, then at their faces. "Joel, got yourself a girl?" he asked frankly, beaming at them.

"Right you are! Sarah Overmiller, this is Mr. Jim Smith. He runs the grocery, he and his brother Bob. Let's go in out of the wet and talk." And Joel took her in as freely as he had brought her into the inn. Mr. Jim Smith set out a chair for her, he and Joel sat on barrels, and gossiped freely. She stayed quite half an hour before Joel got up briskly and said they must be moving on. It had been a pleasant visit.

As they went on down the street, Sarah said rather coldly, "And next time, don't introduce me as your girl! I am not!"

He rounded his gray eyes at her, with mock astonishment. The devilish lights were in the eyes, his thin cheeks showed humor lines down to his wide mouth. "You aren't? But old Adam promised me first chance at you when you came!"

She stared at him. "He did not! He never knew I was coming!" she said severely, to cover her own doubts.

He pulled her to a halt. She waited. His hand dived into his breast pocket, and he took out, a little shyly, a small round locket and chain of gold. He showed it to her, holding it firmly so she couldn't snatch it from him. It showed in the little case the picture of a wide-eyed girl with a ribbon in her hair, a dimpled smile making her seem even younger.

She could not believe it.

"You went all through the war with me," he said, cheerfully, but he gave her a rather dubious look. "Old Adam let me have a copy of your big picture to take with me. I didn't have a girl of my own, and I liked the looks of you. Course, you have changed."

She didn't know whether to be outraged, to laugh, or demand the picture back. She was rather touched that he had carried it all through that horrible war. She could imagine him taking it out and gazing at it before or after a battle, or when he was lonely—She shook herself. He was a stranger to her, and he was being too forward. She should repress his advances, not encourage them.

"You should give that back to me," she said, her mouth compressed.

"Nope. It's mine. Besides—you are different now." And he put the locket and chain carefully back into his inner pocket. "Might be another girl. She's so young and happy. You—well, you laughed for the first time this morning."

She looked up at him, at the gray eyes that saw so much. "Yes—for the first time—in years," she said, in a low tone, her voice rather choked. "I don't know—how I could laugh—"

"People need to laugh," he said. "It's as important as eating food, or lying down to sleep. Come on, next door is the hat shop, chief rival to Clarence Gibson and Maxine's hats."

He took her in and introduced her to the little lady who waited there. "I thought you weren't coming in," said the woman, severely. "I would have given you a tongue-lashing, Joel Walden!"

"Yes, ma'am, that you would. That's the very reason I brought her, because I was so scared." And he grinned down at the tiny female, and Sarah knew they were old friends.

From the hat lady, they went to the bootmaker, and down the street and across to the tavern, where Joel introduced her to the bartender as a matter of course. They went on down a side street to a meat shop, then to a private home where they were urged to stay for tea. After tea they went on to the chapel, which was empty.

"The preacher got caught by the floods up North," Joel explained. "But we do have some powerful preaching on some Sundays, you wait and see. You'll think you're back East, we got such hell fire and damnation."

"Joel!" she scolded strongly, and shook her finger at him, then when he laughed she realized she had called him by his first name. She shook her head at him and at herself in exasperation.

Later in the morning, he made her laugh again. The second time in one day, she thought, and marveled at herself. What reason did she have to laugh? None. And he had little. He was crippled by the war, he had been an orphan, his business was slight, yet he could laugh, and make her laugh. She put the thought aside to ponder when she was alone and quiet.

He introduced her to Northern rabids and to Copperheads, to moderate ones, to ex-slaves in a field, to a shabby man sitting on a chair outside an old tavern. He introduced her proudly, as "Miss Sarah Overmiller, old Adam's granddaughter, come to the Inn of the Golden Goose." And they smiled, and were curious, and friendly, or distant, according to how they had felt about her grandfather.

At one of the stables where they paused, they met Billy Dexter and Hugo Forrester, having a long discussion about horses, she supposed. They paused when Joel and Sarah peered into the stables. Mr. Forrester came forward at once.

"Why, Miss Sarah, what are you doing out in all this mud?" He sounded disapproving and anxious.

"Joel is showing me about town and introducing me to everybody. He knows everyone, I think," she said, smiling up at the kindly lawyer.

"Yep, everybody," said Joel. "If I miss a soul, I'll hear about it to the end of my days. Besides, everybody is curious to see if Miss Sarah is like her grandfather."

"And am I?" she asked bluntly.

He looked down at her thoughtfully, as though she had asked more than she knew. "I'm waiting to see," he said.

"Well, you shouldn't be out too long. It's coming on to rain again," said Billy Dexter, looking up at the watery sun, drifting in and out of some dubious gray-white clouds. "Figure it'll rain by mid-afternoon."

"That's all we need," said Joel. "Anybody around to fix the bridges?"

The two men shook their heads slowly. "Nope. Nobody around to fix anything," said Billy Dexter, looking at Joel significantly.

Joel nodded, and tucked his hand into Sarah's arm. She thought he felt protective toward her, and was puzzled. Were they all conspiring to protect her, did the conversation mean more than she had thought?

On their slow meandering way back to the inn, with frequent pauses for introductions, Sarah began to think again about her grandfather. Finally in one interval, she asked Joel, "Joel, I wish you would tell me—how did grandfather die? He wasn't ill very long, was he?"

Joel stopped abruptly in the middle of a rut in the street and stared down at her. "Ill?" He seemed to explode the word. "Ill! Your grandfather was never ill a day in his life! Strongest man I ever knew!"

She gazed up at him, forgetting everybody in town, half of them probably staring at her and him. "What do you mean? How did he die?" she asked.

"Why—it was an accident. He was driving a buggy, and it overturned. He must have died instantly, but we didn't find him for several hours." He took her arm and helped her around a carriage, apparently stuck in the mud and abandoned. "Golly, Sarah, I thought you knew that. I shouldn't have said it so fast, like that. I'm sorry. You feel faint or anything?"

She pressed her hand to her forehead. "Buggy?—accident? It's funny—no—I'm all right." Something was nagging at her, something that felt important, but she could not place it. She did feel a little queer and funny, as though the blood had rushed away from her brain. Joel stared down at her in concern.

"You're all white, Sarah. You are shocked. Cuss me anyhow. I'll get you a chair—" He looked helplessly about the street.

They were near someone's house. Joel went right up, rang the bell, and cheerfully introduced Sarah to the lady who bustled to the door. He got her inside, and seated, and talked to the lady while Sarah recovered. Perhaps, she thought, it was needing food. It was long past noon, and the tea hadn't lasted her.

"We must be getting back," she finally said, as Joel showed no signs of terminating his conversation with the pleasant lady. "I do hope to meet you again soon—" Then she couldn't remember the lady's name.

Joel covered for her, and got her out of the house. He tucked her hand into his arm in friendly fashion. "All right now, Sarah? Your color is back."

"I'm fine. But we should get back. Justina is probably thinking I have drowned somewhere."

Someone hailed them cheerfully, a light pretty voice. They turned around to see Maxine waving at them, her dainty umbrella signaling for her. It was a violet umbrella, matching her lovely silk dress and matching silk coat. She looked such a radiant vision that Sarah felt a real dowd in her gray. Like a gray dove and a bird of paradise, she thought, as Maxine picked her way daintily across the street.

"I've been looking and looking for you. Justina said you started hours ago! Where in the world have you been? Joel, you *are* an idiot! Sarah is worn out. Have you been showing her the entire town in one morning?"

"That's right. Guess she is tired," said Joel, more soberly, looking down anxiously at Sarah. "We better get her back to the inn."

Maxine put her arm affectionately about Sarah. "You poor thing! Joel should be thrashed. I wish someone in town would do it, but nobody dares!" And she laughed her pretty trill of sound. "Come on back with us. I've been wanting to talk to you about the couches and chairs at the Golden Goose. Are you going to have them fixed?"

"Oh, I want to, Maxine," she said. "But I don't do such fine sewing. All that silk and satin material—and how can I match the fabrics?"

"Easy. I have them all at the shop—or rather, Dad does. He fought with old Adam, but he gave him materials at bargain prices, and old Adam couldn't resist bargains. We can match just about anything you want," said Maxine, and chatted on gaily as they proceeded back to the inn.

Sarah was wondering if she dared ask Maxine to help her do the mending. But Maxine was so busy—

Joel had no such compunctions. "Why don't you offer to sew them for her, Maxine? You know you like that."

"Oh, Joel, I can't ask—" Sarah began, aghast.

"Oh, do let me," Maxine, at the same moment, was saying eagerly. "I'm dying to get my hands on those beautiful things, to restore them the way they should be. Oh, if you had seen them before! And I want to make a new set for the far living room. I don't like the peach satin. Would you mind if I sewed covers in plum color, with gold trim? I have the loveliest material in the shop—"

Sarah hugged her arm against her impulsively and smiled at the beautiful girl. "How can I let you do it? It would be such a long job! You are dear to ask—"

"Only let me! I dearly love to sew, and to work with those beautiful cherry wood and mahogany couches and chairs will be a delight. I bet Pearl could help me, she has such dainty hands, and she does sew the linens."

They settled it on the way back to the inn. Justina shook her head at them severely when they came in. "Miss Sarah, getting all wore out and muddy. Joel, ain't you ashamed of yourself? Look out you don't wear her plumb out. She is that white-faced."

Joel did look abashed. Zeke went up to Sarah's rooms and brought down her black heel-less slippers, and they took off her muddy shoes. Justina set them all down to a very late lunch, and served them hot soup, greens, ham and a scolding all at once.

When she had finally exhausted that theme, Justina informed Sarah that her rooms were ready. "Zeke and Pearl did work all the blessed morning, and Miss Sarah, they do look nice if I do say so myself. All right and bright and fresh for you, just as they looked when old Adam was here. He'd be right proud for you to have his rooms, I know he would, the dear man."

"Thank you very much, Justina. And Zeke and Pearl." She smiled especially at Pearl, and won a very shy scared half-smile in return before the girl ducked her head down again.

Maxine suggested the sewing to Justina, and the woman was quite willing for Pearl to work with Maxine on mending the couches and chairs. Pearl never said a word, just listening with her big anxious eyes going from face to face. She was such a little scared thing, Sarah thought. Would she never recover from her experiences in the South?

How terrible it must have been for the shy dainty little girl to know she was "desired" by the master, by the brutal overseer, to be used and discarded at will. They had been right to fight a war against slavery, thought Sarah.

"She's tired out," said Joel. Sarah looked at him questioningly. "You didn't answer the last two questions. Why don't you go on up to bed and rest?"

She didn't particularly want to, but Joel escorted her

firmly up to her grandfather's rooms. She found that
Justina had followed them, to show her how they had
moved Sarah's belongings to the new room, and hung
up her dresses in the beautifully carved wardrobe. The
bed was freshly made with lavender-scented linens and
a pile of fresh blankets, covered with a gay quilt, of reds
and blues and greens and yellows.

It did look so comfortable. After they had left her,
Sarah looked at the bed a long time. Finally she gave in,
and lay down, and knew nothing more for two hours.

She woke up slowly, feeling warm and contented and
pleasantly rested. Her legs were stiff, probably from so
much walking, she thought. When she got up, and had
washed and dressed again, she looked with pride and
pleasure about her new rooms.

Grandfather Adam had loved books as she did, she
discovered as she browsed along the bookcases. She
found several of her favorites there, Jane Austen,
Henry Thoreau, Rev. Mr. Emerson, Sir Walter Scott,
many of the English poets. How odd, she thought, that
a tough lusty man like her grandfather had been fond of
the poets. The books were well-worn.

Then on the bottom shelf of one of the bookcases,
she found what she had been seeking, a row of account
books. Breathlessly she took them out and stacked
them neatly on the table nearby. She glanced quickly
from one to another, hoping, hoping—

But there was no diary. Just the accounts of the inn,
neatly kept in a businesslike readable fashion of a man
who had not studied accounting formally, but neverthe-
less knew what he needed to keep in his records.

She sat down in a rocking chair, rather large for her,
but comfortable with a thick cushion of knitted wools in
reds and greens. She found she was sitting opposite her
own portrait. She looked up at it, thought of the
evenings when her grandfather must have sat just here,
and looked into her face. Why had he set her portrait
there? She had not thought he had any special affection
for her—yet he had loved her father. Perhaps he had

loved her also, and had thought of her. He had sent her a few presents in her younger years, a doll, a dress, a bonnet, a gold locket. She liked to think that he had thought much of her, and had pondered about her future and her welfare.

She was the only one left. She closed her eyes, and felt the sting of tears against the lids, then blinked them back resolutely. She would not cry. That was over. The war was over. She must make a new life, either here or back East.

As she picked up the first account book to study it, she thought of Joel, carrying her picture with him through four years of agony and battle. She should have taken the picture from him, he had no right to have it, but she could not. After all, he had said it wasn't like her anymore. She felt a little pang over that. Yes, she had changed, she had grown older and much more serious.

"Sometimes I feel I have known you a long time," Joel had said on their trek this morning. She laid the account book on her knees and thought again. Yes, she felt the same way about him. Yet she didn't know him. She didn't know any of them, really—not Joel, or Maxine, or Clarence, or the many people she had met this morning.

She sighed, why, she did not know. She picked up the book, and skimmed it rapidly. It was of the older days of the inn. She laid it aside, skimmed others, until she came to the more recent years. Then she began studying the entries more carefully, both to study how he kept his accounts, and to find out how profitable the inn had been.

She found the accounts easy enough to read. So much for china and linens, and paying the cook, and the grocery store, and the man who delivered fresh fruit. And so much taken in for bed and so much for board and so much for a fine meal given by a gentleman for his friends, and so much for wine bottles.

She went over the accounts rather rapidly. She was

used to accounts, she had kept her father's housekeeping accounts for years, and these were not too unalike. But when she came to some yearly totals, she gasped several times aloud.

It could not be. The inn was much more profitable than she had dreamed. Of course, he had done much of the work himself, registering guests, arranging parties, ordering the foods and wines, supervising the work. Still—the sums he had amassed—

The gold, she thought, and laid down the book she had been studying. There must have been gold. He had not turned back everything into the inn, though he had bought fine furniture and expensive china and glass, and the best foods. He had made a small fortune. And it must be in that gold.

Only—where was the gold?

Chapter 5

~~~~~~

When the light from the window grew much more dim, Sarah knew it was evening. She stood up, stretched, and set the account books neatly back into the bookcase, except the latest one. She must study again how her grandfather had kept his accounts, then continue them as he had.

If she remained.

She studied her pale reflection in the mirror soberly. She smoothed her hair automatically. Several curls had escaped, to lie against her broad forehead. She smoothed them back carefully. She was so thin. If she remained here, would she get more "beef on her bones," as Joel had cheerfully told her? Would she regain her somewhat shattered health? She did not feel quite so exhausted as she had felt last week this time. She had really wondered if she could start on a long journey, she was so weary.

If she remained.

She could run the inn, she thought. She would enjoy doing it. Justina would help, and Pearl and Zeke. And Joel would help her. Even Clarence. And especially Maxine—she was so kind and eager to help out. It would be very pleasant to have a good friend like Maxine nearby, to confide in, to gossip with, to laugh with. Laughter. It had been omitted from her life in recent years. Joel was probably right about laughter—one needed it.

But—what if—She paused and thought of that vicious attack on her life. The murder of Roscoe. Someone didn't want her to remain—not alive—here in the Inn of the Golden Goose. There were dark shadows somewhere in the Inn, some secrets that she did not know yet. She shivered, involuntarily, and reached for a light cashmere shawl to put about her shoulders. Someone wanted her dead.

Who was that someone? How could she protect herself?

The tapping at the door startled her so, that she jerked. She whirled about, stared at the door to her living room with wide apprehensive eyes.

"Miss Sarah? You be awake? Mama says it time for supper, Miss Sarah," came Zeke's cautiously raised voice.

In great relief she flung open the door and smiled at the tall strong colored boy. Protect herself? She didn't have to. She was surrounded by protectors!

"And I'm so hungry I could eat a whole hog, Zeke," she told him happily. He beamed down at her.

"Yes, ma'am. Mama, she got a big supper all fixed and hot for you."

Sarah was not surprised to find Joel waiting for her in the kitchen, standing near the huge fireplace and teasing Justina so that she beamed from ear to ear.

"You'll stay for supper, Joel," she said, glad not to be alone.

"You never have to ask me twice, Sarah," he said, his gray eyes twinkling readily. "You'll think I live over here. Matter of fact, sometimes in the winter I do. That is, I did when Old Adam was here. I paid him some board in recent years," he added quietly, and looked at her.

So he had his pride. She had thought so. He held her chair for her, and they sat down to a feast. As Justina served the vegetables, she said, "Miss Maxine done came three time this evening, wanting to see you, Miss Sarah. She is that excited about some material she wants to use on the couches."

"Already? That is wonderful. We can choose tomorrow—"

"I think she want you to choose tonight, Miss Sarah," sighed Justina. "She be all set to start sewing tomorrow morning! When Miss Maxine sets her mind, you might as well let her move! She be that stubborn."

Joel did not smile. He was looking down at his plate thoughtfully. She supposed he was not listening to the women's talk.

Maxine came before they had finished eating the delicious beef and vegetables, the home-made hot bread and jelly, the pumpkin pie hot from the oven. She sat down with them promptly when Sarah invited her.

"No, nothing—oh, Justina, you didn't make pumpkin pie!" she said, as though reproachfully.

"Yes, Miss Maxine. But if you be too full to eat any—" And Justina chuckled at her own joke.

Maxine shook her golden blonde hair. "If I had any sense—no, I don't. Please, Justina, just a tiny little piece—"

Justina got her a huge piece, and Maxine ate every bite of the custard and flaky crust.

"Oh, delicious," she sighed. "If I could make pies like that, I would die happy."

Sarah started. It made her jump now, to have someone speak of dying. Maxine was rattling on, oblivious to her distress.

"Sarah, dearest, you must come over and see the fabrics I found. Dad had them tucked away, but Leonard pulled them out for me, and they are marvelous. I found the matching fabrics that old Adam used in the blue set and the cream satin. I found the peach satin, too, but oh, dear, you don't want peach, do you? No, of course you don't. I adore bright colors. There is a plum—"

Joel quietly offered to go with them, and Zeke went along to lift the heavy bolts of fabric for them. Joel leaned against the counter of the silent store, lifted the lamp for them to see better, held out a length of fabric so the girls could see it, and generally made himself useful. Sarah wondered if he were curious about how she would decorate the inn. Surely he was not worried about her. She was not alone in the store. There was Maxine, and Zeke.

"Oh, I do like this plum satin," she told Maxine eagerly. "This is a lovely shade. Do you think it would be too bright, with gold braid?"

Maxine lifted a length of gold braid against the plum and all four of them considered the matter seriously, and decided it would be beautiful. Sarah fingered the next bolt. It was a lovely shade of old rose silk.

"That's too fragile for couch material, dear," said Maxine, practically. "We sell that for dresses."

"I guessed that," said Sarah, setting it down with a sigh. "I was thinking about a dress for me—oh, no, that would be foolish."

"Foolish! I should think not!" Maxine cried out eagerly, and lifted a length of it to Sarah's chin critically. "Oh, Joel, look at that! The color is perfect for her, that rose against her pretty skin, and her golden brown hair. Of course, blue goes better with her eyes, but you can't wear blue all the time, darling. Oh, do take some of this. I'll help you sew it, and do let's look at patterns tonight! I have a new book of patterns, and I have scarcely had a chance to look at it—oh, do let's choose some pretty braiding to go with it—"

Before Sarah could catch her breath, Maxine was measuring off lengths of the old rose silk, some black velvet for trim, choosing some buttons of black to go with it. She was cutting, and talking, as fast as she could, as eagerly as though it was a new gown for herself. Joel and Zeke watched with sober interest, as the two girls discussed the matter.

They returned to the bright kitchen, where Justina was sitting in a rocker before the dying fire, reading her

Bible. She smiled at the girls as they sat down with pattern book, fabrics, sewing materials. Joel settled down with them, a pipe at hand. It was the first time Sarah had seen him smoking. She wondered if her grandfather had sat just there, near the fire, in his slippers, with his pipe at the end of a busy day.

It was a very comfortable evening, she thought. Maxine was going to help her start the dress the next day, then she and Pearl would set to work mending and piecing the blue couch and chairs. They had sustained the least damage.

"And something has to be ready for the guests, when the rains let up," said Maxine practically. "Whether you stay or not, Sarah! And you do want to stay, don't you?"

Suddenly, everyone in the room was staring at Sarah. She flushed a little, aware that she had practically made up her mind already. In spite of the dangers, the very real danger of murder, she wanted to stay here. She felt loved and warm and comfortable, among friends, for the first time in a long time. Here, she could forget the long weary war years, the heartaches, the nightmares, the deaths of her father and brother, the many men in the hospitals wounded and in agony and dying.

She could begin to live here, in the Inn of the Golden Goose. Her grandfather had left it to her, and she could carry on as he had, almost as well as he had, she vowed.

"Yes, I want to stay," she said, finally.

Justina muttered happily over her Bible, "Praise the Lord, to His name praise," and chuckled a little to herself.

Joel reached across to Sarah and patted her hand on the table. "Good girl. I knew you had courage," he said, oddly.

Zeke and Pearl were sitting near their mother. Ever so often she read a verse softly to them, and pointed out the words. They said nothing to Sarah, but Zeke was looking pleased. Pearl was still downcast, her eyes on her hands, her little frightened face so tired and gloomy that Sarah wondered at her.

"Good," said Maxine, firmly. "That is good. Now, we ought to plan to fix up the sets soon. Pearl and I will start with the blue, that won't take long. Then we'll do the cream and the summery green one. The plum will take the longest. If the rains keep on, we'll leave the furniture where it is, and work on it in the living rooms. If that dratted rain lets up—and it better before I go insane!—then we can move the unfinished pieces to the back of the store, and Pearl can help me do the sewing there." She rattled on swiftly, making plans faster than Sarah could grasp them.

Joel twinkled his eyes at Sarah once or twice, as Maxine chatted as fast as she planned.

"Oh, do let's have some flounces in the skirt, Sarah," she switched her attention rapidly to the pattern book Sarah was studying. "Like that one. You wouldn't have to have seven flounces, but do let's have three or four. Would you like lace on the skirt?"

"No, I don't believe so. That would be too—too much," Sarah decided. "Just three flounces, and the black velvet trim—"

"And a bonnet to match," declared Maxine happily. "I have the very thing. It's a small darling bonnet in cream, with roses on the brim, the very shade, I declare. I'll bring it over in the morning, and you'll try it on. You'll love it."

Joel got up, went over to the fireplace, and knocked out his pipe. "You girls have planned enough to last a month," he said firmly. "Sarah is white again, and Maxine, you're tired too. I can tell by the way you're talking. Come on, I'll take you home, Maxine."

She sighed, but gave in so readily that Sarah realized she was tired. "I shouldn't have kept you so long," said Sarah, anxiously. "I was enjoying it so much—"

"Me also," said Maxine, as she stood. Unexpectedly, she leaned over and pressed her cheek to Sarah's. "You are very much like old Adam," she said. "And yet such a dear girl—I hope we can be good friends." And she turned quickly, as though to hide tears.

Sarah was deeply touched by this sign of friendship and liking. She went to the door with Maxine and Joel, and saw them as the lantern lighted their way along the back path to the door of the next building. She went back inside thoughtfully. It was raining again, a heavy drizzling rain.

Zeke was going to escort her to her room. But by the time she had folded up the silk fabric, rolled up the velvet, and set aside the pattern book, Joel had returned. "I'll take you up and make sure the lock is fastened properly," he said.

He took her up to her room, looked inside both rooms, and made sure no one was hiding within. Then he started to the door, but paused.

"I know you're tired, Sarah," he said. "But I got to talk to you, and tonight is as good a time as any."

She stared at him curiously. He was much more serious than he was usually. "Of course, sit down here, Joel." She indicated a comfortable chair opposite the huge rocker she had appropriated as her own. They both sat down, the door to the hallway open.

He clasped his hands between his knees, in a gesture strangely uneasy for the confident Joel Walden. He looked down at his hands for a long moment, then up at Sarah, directly, his dark gray eyes looking black in the light of the single lamp with the rose printed white bowl. She remembered afterwards how the lamplight glistened on the cherry wood furniture, on the table and the chairs where they sat, and on the bookcases near them.

"Sarah, I don't think you should stay here," he said, bluntly. "I want to buy the inn. I'll make you a good offer, we'll fix it up, then you leave when the rains let up."

If he had struck her in the face, she could not have been more aghast and shocked. "Leave," she said, very blankly. "Leave?"

"It isn't safe for you here," he said, quietly. "I can't

always be around. You won't always be protected. You are in danger, Sarah, I know this. By a hunch, I suppose. Feeling I have in my stomach. But I want you to get out of here, fast as you can go. Billy Dexter will take you to the railroad, you get the next train back East."

She swallowed back tears. She had thought he liked her, wanted very much for her to stay. How could she have been so mistaken?

"I'll buy the inn from you. I'll run it the way your grandfather did, no need to worry about that. I'll keep Justina and her children. But you must get away!"

"I—I can't think tonight," she said, and it was the stark truth. "I can't think."

"All right, Sarah. Think about it tomorrow. But decide soon. If you sell to me, you won't be in so much danger, I believe. You must go soon." And he stood up, his lean height exaggerated by the lamplight. She looked up at him, and for a moment, a blinding moment, she was afraid of him. He had killed in the war, she thought.

Oh, God, he had killed in the war. He could kill again.

What am I thinking? Oh, no, no, not Joel Walden, he is so gentle, he laughs, he makes me laugh. No, not kill—

"Good night, Sarah." He went to the door, and paused. Why was he waiting, she wondered, sitting very still in the huge rocker. "Come on, I want you to lock the door after me," he said, rather impatiently. She saw that he looked very weary, and his limp was more pronounced than before.

"I'm coming—" She went to the door, and he walked out, turning to look at her. The hall was thick with black shadows. Did something move out there? Or was the man before her the one whom she should fear? She looked up at him, her eyes very wide and frightened.

He reached out to her neck. She went stiff. He patted

her cheek slowly with his hand, then dropped his hand. "Good night, Sarah," he said again. "Let me hear you fasten the lock."

"Good—night—Joel—" She closed the door slowly, and fastened the lock with hands that shook so she could scarcely control them.

She went back to the rocker and sat down. She saw the account book on the table, and finally her brain began to work. All that money. All that gold. Would he kill for that? Did he know where it was?

He was a poor boy, making little money. Yet he had offered to buy the inn! With what money, she thought. Oh, God, with what money could he buy an expensive inn?

She sat in the rocker, moving it slowly with her slow-moving thoughts, until she was so tired she was about to drop with weariness. Finally she stood up, removed her clothes, washed, got into the comfortable bed which had been her grandfather's. Oh, if he could only return for a few minutes, to help her worry out this matter!

Joel was not in the kitchen the next morning. She supposed he was working somewhere, though the rain had not let up. Justina chatted comfortably. Pearl had gone to help Maxine with the sewing. Zeke was mending some harness in the corner, sitting on a bench, absorbed in his work.

Sarah's mind was functioning more alertly this morning. When Hugo Forrester came down late to breakfast, as she was finishing her coffee, she had made up her resolution to one point. She would ask for advice from the one disinterested kindly man she knew.

She said low, as Justina went to get his ham and eggs, "I want to talk to you after breakfast. Will you come up to my rooms for a few minutes?"

"Of course. I am at your disposal," he said, with his usual courtesy, curiosity shining in his eyes. "Thank you, Justina. That looks delicious. I am afraid I am quite late this morning."

"Means you slept good, Mr. Forrester," said Justina. "You be in for lunch, maybe? I can fix it in the dining room. Zeke got it all cleaned up again."

"I would like to come for lunch. But if I may, I will partake of my lunch wherever Miss Sarah does. If she eats in the kitchen, I should like to also."

Sarah smiled at him. He was such a gentleman, and so thoughtful. She decided she liked lawyers. They were smart, and kind also.

"I would like to continue eating in the kitchen, and I would be pleased if you would join me whenever your time permits, Mr. Forrester."

After breakfast, they went up to her room. He left the door open a few inches, as was proper. They sat down, she in the rocker, he sitting where Joel had sat last night.

"Mr. Forrester, I have been studying the account books," she said in a low tone. "I have found that grandfather made quite a deal of money. The stories of the gold hidden about may well be true."

He nodded thoughtfully. "I would not be surprised, Miss Sarah. Whenever I came to the inn, it was frequently crowded, and the dining room was always popular. Good as Justina's cooking is, the cook that Old Adam had was even better. You should have tasted her custards, her baby beef, the veal, the venison—" He shook his head. "If you could lure her back, you would be well served, I think. And of course, the rooms are always comfortable, Adam saw to that."

"Mr. Forrester, do you think—honestly—that I could run the inn, well, not as beautifully as grandfather did, but efficiently enough to make a paying proposition of it?" She blurted out the question hurriedly before she could regret it.

He studied her face, and the matter, with his usual calm. "Yes, Miss Sarah, I think you could. You would need more help than Adam had, I believe. A man to help at the registration desk, and to handle any difficult patrons—such as those who partake too liberally of wines," he added with a slight smile. "As far as the accounts and management are concerned, you would manage most efficiently, from what I have seen of your actions."

"Then why—why would Joel Walden warn me away? Why would he offer to buy the inn and tell me I can't run it? Where would he get the money to buy it?"

He caught his breath as he understood the significance of her questions. His face had sobered a great deal.

"Joel Walden offered to buy the inn? But he is poor—and warning you away—Yes, yes, because of old Roscoe, and the attack on you—But I wonder—" He fell silent, still studying her face in a worried way.

"Where would he get the money to buy?" she asked again.

"I don't know that, Miss Sarah," he said simply.

"You have talked to Billy Dexter. He trusts you, I believe. Does he think I am not safe here?"

Mr. Forrester nodded. His face was screwed up now in a frown of concentration and concern. "Yes, he thinks so, and so do I. We have been most concerned. The sheriff is away. Of course, Zeke and Joel have been protecting you—"

Then the names hit him. They sat and stared at each other. Zeke, with whom Joel was on the best of terms. Joel, who had offered to buy the inn, who had warned her away.

Mr. Forrester finally stood up. "Miss Sarah, I'll ask about town, talk some more to Billy Dexter. I'll let you know what I discover. And I must have time to think about this matter. I would not want you to remain if you were in grave danger. Your life is much too precious to risk for that."

"Thank you, Mr. Forrester." She put her hand out impulsively, and he clasped it warmly in his big hand. She saw him to the door, and he went down the back stairs.

"Sarah!" The voice beside her startled her wildly. It

was Joel, coming along the hall, limping. She pulled back into her room, frightened involuntarily. "Sarah! I have to talk to you."

She was closing the door, when he pushed on it strongly and came into her room. His face was dark and stormy, the gray eyes black and furious.

"Don't shut me out!" he raged. "How dare you talk to that man about me? How dared you tell him—"

She drew herself up, fright bringing out her courage. She faced him fully. "I dare talk to anyone I please! I trust Mr. Forrester, he has been kind and a gentleman to me!"

"You told him I wanted to buy the inn! You asked where I would get the money! Did you think I would rob somebody? Have you never heard of banks loaning money on a man's future?" He raged at her.

She stared at him. She had never dreamed there was such a volcano of fury under his usually sunny disposition. Now she saw how he could have killed in the war. His passions were there all the time, usually concealed under his humor and calm. But they were there—the volcano and heat and storm.

"Or did you think I knew where old Adam's gold was? Did you think I had stolen from him, that I would pay you with blood money? Answer me, what did you think?" he blasted the words at her.

"I did—not think—Joel, I don't know what to think. Old Roscoe is dead, so is my grandfather. And an attempt was made on my life. And you are all strangers to me," she finished, with quiet dignity, staring him right in the eye.

"We are all strangers to you! Sure, I understand that! But so is Forrester! So why did you confide in him? Why do you trust him? Maybe he found the gold! Maybe he wants you done away with! Slick lawyers always head for money—"

"That is unkind and untrue," she blazed back at him. "You have no right to say such things of Mr. Forrester!"

"And you two had no right to discuss me as you did! Sure, I listened to you! Ripping me apart as though I was a rag doll! What makes you think Forrester is so great? We are all strangers to you! All of us! How can you trust any of us?"

"I can't. That is it, I can't." Her tone quivered. She bit her lips, fighting back her loneliness and grief. He was tearing apart the shell she had built around herself these years. He was making her feel, making her know the deep emotions she had tried to avoid all this time. She could not endure more pain. She must have her shell.

He muttered something, staring down at her, his eyes still black with fury. "Trust—damn it all—he trusted—"

"What did you say?" she asked.

"Never mind. Sarah, you have to trust me. Old Adam did, he never regretted it," he said, with a little more calm. "I want you to trust me completely. I'll pull you through. I can protect you, I know I can. Zeke will watch over you. Trust me—"

"No," she said, perversely. "I will trust no one. I don't know any of you! I'll keep my doors locked—"

"Sarah, you stupid little pretty idiot, locked doors won't keep out a murderer and a thief! You have to trust some of us! I can help you, I will. Just listen to me—" He grasped her arm, half-shook her with the force of his gesture.

She tried to pull away. "No, Joel. Let me go. I have looked after myself for years, I can again. No one is going to drive me away. I shall look after myself. You have no right to try to bully me!"

"Bully you! It's for your own protection!"

She looked up stormily. She had never felt so torn apart by confusing emotions. Her shell was gone, swept away, perhaps never to return. She was open again to pain, to love, to fear, to hate, to confusion, to doubt—

"You let me alone. I will not be dominated by

anyone! I can look after myself—" And she was foolish enough to try to pull herself by force from him.

He too seemed swept by strange emotions. As she tried to pull away, he held her the more strongly, staring down into her blue eyes. Then he said something, and pulled, yanked her to himself.

She was caught off balance. She fell against him, felt the hard warmth of his body against her whole length. He had her hand in one arm, his other hand went up to her head, his fingers thrust through her hair, mussing it, tearing the neat arrangement into loose curls. He held her head so her face was just under his. Then he bent his face closer, closer. She saw his dark stormy gray eyes changing, changing, like the sea under a hard fierce wind. Then his mouth was on hers.

He held her lips with the pressure of his. He hurt her for a moment, before his mouth gentled. She felt the lips pressing fiercely against the half-opened mouth she was helpless to close. She had been gasping—then his lips had pressed on hers—and now he was kissing her with a fierce possessive heat that sent alarm and warmth both raging through her whole body.

He turned his head slightly, so that his lips moved on hers and learned hers, and his hand held her head still under his attack. He was angry, she felt that with her whole body, but there was something else there too. Possession? Some—and love? perhaps—and need—need of a woman, hunger, a raging hunger for a woman—

She knew all that, and was limp before the knowledge. If he had raped her, she would have been helpless. She could not move or stir. In the hospital, they had taught her how to protect herself from a crazed patient. She could not move one finger to use her knowledge.

Finally his lips left hers, and she could draw a ragged breath. His mouth moved swiftly to her cheek, down to her throat, back up to her ear, over her soft flesh, as though learning her, possessing her, taking her to himself.

And she could struggle. She had her breath, and her voice.

"Let me go—Joel! Let me go—how dare you—let me go!" One arm came loose from his rough grip, and she pushed against him vigorously.

Finally, then, he let her go, to arm's length, and stood looking down at her. She found she could not meet his eyes. They were so glowing, so alive, like coals, fierce, hot, with a message in them she did not want to read. Not yet.

"You belong to me, Sarah," he said, his voice rough. "You belong to me." He set her down in the rocker, and went out and shut the door softly behind him.

She was completely limp. She thought he had taken all her strength from her, by the power of his body, draining her, using all her will to take it to himself and keep it. She could still feel against her flesh and bones the hot possessive touch of his body and his lips and his hands.

Chapter 6

〰〰〰〰〰〰〰〰〰〰〰〰〰〰〰〰〰〰〰〰〰〰

Sarah sat still in the rocker for a long time. She was ashamed of herself, shocked. She had—liked it! She had liked the way Joel had kissed her, so hard, so possessively.

Yet he had no claim on her, none at all. Why, one week ago they had not even met each other! Now he acted as·though he owned her, he said it! She rubbed her hands over her flushed cheeks again and again, touched her lips wonderingly. He was the first man, outside her family, who had ever kissed her mouth.

She washed her face, to cool the flush and heat of her skin. She must, must stop thinking of Joel. He was too possessive, too soon. And the way he had acted toward her—why, he must have no respect for her at all.

She tried to whip up her anger against him. He had no right to act that way. Of course, she added honestly, she had provoked him, made him furiously angry. Maybe that was it. He did not love her, he was just so angry, it was like hitting a man, to kiss a woman like that.

But his mouth had been so hard, yet so sweet and hungry.

She would have to avoid him, act cold to him. He must not think he could do things like that freely.

She could hear Justina singing in the kitchen, one of the low plaintive hymns of her people. It was such a peaceful sound, on that rainy cold October day.

Sarah decided to work on her new dress. It was something quiet to do, something her hands could work on without too much bother to her mind. She laid it out on a small table, studied the pattern. It didn't look too bad to do. She took her gray wool dress, laid it against the cloth, and finally figured out how to cut the old rose silk. It was such a beautiful shade of rose, so pretty. She wondered if Joel would—

No, forget Joel!

She found some good scissors in a drawer, finally decided to dare to cut the fabric. She cut, measured, cut again, laid it against herself. It looked right. She had made several dresses in her younger years, following the directions of an older friend of her mother who sometimes came over to sew for them.

When the soft swishy fabric was cut, she pinned it all, and then carefully tried it on. Oh, it did look pretty. That rose color did look right with her pink and white skin. And with the black velvet ribbons on it, it would be smart and modern. Joel might like—

Forget Joel!

She sat down in the rocker, and began to sew the seams, humming softly to herself the same melody that Justina was singing in the kitchen.

By noon, she had most of the major seams sewed up. She was pleased with herself when she went down to lunch. Again Zeke was waiting for her in the hall, padding quietly down the stairs after her.

"You been asleep, Miss Sarah?" asked Justina, with friendly interest. Her smooth brown face was happy and contented, as she began dishing up the ham and brown beans. "You so quiet all morning, I thought you been asleep."

"No, I was sewing my new dress, Justina. I can finish it in another day or two, I think."

"Oh, my, that's nice. You should wear something

bright and pretty, Miss Sarah. Old Adam, he liked bright colors. He be sad if he see you all in dark colors."

Sarah looked down soberly at her dark blue dress. She had not realized how in the past couple years she had chosen all dark dresses. They had been reflections of the sadness of her mind, she thought. From now on, she decided, she would wear brighter colors. Her father had liked for her to wear bright red, rose, bright blue the color of her eyes.

Mr. Forrester came as she was beginning to eat. He smiled at her, his pleasant brown eyes lighting to see her. "I thought I might be late, Miss Sarah. I have been all around town, listening to the gossip."

He looked significantly at her, and she nodded her understanding, her heart giving a quick thump of apprehension.

They talked only casually through lunch. Joel did not come, and Justina wondered aloud several times what might be keeping him. Pearl had not returned. Zeke had reported that she was eating over at the Gibsons, that Maxine was going right after the sewing and had finished the first couch cushions.

"Give her something good to do," said Justina. "That is fine. That poor woman, she about crazy when her beautiful husband, he died."

"Beautiful husband?" Sarah was surprised at the expression.

"Oh, yes, ma'am, Miss Sarah. That Mr. Tim Gibson, he one of the best looking men you ever do see. Fine yellow hair, he had, and dark blue eyes, some darker than yours. And tall, and straight and handsome. Oh, my, how she did cry and carry on when he reported gone, and then they said he was truly gone, and poor Miss Maxine, her heart was done broke."

"His father is very handsome also," said Sarah, thinking more about Maxine and her grief. She must have loved him deeply.

"Yes, but not so handsome as Mr. Tim. He got his

mother's good looks and his paw's. And my, how his paw was mad at him when he enlisted! His paw and Maxine, they try to talk him out of going, but he listen to old Adam, and he gone to help free us colored chillen, he did. Good as gold, he always was, a fine boy he was, to be sure." And she sighed heavily.

Mr. Forrester looked keenly at Sarah, and she returned his look. This was interesting gossip to her. The town was badly divided over slavery, and even the Gibson family itself had been divided, with Tim siding with the North and his father with the South. Probably Maxine had been ripped to pieces in her loyalties. She seemed to adore her husband's father.

After lunch, she went upstairs with Mr. Forrester. This time, they defied conventions and closed the door to her rooms. She wanted to talk privately to him. She did not tell him that Joel had overheard their conversation. She was in no mood to confess what Joel had done to her, and how she had felt over it.

"Well, Miss Sarah," he said, settling down in the chair, his face lighted with interest. "I have been learning a great deal about Paintsville the past few hours. And about Joel Walden."

She looked eagerly at him. "What—what have you learned? How could Joel offer to buy the inn?"

"Well, my best guess is that he has been offered credit, a loan from the local bank. They would back him. He is much respected in town, even by the Copperheads. He has been here all his life, knows everyone by name."

She was so relieved, she gave a big sigh. He smiled at her. "Oh, I am glad. I didn't want to think that Joel—that he—"

"I am quite jealous, Miss Sarah," he said, unexpectedly with a funny little twist at his mouth. "After four days, you call Joel Walden by his first name. But I claim prior acquaintance by one day, and you still call me Mr. Forrester. My first name is Hugo. I beg you to use it."

She colored a little. "Why—I would be delighted. And you have been so extremely kind to me. I'm sure I don't know why, but you have made me feel—well, very protected. It is very good of you, Mr.—"

"Hugo," he said, firmly.

"Hugo," she agreed. "May I beg for more advice?"

"I should be honored!"

"I—I should say—please don't be offended—that I would like you to give me some legal advice, and I will pay for it—"

"Never!" he said. "I shall be only too happy to assist you in any way I may."

"But Mr. Forrester—"

"Hugo!" he corrected, his brown eyes laughing, a little like Joel's at his most mischievous.

"Truly, I do wish some legal advice, about the inn, and the accounts," she went on, rather shyly. "You see, I have been studying my grandfather's accounts, and I have some questions—" She drew the latest account book to her. He pulled his chair briskly over closer to her, and looked at the book.

They discussed the manner of keeping accounts, and he advised her to continue them, at least for the present.

"Later, you may wish to turn to a more systematic manner of bookkeeping, but this looks quite usable, quite orderly," he said, with approval, studying the entries.

"You see, the totals at the end, Hugo— And how much there is. I think—I think grandfather must have had some gold put away. I believe he did pay a great deal for some slaves, to obtain their freedom. But those entries appear here and there in the earlier books. So these totals, large as they are, must be the sums he had amassed."

"Hum." He frowned over the totals, studied two of the earlier books. They discussed the matter in some detail, he told her some ideas about following up on the entries.

"Do you suppose," she finally asked, "that he did the sensible thing, and put the money in the bank? Do you suppose I might ask—"

"Of course, you should ask at the bank. The banker will be happy to explain your grandfather's accounts. I think there would be no difficulty in turning over his affairs to you, and it would be mere formality, signatures, etc. However, I should be much surprised if you find more than a comfortable savings in the account, Miss Sarah. The rumors about Old Adam's gold are quite strong. Gossip mentions it every other word," and his mouth twisted again, and his eyebrows quirked.

They talked for a long time. Hugo Forrester was very much a businessman and lawyer. He gave her some practical advice about running the inn, "should you decide to remain here, Miss Sarah," he added. He suggested methods of hiring and firing employees, paying regular wages to Justina and her family.

"Since the war is over, things will be different. There should be no hint of slavery, no matter what your intentions. Even though you furnish them room and board, they should receive salaries as well, even Pearl."

He talked about inventory, and how to take it. He discussed payment to Maxine for doing over the couches and chairs. He suggested that she consult with Clarence Gibson about her account with him, and that she should find out from all the merchants in town what debits might be owing. Her head was spinning, and finally she took notepaper and pencil and began writing down some of the things he was saying.

Running an inn was not quite so simple as she had thought, from her grandfather's accounts. Hugo Forrester reminded her about getting cash in advance from transient guests, not letting important people run up huge accounts. Wealthy people, he said, were sometimes reluctant to part with that wealth, even for honest debts. She would have to be firm. Or she might hire a manager for the inn, if she could find a dependable person to do the debt collecting for her.

His advice ranged over a wide area. He spoke of rehiring the cook whose food was the talk of several counties. He spoke of the advisability of building up the reputation of the inn even higher, since the railroads were now so far North. She would need a heavy incentive to get people to come to Paintsville for the night, to come that way instead of another route. She should hire more servants, choosing them carefully, so that the rooms would always be fresh and clean, with clean linens.

He would go to the bank with her, he said, and introduce her to the banker. She should bring all her papers with her, to prove her identity and her ownership of the inn and Adam's other properties.

As they talked on and on, into the late afternoon, and the shadows began to fall in the room, they drew nearer to the table, and its pretty rose-painted lamp, to speak more comfortably. Twice he patted her hand soothingly, when she expressed doubts over her ability to carry on. She caught an expression in his eyes, a tender gentle look, that indicated he was more interested in her than as a possible client.

Yes, he did like her, and that was very nice, she thought. He was a kind intelligent man. A young lawyer, from a good family, on his way up in a career of importance in this frontier area. She could do worse— She seemed to hear an older woman saying this to her in authoritative tones. *You could do worse, Sarah, my dear!*

She did like Mr. Forrester—Hugo, she corrected herself mentally. She liked him, and he seemed to be becoming fond of her. Surely, he had stayed on in Paintsville, when he could really have gotten out by boat. He was strong, and not a coward. He and Billy Dexter could both have gotten out by boat, if they had decided on that course. She had the feeling that Hugo had remained because he was uneasy about Sarah and her safety.

Their talk turned to her grandfather. Hugo told her what he could remember of the man, though he had met him only casually as the owner of the inn where he had stayed on a number of times.

"But you do remind me of him, Sarah, the more I talk to you. He had a good quick mind, a thoughtful turn, considerate of others. And a little stubborn, in a good way," he added, with a smile. "I think you will need all your courage to manage here. I would hope that before long you will marry, and have a helpmeet for your burdens here."

She did blush then. "I expect—that might happen in time," she said, rather primly, looking down blindly at the account book. Could he read her thoughts? She had been thinking how kindly and helpful he was. "But for now, I must consider how I can carry on alone. I do appreciate your advice."

"I am glad to be able to give it. I am happy that you turned to me for such advice, Sarah," he said, his tone deepening. He put his hand on hers again.

Someone knocked sharply at the door. Sarah jumped nervously, like a cat on a hot hearth. Hugo got up and went to the door, his right hand at his trouser pocket. Sarah looked at that hand. Did he carry a weapon, a small pistol, or a knife? She would not be surprised.

Hugo opened the door. Clarence Gibson stared at him, then beyond him at Sarah. "Well—sorry to interrupt," he said, with surprise, then a little grin. "I'll go away. Maxine was trying to find you. Justina said you had gone out in the rain, and I couldn't believe it. It's pouring down hard,"

Justina had been protecting them, Sarah thought. She probably knew quite well that Sarah and Hugo Forrester were conversing seriously here.

"Oh, please come in, Mr. Gibson. We were talking, but we are talked out for now, I think. Do please come in." She stood up, urging him, not wanting him to think he was shut out, or that she had been having a secret rendezvous. She really should guard her reputation in this small gossipy town, she thought.

Though Hugo glared, Clarence Gibson came in, and sat down in the chair Hugo had sat in. Hugo had to draw up another, more uncomfortable straight chair.

But he did draw it up, and remained, glaring some more at the older man.

"I hope he was giving you some good advice," said Mr. Gibson, his mouth turning down sarcastically.

Hugo frowned heavily. Sarah thought, he was probably thinking this was violating the privacy of communication between lawyer and client! Besides meddling in his private matters!

She said quickly, "He was. Quite good. He was telling me details I need to know about running the inn. And about grandfather's affairs."

"Running the inn?" Mr. Gibson took that up fast, leaning forward and staring at her. "You mean to stay then? You mean to run the Golden Goose?"

She hesitated. She was still not quite sure. "I don't know yet, Mr. Gibson," she said, more quietly. "I want to think of all possibilities. It is quite a big job to run this place, isn't it?"

"Big job, yes. Pretty big. Tough job," said Clarence. He leaned back, his long fingers tapping, tapping at the arm of the chair. When he noticed that Sarah was looking at his hand, he stopped the tapping, as though by an intense effort of will. "Your grandfather had quite a time of it, getting started," he said, absently.

"Yes, you probably knew him in those days, didn't you?" she said, encouragingly.

"Well, early enough. He was considerably older than I. More the grandfather sort," he said, and frowned heavily. He bit his lips, seemed to be struggling with himself. "Liked to meddle, the way grandparents do," he said, as though forced.

Suddenly she had the feeling that Clarence Gibson was saying something important to her. She strained to hear his words, and the meaning behind them. He had paused.

"I don't know, really," she said, softly, not to interrupt, but to encourage. "I didn't know my grandparents, you see."

"He did, though. Meddled. Everyone in town. Had

to know what was going on and why. Mad as fire if someone meddled in *his* business, though. Yep! Mad as fire," he said, with some satisfaction. "Started some trouble he couldn't stop, often enough."

"Oh, tell me about it," she said.

He frowned. "That is past history. Maxine won't like it if I gossip too long," he said. "Got to get back to the store. Left her and Pearl sewing like crazy. Leonard looking after the store, selling hats, which he hates. Good for him to do something he hates. Has to learn to do that. Might get the store someday, if Maxine marries him."

She did not know what to say. She didn't really know Leonard, but she felt he was rather a gloomy somber person beside Maxine's gay brightness. Perhaps Maxine could do better for herself than Leonard. Maxine did not seem overly keen to spend much time in his company.

She wondered about Maxine. There was probably a dearth of marriageable men in the community, and of course she had been intensely in love with that attractive Mr. Tim. She was probably not yet ready to marry. But when she did, Sarah rather hoped she would find someone more cheerful than Leonard.

"Your grandfather made many enemies, in town and outside," said Clarence, gazing at the bookcase intently, as though reading all the titles. His dark blue eyes were unfocused though, she saw. "Many enemies. Kind that did. Stubborn, strong-willed."

She held her breath. She dared not say a word, and she hoped Hugo would not. She glanced at Hugo, and saw him looking very thoughtfully at Clarence, a distant intent look in his brown eyes.

"Yep. In the days before the war, many years of them, this town was bitterly divided. Lots of talk about slavery, rights of states, and all that. We fought the war many a time, long before the war started."

She kept her mouth shut with an intense effort of

will. Clarence Gibson had started to talk, and what he said was immensely important to her, she knew, she had that funny feeling in the bottom of her stomach.

"Paintsville is a small town, holds its loves and hates," said Clarence. His gaze finally came back to her. "I admired old Adam, though we fought. You ought to find the gold, you know. There is gold, I know it. He taunted me about it, said if he went, I'd never find it. But it was hereabouts, I know that."

"Hidden," she said, softly, not to interrupt him.

"Yep, hidden. Somewhere. That was old Adam, never told his secrets. Mad as fire if they were found out, though. He always could get mad. Real angry." He paused for a long moment. "You ought to find that gold, Miss Sarah," he said, very quietly, his words almost whispered. "You find it—go back East, spend it, have a good life. Safe. Buy yourself some pretty clothes and hats, and get yourself a fine beau. Nice back East, not so violent as here."

She wanted to cry out, at the hidden threat in his tone. She stared at him, her eyes wider and wider.

"Yep, old Adam made enemies," he said, standing up, looking about in a troubled way, uneasy somehow. "Lots of trouble left over, I figure. You think about it, Miss Sarah. Don't make up your mind about staying 'til you think about it. Huh?" He looked down at her, his eyes shuttered and dark. He nodded abruptly, and went out of the room, almost stumbling over Hugo's long legs stretched out near the door.

They were both silent, listening to Clarence going down the stairs to the kitchen, his cheerful loud greeting to Justina. "How are you Justina? Miss Sarah is upstairs in her room. How about that! Thought you said she was out in the rain! Now, I knew she had more sense than that! Sensible girl, Miss Sarah!"

They did not hear Justina's low voice answering. They heard Clarence laugh, in a hard way, then the slam of the outside door.

Hugo finally stirred and got up. He peered steadily out into the dark hallway, as though looking for someone.

"No one here," he said, low. He turned back to Sarah. "Well, you have much to ponder, Miss Sarah. If there is anything I can do to help, anything at all, you have only to call upon me. I hope—I hope very much that I have given you some wholesome advice. I should hate to believe I was causing further trouble to you." He looked down at her in a very troubled way.

"Thank you very much—Hugo." She got up and went to the door with him, and put her hand in his outstretched large warm hand. She felt as though she wanted to cling to him and cry out for assistance. She could not do that. She forced a smile. "I have much to think about. Your advice, and Clarence Gibson's advice." She looked at him steadily.

"Yes, you must think about it. I'll go now. You will lock the door after me, won't you?"

She nodded, and he left. She locked the door firmly, and turned back into her lovely room, which seemed empty and somehow dark and shadowy, now that the two men had departed.

She did not feel like doing any more sewing, or studying of accounts, or even reading the comforting poems in the books of the huge bookcases. Yes, she had much to think about.

Joel, last night. His offer to buy the inn, his warning to leave. His hard anger, and possessive kisses.

Hugo, and all his advice, so confusing, so overwhelming, the duties sounding so very much. She did need help, a helpmeet, as he had said. She sighed heavily, and leaned her head back against the wide headrest of the rocker.

"Oh, grandfather," she whispered. "I wish you were here to help me! I'm so mixed up, and bewildered. Who are your enemies? Who are your friends? For they are mine also."

Clarence Gibson, with his thinly veiled warnings. She

should find the gold and go back East, where it was not so violent.

Roscoe, the blood streaming over his body, from the cut throat. The lovely braided rug saturated with his red blood.

Choking hands around her throat on the stairs. Whose hands? Joel? Clarence? Leonard? Zeke? Even Hugo? No, no, not Hugo, he had come running down the stairs with Billy Dexter and rescued her. He could not have—

Then who? Why? Did someone know the secret of the gold? Did they have to have her murdered, to find the gold and take it? Why did someone want to kill her? Why had Roscoe been murdered?

That horse don't never shy, he had said. That horse, she thought, that horse don't never shy. What horse? Had it been the rambling remark of a senile old man? Or something terribly vitally important?

Zeke came, and took her down to supper. He was still on guard. Somehow she felt terribly depressed that night. Joel did not come. Was he furious with her? She supposed it was just as well she did not see him. She should be angry with him, cold and haughty. And she didn't want to be angry with Joel, she really did like him.

He was so cheerful. He had made her laugh twice.

"It's quiet tonight," said Justina. "Too bad Mr. Joel, he had some work to do at the stage office. There a bad leak, he done told me."

"He should have come for dinner," she said, finally. "He needs a hot meal. He is so thin."

"That he is," said Justina, heartily. "He terrible thin. I'll send Zeke over with some food pretty quick. He needs his vittles."

Zeke was duly sent on his errand of mercy, which he did with great willingness. He did not return. He was very fond of Joel, said his mother, with a sigh. He was probably working with him, fixing the leaks.

Sarah was weary, and she wanted to think some

more. After dinner, she said, "I'll go on upstairs, Justina. I'll work in my room tonight. I want to go over grandfather's account books."

"Now, Miss Sarah, you wait till my Zeke gets back! You don't go upstairs alone." Justina sent an apprehensive look up the back stairs, and it sent a shiver through Sarah.

"I'll be okay. You wait at the bottom of the stairs, Justina. I'll sing out when I get to my room and get the door locked."

Justina didn't like it at all, and said so. But Sarah insisted. She could not go all her days followed by a black shadow of fear. She walked bravely up the stairs, repressing a shudder as she passed the closed door of the room that had been Roscoe's. She went on up the stairs, to her own room, and unlocked the door. The lamp on the table was still burning well.

"I'm okay, Justina," she called down.

"Okay, honey, lamb, you just lock your door so I can hear you, then you holler again that you all right!" Justina called.

Sarah went in, locked the door firmly, then yelled down again. "I'm fine, Justina!"

"Yes, ma'am! You have a good sleep, honey!"

"Thank you, goodnight, Justina!"

She sat down in her rocker again. She was shivering. It was all her imagination. As she had unlocked the door, she had seen a black shadow down the hall, toward the front of the inn. It had detached itself from the wall, she had thought, and had started slowly toward her. The figure of a man? She had thought it was a figure of a man, a black shadow moving toward her.

All her imagination, she said bravely to herself. It was silly to imagine—

She went still, the rocker stopped. She was looking at the door. Had she imagined a sound at the door? A faint brushing sound. She was looking at the door knob.

As she looked, she saw the light glistening on the shiny knob. It was turning, turning, slowly.

She held her breath. She was so scared she was cold.

It was turning, then slowly back again. Quiet. Then the brushing sound again, as though someone was there.

"Oh, God," she moaned to herself. "Oh—God—"

She waited, a long time. But there were no other sounds, nothing else at the door. But her mouth was dry, her heart racing. She could not bring herself to move, to think, to try to go to bed.

It was late before she could relax, and force herself to move from the rocker, to go to the bedroom, and go to bed.

Someone had been there, at her door. Someone had tried the knob. Someone—someone had tried to get in to her. Who?

Chapter 7

~~~~~~

Morning usually made things look brighter for Sarah. It was that way the next morning, her fifth day in Paintsville, she thought, with some surprise. It seemed as though she had been here much longer, maybe months.

She washed, dressed in her brightest blue wool dress, and went down to breakfast, followed by Zeke, silent, but grinning with pleasure at his role of guard. Justina greeted her happily, even Pearl looked up with a shy half-smile.

"There, now, you look more rested, Miss Sarah," said Justina. "You like it here, don't you, ma'am?"

She looked so eager and hopeful that Sarah had to say, "Yes, I like it here very much. I do hope it works out that I am able to remain."

"Lord, Lord, I been praying that very thing, Miss Sarah. Have some fresh ham, ma'am. I mixed up some biscuits, they be ready in a few minutes. You like your coffee like this, or a mite less black, or maybe some cream in it?"

She was obviously anxious to please, fussing about in her kindly way. Sarah could not help but be flattered at all her attentions. If Joel bought the inn, Justina would be well off, even better than with Sarah, for Justina and

96

Joel seemed to be good friends. But, of course, if Clarence Gibson or some other Copperhead bought the inn, she would not be doing so well.

Still, it was nice to believe that Justina liked Sarah for herself, and for her relationship and resemblance to old Adam, whom she had seemed to adore.

The eggs were delicious, in a small omelette, so light and fluffy it was like eating flavored air. The ham was cooked to perfection. When the biscuits were ready, small, hot, light, smothered with fresh butter and honey, Sarah sighed.

"I'm going to get fat, Justina!"

"Oh, no, ma'am," Justina chuckled. "Your kind, you never get fat. But you need some beef on your bones, like Mr. Joel say."

"That's right," said Joel, coming in from the back door. Sarah looked up, startled, met his straight-gazing gray eyes, promptly blushed, and looked down at her biscuit. "She looks better already, doesn't she, Justina? You keep on feeding her."

Maxine chimed in from behind him. Joel was holding the door for her, Sarah finally realized. She fluttered in, holding needles, threads, fabrics. "But not too much! Not to spoil that lovely figure! How are you, Sarah?"

"After all the compliments, Maxine, I'm floating up in the sky," she said, a little drily.

They all laughed, even little Pearl. Maxine sniffed the biscuits, and was promptly invited to sit down by Justina.

"Oh, I shouldn't," said Maxine, sitting down in front of a place, so eagerly that Sarah smiled at her.

"No one can resist Justina's cooking, Maxine, so don't even try. Do have some of the honey, it is so delicious! What is the heavenly flavor, Justina?"

Justina was busily dishing up ham and eggs for Joel, and Joel replied for her. "Clover. The bees are let loose to feast in it, then we feast in their honey. And I think sometimes they get into some of the wild flowers."

Sarah had thought she would feel very awkward

when she met Joel again. This was the first she had seen him since his passionate possessive embrace. But he seemed so easy, so humorous and calm, that she could almost imagine she had dreamed the embrace. Until she met his glance, fiery hot and dark gray. His words might be calm, but he was not inside, she thought. She turned back to Maxine, hastily, glad the girl had come.

"Oh, Maxine, I've been working on my old rose dress. I do want you to look at it, and see if I have done it right."

Maxine's delicately pretty face lighted up, and so did her large violet eyes. "Of course! What fun. Do let's work on that this morning instead of the couches. Do you know, I've finished one complete set of couch and chairs? Pearl was a marvelous help." She bestowed a gracious smile on the tiny dark girl, who stared down at her legs in embarrassment.

They discussed the mending, and repairing jobs. "I really should settle on a price to pay for the work," Sarah said thoughtfully. "Please don't protest, Maxine. Of course, I must pay for it. I talked to Hugo, I mean Mr. Forrester, and he said I must do this. It is only businesslike," she said firmly, as Maxine began to protest.

"But I enjoy doing it! If you knew what a pleasure it is to have something besides the same old things at the store! And the fabrics are so pretty. Don't pay me, Sarah, that is foolish. You'll need your money for other things. Besides—" Maxine paused thoughtfully, licked the honey from her small delicate fingers absently. "Dad said you might not stay. He said he didn't think you should, that the work was too much for you. Do you think it will be, Sarah?"

She hesitated, so long that everyone in the room was finally looking at her. "I really don't know, Maxine. I haven't decided whether to remain or to go back— home." She used the word "home" though she actually had come to feel more at home in the Inn of the Sign of the Golden Goose than she did back in Pennsylvania. And the Pennsylvania home had so many stricken memories in it, that she winced from the thought of returning. "In any event, things ought to be mended and polished and in good condition before I sell, shouldn't they?"

Justina's face darkened, she turned back to the huge fireplace and her heavy iron stove without speaking. Zeke and Pearl were listening in silence. Joel was staring down at his plate, eating ham and eggs as though life depended on it. Only Maxine spoke up.

Her pretty face seemed to cloud up, her figure drooped. "Oh, Sarah, I wish you wouldn't talk like that! You're the first good friend I've had in years—"

"Thank you, dear Maxine," said Joel, rather humorously.

"Oh, you know what I mean! The first girl friend! Everyone was so awfully jealous of me—because Tim preferred me, he always did, right from the time we were little. And after we were engaged, they wouldn't speak to me. That's true, isn't it, Joel?" She turned impatiently to Joel who grinned at her.

"No, it isn't, Maxine, and you know it. You're exaggerating as usual," he said, his gray eyes twinkling with fun. "The girls were very nice to you, they gave you parties—even though they were crying the whole time. You should have heard it, Sarah, the girls crying and crying, you could hear them all through town."

Even Maxine smiled a little, though she flipped her hand at him crossly. "Well, I mean it. I feel as though we could become very good friends. You are very much like Adam, and he was one of my *dearest* friends. He was so strong, and sure of himself, and he did give one advice, and he seemed to understand." She poured it all out in a breath, gave a deep sigh, and stuffed her mouth with hot biscuit.

Justina brought a fresh platter of hot biscuits to the table. She said, "Yes, sir, that Old Adam, he did understand people, he sholely did. Black people and white people, he did comprehend them, he sholely did, may he rest in peace."

Sarah wondered where Justina had learned the big

word, "comprehend," and was thinking about that when Zeke spoke up.

"Mr. Joel, you want to put the locks on today? I got the nails ready, like you say."

"Oh—yeah. That's a good idea. Sarah, don't lock your door, if you and Maxine are going up to your rooms. We'll come up and put fresh locks on."

"Fresh locks?" asked Maxine, alertly.

"That's right. We'll use all new keys, just in case some are still around here." Joel shoved back from the table, excused himself and was about to leave the room.

"Joel?" Sarah said, and was surprised at the little shock that went through her as he turned around quickly and looked right into her eyes. She felt confused whenever he looked directly at her. A funny feeling in her stomach made her dizzy, and she felt warm. Maybe it was the coffee—but she knew better. "Could you put on a bolt also? Then when I'm inside, I'll have double protection."

"I intend to put on a bolt." he said, brusquely, and left.

Maxine looked cross. "That's the kind of talk I don't like! No wonder you're scared and want to leave! Sarah, don't listen to them. I'm sure the danger is past. Why, it was probably some transient who came, some bum who killed Roscoe. There used to be men who'd stop in, and sleep in the rooms without old Adam knowing it. He got so mad at them, mad as fire."

"It could be," said Justina, pausing thoughtfully. "Sholely, they could have got in, with so many doors about. Bums looking for that trouble-making gold. Everybody done heered about that old gold, and go looking for it, thinking they be rich." She sniffed. "I wish I had a bit of gold from someone who *talk* about that gold, I be rich."

Sarah laughed, but she was the only one. Maxine still looked outraged and troubled. After breakfast, the two girls went up to Sarah's living room. Maxine looked at the dress, criticized one seam, offered to rip it out and

redo it, then started in again on Sarah. She wanted
Sarah to promise to stay, she hadn't met anyone in
years whom she liked half so well, she was sure Sarah
would be safe, and in any event there were plenty of
men about to protect them.

Sarah was pleased that Maxine felt so strongly about
this. She too had not had a good close girl friend for
years. It would be good, she thought, to have a friend
living next door, a nice friendly girl like Maxine, with
whom to share confidences, and work, and sewing, and
advice.

They shut and locked the door while Sarah tried on
the old-rose dress. It did look fine now, that Maxine
had shaped the seam so deftly over the bustline.
Maxine praised her, and criticized in one breath, telling
her to gain a little weight in her hips. and lose some in
her waist. She told her to wear brighter colors, offered
to run over to the store and get a beautiful blue she
had.

Sarah refused, laughing a little, but immensely
pleased at Maxine's frankness and help. "No, no, one
new dress is plenty for now, Maxine. And when will I
ever wear this? Nothing goes on in Paintsville, does it?"

"You'll be surprised! Wait 'til the rains let up, and
the winters begin. We have dances every Saturday
night! And even singing socials. You should hear Joel
sing, he is fine. He has a good voice."

Joel knocked brusquely on the door, and scowled at
Sarah when she opened it. "I thought I told you
to—oh, you have on your new dress." He looked at her
up and down, and she blushed hotly again. He had no
right to look at her like that. "I like it," he said, more
pleased. "That color is good. You should wear brighter
colors."

"Just what I told her. Now, you get out so Sarah can
change back, and we can do some sewing while you
work!" Maxine put her hand on his chest and pushed
him back into the hallway.

It was a happy morning, for all the drizzling cold rain

outside, and the dark storm clouds which kept drawing up and unloading their unwelcome lightning and water. Maxine and Sarah sewed the trim on the dress, each working at one sleeve and one side of the hem, making the work go more than twice as fast.

Joel and Zeke ripped out the old lock, and put a new one in. Then they worked at putting the bolt on, a huge heavy bolt which made Maxine exclaim in scorn.

"Sarah will just lock herself in, and someone will have to climb in the window and rescue her! Joel, it's just like a man, so *thoughtless!* What does she want with that ugly heavy old thing! And you've been scaring her to death! She won't stay if you keep scaring her."

"Reckon she is still in danger," said Joel, quietly, when Maxine gave him a chance to get a word in.

"Oh, poof! I explained it was probably a bum who got in, and maybe Roscoe surprised him in the rooms trying to find the gold. That old gold. Sarah, I wish you would hurry up and find it, and stop all this trouble! You are very much like Old Adam, you think like him. Why don't you figure it out?"

They all looked at her. She shrugged, smiling. "I'll put my mind to it, you all seem to think it matters so much! But I wish you would tell me more about grandfather. How can I figure like him if I don't know what he was like?"

Maxine promptly started a long enthusiastic monologue about Old Adam, and what he did for people, and how much everyone had loved him or hated him through the years. She stopped talking only long enough to go over to the store and bring back a bright blue silk fabric, which she declared firmly would be their next project, another new dress for Sarah.

Joel looked at the blue fabric critically as it was held up to Sarah by the enthusiastic bubbling Maxine. "Yes, it's the color of her eyes. I vote for it."

Zeke was grinning ear to ear. Sarah sighed and gave in, and agreed to let Maxine cut it out for her. She went on sewing the black velvet trim on the old rose material while Maxine took one of Sarah's dresses and cut out the blue silk. The girl could talk as fast as she worked, Sarah thought. And she was certainly determined! Once she made up her mind, not much could stop her.

Joel had Sarah try the bolt several times before he was satisfied with the fit. She would try it, declare it was too heavy to handle. He would work and work at it, then have her try it again. He was very careful in his work, she thought, careful and precise as Maxine in her sewing and fitting.

Joel completed his work, and he and Zeke left after making Sarah lock and bolt the door after them, to Maxine's open scorn.

"Those men!" Maxine complained bitterly. "Leonard is just as bad. Why, I went out alone in the dark the other night, and you would think I had gone out to steal! Leonard was just awful! He bawled me out so—and Dad was almost as bad. Surely they don't think there really is any danger about, do you?"

Sarah replied carefully, not liking the worried shadows in the lovely violet eyes. "There probably is some danger, Maxine, because poor old Roscoe was murdered. But as you said, it might be a bum, and the men want to be careful of us. It is good of them, isn't it? Joel was kind to take so much trouble."

"Oh, he's stuck on you already," said Maxine, with her devastating frankness. "I can tell by the look in his eyes every time he looks at you! He used to listen to your grandfather tell about you, and he read all your letters to your grandfather. And he adored your picture." She paused and looked at the startled Sarah critically. "It doesn't look *much* like you anymore. But the war—" Her voice quieted, moodily. "The war aged us all, I guess. Terribly. I think I grew thirty years older, when I—heard—about—my darling—Tim." Her voice cracked, and she put her head down on her hand for a moment.

"Oh, Maxine—I'm so—sorry." How futile words were, Sarah thought. She wished she knew the girl better, whether it would help to put her arms about her, and comfort her, or be brisk and cheery and help her forget. She was silent then, not knowing what to do.

Maxine finally wiped her eyes carefully, blew her nose, and sat up determinedly. "I have to begin to forget," she said, her voice still broken. "I have to—I have to forget. It is past, it can't be helped. But whenever I think—of the future—it is so empty—I can't bear—"

Sarah was immensely relieved to hear Joel's voice at the door. "Sarah. Try the bolt! Come on, girls, stop gossiping and come down to lunch. Justina has some heavenly chicken, and I am starving!"

"Men, always thinking about food," said Maxine, in an almost normal voice. She wiped her eyes carefully once more. "Come on, Sarah, we'll eat. You ought to rest this afternoon—unless you have some bright idea about where to find the gold," she added in a joking tone as Sarah slid the bolt open. It worked very smoothly now for such a heavy bolt.

They went down to lunch, and talked some more. The chicken was heavenly, as Joel had predicted, boiled with some herbs and spices, with onions and carrots and other fresh vegetables and potatoes added. So tender and succulent it was, Sarah ate much more than she had intended, to Justina's satisfaction.

Dessert was a delectable raspberry custard, made with some canned raspberries from Old Adam's garden, said Justina. Maxine said she had eaten too much, and was going home to sleep. Zeke was yawning too. Joel said he was going to work on mending the roof.

They looked at Sarah. "Sleep," she finally said, with a sigh. "Justina, could you be persuaded not to cook so well?"

They all laughed. "No, no, don't suggest that," said Joel. He patted Justina's brown hand as she put a hot steaming cup of black coffee before him. "You just keep right on the way you are. You're perfect."

She chuckled with pleasure, beaming down at Joel. He was really her favorite, Sarah thought. No wonder, he could be so charming and so pleasant. He seemed so cheerful and so calm, as though nothing ruffled or upset him. But she knew better now.

He could be violently passionate, angry, loving, full of desire, full of hungers that made hard demands on a woman. She wondered what he would be like if a girl married him, what he would be like if—Then she found herself getting hot and flushed, and she shut off the thoughts as well as she could.

She went up to her suite of rooms, locked the door, shot home the bolt with a sense of satisfaction. No one could get past that bolted door, Joel had done his job too well.

She removed her dress, put on a robe, and lay down under a blanket to sleep. But sleep would not come. She kept thinking about Joel, the way his dark gray eyes stormed, the way he had stared at her, the way he had held her against his warm body and forced her with his strength, until she had been weak and helpless under his warm mouth. His kisses, they had been so hard—yet so sweet.

She rolled over on the bed, tried not to think. She wanted to sleep. Gold, she thought, she would try to imagine where her grandfather had kept the gold.

She remembered about the slaves. He had prepared a room in the basement, behind the walls, Joel had said. She had not looked carefully at that. She hadn't been in the basement much at all. Suddenly she was very wide awake. What if old Adam had sealed off that room—after putting the gold in it? That might be the sort of clever idea he would have, a rather obvious hiding place which everyone knew about, because the slaves had been found and betrayed.

Mad as fire, he was, Clarence had said. *Mad as fire when his secrets were discovered—mad as fire when someone else meddled.*

She wondered who had betrayed the slaves.

She could not sleep. Her mind went around and around. Maxine had urged her to find the gold, then no one would bother her. Was that true? If so, the best thing she could do would be to find the gold, deposit it safely in the bank.

"Oh," she whispered to herself, exasperated. "Oh, I wish I could sleep—"

It was intensely quiet in the inn. She could faintly hear the pounding from next door where Joel was working on the roof. How he worked and worked. He was probably out in the pouring rain, oblivious to it as he pounded on fresh shingles.

No one would be out in this weather, she thought.

Finally she got up, put on her plaid dress and wrapped her shawl about her. She would just go downstairs and look in the basement a few minutes. That would not hurt. She didn't want anyone with her in case she found the gold, and the wrong person had accompanied her. She didn't add up in her mind whom that wrong person might be.

Quietly she opened her door, locked it after her. She crept down the stairs to the kitchen. All was quiet. Justina and Pearl often slept in the afternoon, they got up so early in the morning. Zeke went down to the stables every free hour he had, to groom his beloved horses.

She hesitated a long moment as she opened the door to the basement. It was rather dark down there, on that gloomy afternoon. But she found a candle on the shelf, took a flint and lit the candle, then started down the stairs.

The stairs were firmly made, with a railing on each side. How like her grandfather, she thought, to do something well and solidly, to last. She walked on down slowly, the candle casting flickering lights and shadows around her.

She came to the bottom of the steps and paused. She could see a few basement windows, and beyond them was a torrent of water. The flood waters were pounding against the windows, she saw, and only the glass held them out. Trickles of water ran down the walls of the basement. The walls would need more whitewashing and calking after the rains finally let up.

She saw the bookcase and pantry shelves, studied them curiously, finally found the shelves behind which the little secret room was supposed to be. She pulled gently, then more firmly.

Finally she set down the candle on a nearby work table, and yanked more firmly. The shelves were supposed to swing back when a spring was touched. She bent down, trying to find the right way to touch it.

She didn't hear anyone until it was too late. A step squished behind her, then she felt a sharp blow on her head.

She sank down into black painful darkness.

She wakened slowly, knowing first a throbbing painful hurt in her head and shoulders, The nerves in her neck throbbed in jerks. She turned her head, moved to get out of bed—

She found herself lying on the watery floor of the dark basement. It took a long time to think. Her brain seemed so foggy and numb, and the pain kept shooting through her neck and shoulders and head. She finally moved, and found that the reason she felt so stiff was that she was tightly bound, her hands fastened, and her feet tied. She was lying near the shelves she had been trying to examine. The candle was gone, so was her shawl.

Panic leaped through her. She struggled until her breath was gone. A gag over her mouth was stifling her. She moaned, tried to cry out—it was no good. Someone wanted her bound and helpless—was someone going to return and finish the job? Murder? In her own basement, of her very own inn?

She managed to turn her head, stared about the dimness of the basement. No one was there. But her eyes widened in fresh fear. Someone had opened those windows; the water, which had been held back by the glass, was pouring in.

The basement was flooding. The water was rising rapidly about her. Her dress was soaked and her feet were lying in water, her hips and her hands were inches deep as the water rose about her limp body.

"Must—get—up—" she told herself. "Must—Sarah, must—get up—"

She tried to wrench the ropes, but only hurt herself, her wrists stinging painfully where the ropes tore them and the waters soaked them. She tried to struggle to her feet, they would not hold her, she was too cold and stiff.

She saw the edge of a small table, perhaps a workbench of a child. It had sharp edges. Sharp enough to cut the ropes? She edged over to it, almost swimming in the deepening waters. She was panting for breath, as the gag was cutting off her breathing as well as cutting into the sides of her mouth. She lifted herself enough to put her hands at her back to the edge of the workbench. She sawed desperately. The wood was too smooth to cut the rope.

She leaned back against the bench, half-crying with effort and fear. Someone wanted her dead—someone wanted her dead— It was no bum, after the gold. Someone wanted to kill her, Sarah, to kill—

She would drown down here, unless she had help— Help—

She slid down carefully against the bench. She worked and worked at the gag, rubbing the back of her sore painful head against the small workbench. And finally the gag began to slide upward, painfully, hurting her mouth. Better the pain than death, she thought, closed her eyes, and pushed hard.

The gag came off.

And she began to scream. It was feeble at first, her breath choked and coming hard. She wanted to yell "Help," but she couldn't manage any words. But she could scream, the yelling ripping her throat with the effort.

She screamed and screamed, paused, got her breath, and screamed again.

And finally heard the pounding of heavy-booted feet. The murderer coming back? Oh, God, oh, God, she thought. And she screamed again for good measure.

The door to the basement was ripped open, a man pounded down the stairs. She heard Justina call fearfully, "What is it, Mr. Joel—what is it?"

Joel splashed through the heavy deep waters to Sarah, lying against the bench. He wasted no words. He picked her up bodily and carried her to the stairs, and up them. He was like a giant, she thought. Funny, he didn't seem like a giant, he was slim, but he was so strong—

He carried her as though she were a feather, but she must have been heavy. She was so soaked that she dripped with water, and her dress was hanging so heavily that it kept catching on the steps and the railing. He carried her up the stairs, and she saw Justina's scared face and wide eyes.

He brought her into the lighted warm kitchen, and over to the fire, and set her down on the bench. "Get a knife, Justina," he said curtly. "She's tied up tight."

"Lord—have—mercy—" Justina brought two knives. Joel worked on the bonds on her feet, Justina worked carefully, tenderly at the bonds on her torn hands.

"Who did it, Sarah?" Joel asked her tensely, pausing for a moment. His dark gray eyes were very stormy now, he was panting for breath, his tanned face seemed almost green in the firelight. "Who did it?"

She shook her head, then began to cry because it hurt so much, and she was so relieved. She could not speak, her throat hurt too much. She was shivering with the chill and the reaction.

But she was safe. Justina and Joel had her, and she was safe. She closed her eyes and wept silently.

Chapter 8

〰〰〰〰〰〰〰〰〰〰〰〰〰〰〰〰〰〰〰〰

Sarah could not talk for a long time. She felt numbness all through her, even her throat and tongue. Joel brought clean clothes from her room, then left the kitchen briefly while Justina stripped her, dried her with huge towels, put the long nightgown and robe on her.

By that time, Hugo Forrester, Billy Dexter, Zeke, Maxine, and Leonard had all come, demanding to know what had happened. Pearl lingered near the door to their rooms, as though ready to dash inside at the least hint of danger.

"What happened?" everyone was asking Joel.

"I don't know. We'll have to wait until Sarah recovers to find out." He was cross and brusque. Justina finally let them come near Sarah who was sitting in a big chair, her feet on a stool.

She was dried, warmed, but she still shivered. The fear had been too great. Justina fixed her all-cure favorite, herb tea, and brought Sarah a steaming cup. She could not hold it. Joel took the cup from Justina, and crouched beside Sarah to hold it for her.

"There, drink up, that's my girl," he said, in a low tone. His gray eyes were dark and stormy. She took one sip, and shook her head.

"Hot," she managed to say.

He reached for a spoon, dipped out some liquid, blew on it, put it to her lips. She swallowed it slowly, painfully, past the thick lumps in her throat.

Maxine came up behind her, began stroking her wet hair. She took a towel, rubbed very gently. Sarah winced, moved from her. "What's the matter, Sarah?" asked Maxine.

"Hurt," she said huskily.

Maxine bent over, parted the hair, examined her head. "There's a big lump here, and it's open. Oh, dear. She must have hit her head when she fell. Did she fall down the stairs, Joel?"

"Sure, she fell down the stairs, and while she was unconscious, she put ropes around her feet and hands and a gag at her mouth, so she couldn't move," he said, very sarcastically.

Everyone gasped, and was silent for a moment. Justina's face was sad and troubled as she moved about the kitchen, gathering up the wet clothes. She shook out the soaking wet dress, studied it gravely as though all her attention was on how to restore it to cleanliness and beauty.

"But then—someone—meant to kill her," said Billy Dexter bluntly. Sarah shivered violently inside the warm nightgown and robe. Hugo Forrester brought over a blanket from a pile Joel had brought down. He unfolded it, put it about her tenderly.

"Sarah, can you tell us who it was?" he asked, his face concerned. His big hands were shaking a little, she noted.

She moved her head slowly from side to side. Even that little made the pain go ringing through her head and neck once more. She winced.

"Justina, get some of that ointment," said Joel. Maxine was still gently examining the bump and cut on the back of her head. Sarah felt surrounded by love and attention, but even that did not help the crazy fear inside her.

Someone had tried to kill her. Someone had meant to kill her. Someone had struck her on the head, tied her up, opened the windows to let her drown.

"Someone is crazy around here," said Leonard, suddenly, positively. "That's it. There is a bum around loose, and he's crazy. He's heard about the gold, and he is hiding in the inn to try to get it."

Joel spooned a little more herb tea into Sarah's mouth, then laid aside the cup. He stood up, took the ointment from Justina, and moved Maxine over. Very gently, very carefully, he applied the ointment to the cuts. It stung violently for a moment, then subsided to a throbbing. When he had finished, he set aside the ointment. Very slowly, not to hurt her, he unbound her hair from the neat braiding and unfastened the hair to spread it out on her shoulders. The golden-brown hair was spread down and around her. Then he took a towel, and wiped each strand of hair with it, so carefully that she did not even feel any pain over it.

She leaned back with a sigh of relief. Joel was looking after her, he would not let them hurt her. Then. Him. The bum looking for gold. Had it been the gold? Or was there something else? Why hurt Sarah? Why attack Sarah? Why not search for the gold quietly? Or had she been close to finding it, and the bum was afraid she would get it before he did?

Or was it not a bum? Was it someone she knew, but did not really know? Could it be Joel? Or Justina, or Zeke? Or Leonard? Or even kindly, friendly Maxine? Could it be strong sturdy Billy Dexter, working hard, frankly tired of his runs? Could it be suave Hugo Forrester, just starting out in his law practice? It could be anyone, anyone at all. Clarence Gibson, the banker, the sheriff who was supposed to be out of town— anyone at all.

She closed her eyes and tears trickled down her cheeks. The talk in the room was running on around her, the exclamations, the attempts at explaining. Only she and Joel and Justina were quiet, and of course, little Pearl, standing big-eyed at the door to her rooms.

"I'll take her up to her rooms," said Joel, presently. "All this chatter isn't helping her head!" he added rudely.

At once they were all solicitous. Hugo Forrester wanted to carry her upstairs. Billy Dexter was sure he was the only one strong enough. Joel brushed them all aside, and carried her up the stairs himself. Justina unlocked and opened the door, the others crowded after her.

Joel laid her down on her bed. The quilt was laid back neatly, just as she had left it when she went down to the basement. She shivered again, as she thought that the mere act of leaving her rooms and going downstairs had been close to killing her.

He settled her on the bed, took off her slippers, laid one blanket on her. "It that warm enough, then, Sarah?" he asked, gazing down at her.

"Another—blanket," she said thickly.

He unfolded another one, and laid it tenderly about her, brushing the soft wool up about her aching throat. She cuddled down inside the warmth. Would she ever be warm again? She shivered and shivered.

Justina brought some more herb tea. Maxine wanted to remain, but she was chattering. Sarah closed her eyes, her brows drawing into a frown of pain.

Her head ached and throbbed. Even lying it on the pillow hurt. She wanted to be alone and safe. But she felt too tired and weak to get up and shoo them all away, and bolt the door to her room.

Joel sent the protesting Hugo and Billy and Maxine and Leonard away. "Justina, you sit here with her 'til she sleeps," he said. "I'm going down to the basement with Zeke and get those windows closed. We'll have to get the water out. You got a hose about?"

Billy offered to help, so did Hugo. Justina settled down in the rocker near the bed, folded her hands on her lap, and looked like it would take an earthquake to move her. Everyone else was gone. Silence descended like peace on Sarah.

She closed her eyes. Somehow Justina was comforting. She would never hurt Sarah. Never.

She would half-sleep, then her mind would jolt her awake, and she would shiver again, cuddling deeper into the blankets. Someone wanted to kill her. Someone had tried to kill her.

That water creeping up about her, that cold chill water.

And the ropes that had burned her legs and wrists—the gag at her mouth, cutting her lips. She reached up tentatively, and touched her lips. They felt raw and bruised, but there was no blood.

"Miss Sarah?" Justina's soft voice breathed the words. "You want me to sing you to sleep? Get your mind off your troubles?"

"Yes—please—"

The soft mellow voice spread balm on her. Justina's singing was so calming, so soothing. She sang the old spirituals, the rhythmic gentle work songs, slowly and deliberately, drawing them out in a lulling way.

And finally Sarah was able to close her eyes, and relax, and fall into a restful sleep. The words of the songs followed her into her dreams, the healing plaintive acceptance of trouble.

She slept until dusk. When she wakened, Justina and Pearl were sitting near her bed, quietly, not saying a word. Pearl's big eyes were the first thing Sarah saw as she stirred and opened her own eyes. She wakened slowly, not remembering anything, but the memories began to come back slowly.

Justina was gazing at her anxiously. Sarah smiled at her.

"Oh—I slept—so hard," she said, huskily. Her voice had come back.

Justina's smile showed her relief. "Good, Miss Sarah, that be good. I bring you some eggs, some tea, something easy on you. Pearl, you stay right here, don't you move. If anybody come, no matter who, you scream like you was killed! Hear me?"

Pearl nodded her small dark head, not stirring from her place. She seemed to crouch back in the chair as her mother bustled from the room. She kept glancing from Sarah to the door and back again, like a scared alert little animal.

"Pearl, you don't—need to be—afraid—ever again," Sarah was moved to say. "You're safe. Why are you so frightened?"

Pearl stared at her, her velvety dark eyes big. Then to Sarah's shock, she spoke. "Oh—miss—I be scared. I saw—I saw things—I saw—"

Then a little shock seemed to go through her body, at her own daring. She closed her mouth, looked more frightened than ever.

"You saw things—where—down South? They can't come for you here, Pearl," said Sarah, very carefully. She wanted so badly to soothe the girl. The evil past was behind her. Would the terror of it remain with her all her life?

Pearl nodded, then shook her head. "Not South. No, that over, that done," she whispered in her soft voice. "Here. In the inn. I saw—I saw—" Again she stammered to a halt.

Justina bustled back into the room. She saw Sarah half-sitting up, leaning toward Pearl. "Now you lie right down, honey lamb! You mustn't get up. I got some omelette, and some tea, and a bit of soft biscuit for you. Pearl, you go down to the kitchen and see to the biscuits."

Pearl fairly ran from the room, her scared little face peering back from the doorway toward Sarah for a moment. Sarah lay back, disappointed, puzzled. What had Pearl seen, or thought she saw? Why was she so terribly fearful? Was it anything to do with Sarah, and the inn? Or did she have nightmares of the South?

Justina fed her, refusing to allow Sarah to be more

than propped slightly by pillows. She fed her some delicious plain omelette, light and fluffy, some more herb tea, bits of soft biscuit from the centers of her own crisp ones. When Sarah was finished, and lay back down again, the rough work hand gently smoothed her soft hair for a moment.

"There, Miss Sarah, you rest some more. We look after you, don't you never fret."

Sarah caught her hand, pressed it to her cheek gratefully. "Thank you, Justina. What would I do without you?"

"And Mr. Joel, don't you forget Mr. Joel," said Justina. "He save you. He always look after you, just like he look after old Adam. He a good fine man, that one."

Sarah closed her eyes. She was remembering that afternoon, when Joel had raced down the stairs to rescue her, the strength of his arms as he had picked her up and carried her up to safety.

She fell into a light sleep, comforted by the fact that Justina had settled down into the rocker again. Justina told her that Pearl would fix supper for the men, she would remain with Sarah.

She finally slept hard, wakened to find a small candle burning on the table near the door. She turned her head, aware of the dull pain and throbbing in her neck and forehead. This time she remembered what had happened.

Someone was sitting in the rocker, his head back. Not Justina. No, this was someone more slim, and alert, his eyes watching her.

She half-sat up. "Joel?" she said, aghast.

"It's me. Lie down, Sarah. It's about three in the morning."

"What are—you doing—in my bedroom?" she stammered.

"Watching over you," he said, grimly, not smiling. "Lie down. Get some sleep. No one will bother you tonight."

"Well!" She lay back, blinking. No man had ever

invaded her bedroom as Joel had done! He seemed to feel he could come and go where he pleased. She thought of his words, *You belong to me, Sarah!* Did he take them literally?

Joel set his head against the back of the rocker, and watched her calmly, his mouth twitching a little as though in some hidden amusement. She lay there, feeling a little heat fuming through her. The nerve of him! Did he think saving her life gave him special privileges?

And what of her reputation? What if word got out, as it surely must, that Joel had spent the night in her bedroom? This small town was full of gossip. What a juicy morsel this would be!

She gathered up her strength and her anger. She would not let gratitude to him govern her judgment.

"Joel," she said, very firmly and coldly. "You must go. I'll get up and bolt the door after you. You can see that it certainly is not the proper thing for you to remain. How Justina could permit it—"

"Hoity-toity," he said rudely. "You stay in bed, or I'll put you back under the covers myself! I'm staying here the night, because it is either me or Justina, and she needs her sleep. So you just stay put, young lady from the East, and forget your society manners and your polite ways. It isn't polite or nice to be murdered, either, may I remind you!"

She shuddered. The memory of her awakening in that water-filled basement, bound hand and foot, gagged, helpless, swept back over her like a shock wave. It would be a nightmare for years, she thought. She would always recall that horrible time, as the minutes ticked by, and she fought to force the gag off her head, to be able to scream.

"No," she said faintly. "It isn't very—nice—"

Her voice dragged.

"So lie back," he said, more gently, "and let yourself be looked after. In the hospital wards, you often were in the same rooms at night with men, weren't you?"

"Well—yes—"

"Just pretend you're in a hospital, and I'm your nurse," he said, definitely.

There was silence for a long time. She lay back, thinking about it. Would the proper gossipy town of Paintsville think of Joel as a nurse in a hospital? Or as a terribly attractive young man in the bedroom with a girl?

Her thoughts wandered to other matters. Who had hated her enough to try to kill her? Why had she been attacked those two times? Was it connected with the murder of Roscoe?

Her mind went round and round, restlessly. She had slept enough so that it was difficult to return to sleep, particularly since Joel was in the room with her, watching her, listening for any sounds.

She wondered if she would have minded if Hugo Forrester had been the man in the rocker. What if she had wakened to find Hugo there? Would she have felt the same way? He was so safe, so fine and intelligent. He too liked her very much, yet he was such a gentleman, courteous and never rude. He wanted to look after her interests, he was concerned about her. She liked him.

Yet she could not imagine him sitting in the rocker, awake all night, rudely invading her bedroom to guard her. She simply could not picture it. He would have too much concern for her reputation to do that.

Joel, now, he never let conventions stop him, she thought. She frowned a little, her mind all mixed up. What did she want? Did she want Joel to leave, and preserve her reputation? Or did she want him to remain, and protect her?

Her mind went around and around, not helped by the fact that the wound on the back of her head was throbbing more painfully. She rubbed the back of her neck, and sighed a little. Joel turned in his chair.

"More ointment, Sarah?" he asked, softly.

"Yes. Is there any around?"

"Right here." He got up, brought the small box to

the bed. Then, to her shock, he sat down on the bed, and helped her sit up with his hand around her shoulder.

"Joel—really, I can put it on—" He was disturbingly close to her, and she only wore her nightgown. It was high up about her neck, and very prim and proper, the sleeves down to her wrists. Yet, he was a man, and very close—

"Don't be foolish. Turn your back so I can get at it. I should have cut your hair around the wound," he added thoughtfully, and put a very light careful touch of ointment on the wound, "but I couldn't stand to cut it. Your hair is too pretty and soft. There—how is that?"

Between the ointment and the flattery, she thought, she felt much better! "Thank you," she said meekly.

He pounded her pillows vigorously, probably his version of plumping them, she decided. "There you are, lie down again, Sarah." And he added impudence to his other crimes, by stroking his hand against her cheek and throat as she lay back. "You are soft, your skin is soft as silk," he said.

"Joel—don't," she said, catching her breath. "I really think—you should go—let me bolt the door— that will be all right—"

"Nope. I'm staying the night." He got up, set the ointment on the table, and sat down in the rocker again. He put his feet up on a small footstool, and leaned back. "And if you're quiet enough, I might even get some sleep," he said, rudely, with a little chuckle.

Anger flared up in her a moment, then amusement. He surely did know how to stir her up! And his sense of humor was never quenched for long. She thought idly about him, as silence settled on the bedroom once more. Joel, fighting for four years in the mud and swamps and fallen trees, killing, shooting— She could practically see his grim determined face over the sights of a rifle. She thought, he is so thorough, he would be a good shot, he would kill very efficiently. And he had lived through it, though he had been wounded, and his hip crippled.

He had killed. She knew that. And Joel always did everything very completely and thoroughly. He would be a good shot, and he would be good with a knife, and good with his hands—

She shivered involuntarily, afraid of her very thoughts. He could kill with his hands—of course. She remembered what soldiers had told her, how they had raved in their fevers, telling of killing men with their bare hands when their bullets were gone, when the heat of battle made them mad. One man had been half-crazed with the battle lust, his eyes bright and reddened, telling her how he had killed men with his bare hands, forcing them down in the swampy waters, holding them under 'til all the fight was out of them.

She shivered again and again. Someone might have returned to the basement—Joel?—and held her under the rising waters, gagged and helpless as she was. Someone might have held her under, choking her efficiently, thoroughly, until she was quite helpless and dying, and then she would—die—

She turned in the bed, restlessly, until she could see Joel again. His eyes were open, watching her in the flickering light of the candle.

Had he come to help her, to save her, to protect her? Or was he waiting the moment to kill, more efficiently than had been done in the basement?

Did he love her, or hate her? Did he want the inn, and the gold, enough to kill her? If he couldn't have her, if he thought that she liked Hugo Forrester well enough to marry him, would Joel kill?

She lay there, her eyes half-closed, watching Joel alertly. He had overheard her conversation with Hugo Forrester. He had been fighting mad, furiously angry, his gray eyes almost black, so grimly angry that he had pulled her to him, kissed her possessively, told her that *she belonged to him.*

She belonged to no one, she thought proudly. She was herself, Sarah Overmiller, proud and independent, making her own way. She had inherited the Inn, at the Sign of the Golden Goose, and she could run it. Hugo Forrester thought so, and he was a very smart man.

It would take a lot of work, but she could run the Inn.

If no one killed her first.

She sighed again, turned over to her other side, away from Joel's watching look. If he wanted to kill her, he could do so. She was too weak to fight him. He was strong, she knew that now. He had more strength in his lean arms than one could imagine. He had carried her, dripping wet, up the basement stairs to the kitchen, later on up to her bedroom. And she was no light-weight. Even though she needed "beef on her bones," she thought drowsily.

Joel stirred. She was alert in a moment. He got up and came over to the bed, and sat down beside her.

"Can't you sleep, Sarah?" he asked, softly.

"No. My mind goes round and round," she said, weakly. She turned over to her back and looked up at him. She was so limp, if he wanted to kiss her—rape her even—she could not fight him off. If he wanted to kill her, he could, easily.

"Let it slow down, then, Sarah," he said. His tone was so tender, that *Sarah* sounded more like *Sarie.* He put his big hand on her forehead, held it there a moment. "No fever," he said. Slowly, he began to stroke her hair away from her forehead. "Does that hurt, Sarie?" he asked.

"No." It felt good, though she would not admit it. She closed her eyes with pleasure. His hand was rough with work, like Justina's hand, but it was so gentle, so soothing.

"The weather is so bad now," he said, after a pause, in a low soothing drawl, "that you can't imagine how pretty it is here in the winter. When the rains let up, and the fields dry, pretty soon it's snowing. All the little white flakes start filling up the fields, and covering the corn shocks. And the snow sticks to the trees, 'til they're like fairyland. All pretty and white and shining in the sun. The bushes get covered with the white, and the red berries shine out like a Christmas tree."

He went on talking, softly, like that, his hand stroking and stroking over her forehead. She had her eyes closed, listening to him, her thoughts following his words, instead of her own worrisome troubles.

He was certainly unconventional about remaining in a lady's bedchamber, she thought once. Joel—he didn't care—about conventions.

"And the spring, you won't believe the spring, here, Sarie," he was almost whispering. She had to strain to hear him. "The bushes bloom with yellow, all over the back yard. The bees start singing around, and whizzing, and building more beehives. The flowers are blooming, all red and yellow and purple. You'll like the violets, they are so beautiful, so purple and yellow, we got yellow ones as big as your eyes. In the woods, the little wild flowers will be perking up their heads, so fragile and pretty, like the wind would blow them down, white, and stripey pink, and blue—as blue as your eyes. The farmers will be plowing their fields, turning up the dirt so black and thick and fertile."

Her mind was blurring, pleasantly. She could picture the things he was saying, the little wild flowers blowing in the wind, the black fields, turned up by the plow. His hand was like magic, smoothing away her troubles and her worries.

She sighed a little, softly, and her mind seemed to sink down, down, into a pleasant brown darkness, lit with a little flickering candle. His voice was going on, and on, but she couldn't hear the words much longer. Pity. She wanted to hear what Joel was saying—but she couldn't keep on listening—her mind was blurring, blurring—

She thought once of the wild swirling waters of the basement, but the memory had dimmed. She remembered more the strength of Joel's arms as he had carried her up, and up, and up—

Into darkness, and safety, and quiet, and peace. With his hand stroking over her forehead and her hair, so soothingly, and his voice going on and on, murmuring now—

And she was finally deeply asleep.

Chapter 9

~~~~~~

She wakened several times in the night. Joel was still there, half-asleep, coming alert when she stirred, silent unless she spoke to him.

When Sarah finally became aroused, the dull gray dawn was creeping through the windows, and she heard a bird singing. She looked out at the bleak darkness of the back yard, and thought of how Joel said it was so pretty with yellow bushes in the springtime. Would she be here to see the spring in Paintsville?

Would she be back East, safely in Pennsylvania? *Or would she be dead?*

She turned slowly in bed, and saw Joel sleeping deeply, his head against the back of the rocker. The lines of his face were deeply carved, she could see the high cheekbones, the sharp planes, the hard chin. Sleeping, he seemed so vulnerable, yet strong also. Like a mountain cat that could come alert and snarling in a moment.

Someone cautiously opened the door to the room, and a draft blew a chill with it. Joel was awake in a moment, lunging up and out of the chair, facing the door.

"Lawdy, it's just me!" wailed Zeke, cringing back, his eyes wide in alarm.

Joel stared at him, shook his head hard, rubbed his hair back sheepishly. "Must have been asleep," he said. "Lord, thought I was back in the war." He shook himself like a cat, and seemed to come alert in a few seconds.

"Mama sent me up to watch over Miss Sarah whilst you get some breakfast," said Zeke, still watching his mentor with cautious wariness.

"Right," said Joel. He turned around and stared down at Sarah. "You awake, Sarah?"

"Yes, I'm awake." She felt suddenly shy of him. He had watched over her while she slept, studying her face, seeing her limp and helpless and warm in bed.

"Fine. I'll go down now. Zeke, you yell out like crazy if anyone comes in. And I mean anybody!" He saw Zeke settled down in the front room, then went out, looking back one more time at Sarah, before he closed the door.

She snuggled down in bed again. She didn't want to move. Her head throbbed dully, except when the sore place on the back hit the pillow, and then it hurt like crazy. Her limbs felt achy and tired, as they had when she had worked for too many hours without sleep in the hospital.

She was slept out. She couldn't sleep now, but she lay with her eyes closed for a long time. Presently, Justina came up. Zeke did not yell like crazy when his mother came in, she thought with some amusement. They conferred in low tones, then Justina came into the bedroom.

"Miss Sarah, you want me to help you wash, get ready for breakfast? Mr. Joel, he thinks you should stay in bed today."

Sarah thought about it, and decided that Joel was right. Justina helped her wash, and put on a fresh nightgown, then settled her back into the bed again. She was glad to sink back against the pillows. Her head was achy and dizzy again, and the world was going around and around in slow spirals.

Pearl brought up a tray, as neatly arranged as her mother would have done. Justina cast a professional eye over the food, and finally nodded. There was bacon, already chopped up in crisp bits, omelette as light and fluffy as whipped cream, fresh bread cut and buttered, a little pot of yellow honey, and a large steaming pot of tea.

Sarah had not thought she was hungry, but before long she had eaten every morsel on the tray, to Justina's pleasure. Pearl had arranged all on the best china from the china cupboards, and she enjoyed eating the good food on the pretty flower china.

"Old Adam," said Justina, complacently, beaming, "he always liked that there pattern of the china. He liked the pretty blue sprigs of flowers on the white, and that little band of gold. Do you like that one, Miss Sarah?"

"Yes, I like it immensely," said Sarah, reluctantly finishing the good flavorful tea.

"Then we fix your meals on that china, from now on," said Justina, casting her a little glance out of the sides of her eyes. Sarah hid her amusement. Justina was broadly hinting that Miss Sarah was going to stay on, and on, and on.

She hoped she could, she thought more soberly, as Justina took the tray away, and Zeke resumed his guardian post.

Sarah did not think she could sleep. It was just as well. A small stream of visitors began to arrive. Maxine came first, "just to see how you are getting along, darling," she said.

She stayed for an hour, sewing busily on Sarah's blue dress, chatting as fast as she sewed. Joel came in and out, scowled at Maxine, and finally said rudely, "She can't sleep while you talk like that, Maxine!"

"I don't expect her to sleep, Joel. Go away. We are gossiping." Maxine made a face at him, and stayed where she was.

Presently, a small elderly lady was announced rather

ceremoniously by Hugo Forrester. He ushered her in, little and frail and white-haired, but her bright black eyes were not missing anything, from the beautifully furnished room, to Sarah's appearance, with her blonde hair spread out, and the dress that Maxine was sewing.

"Miss Sarah Overmiller, this is a little lady who has been wanting to meet you. She heard about your—accident—and insisted on coming at once. Mrs. Mandy Hunsberger, this is Miss Overmiller." Hugo Forrester did the honors very formally, Sarah thought.

The little lady hobbled over to the bed, managed to shake Sarah's hand and put a round cool dish of custard into it all at once. "How de do! I knew your grandfather well," she said, in a high shrill voice. "Old Adam and I grew up in this town. Had to come see his granddaughter! My, you're pretty. Wouldn't have thought Old Adam would have a pretty grandchild. He was homely. Had blue eyes like yours, though!"

Maxine rescued the dish of custard and took it down to the kitchen to save for Sarah's lunch. Mrs. Hunsberger perched in the large rocker, her feet swinging free, and studied Sarah with lively curiosity as she chatted.

She inquired about Sarah's father, her brother, the war and her nursing, finally got around to the inn. "After the gold, are they?" she said, in her lively manner, her black eyes snapping. "You better hurry yourself and find it first! You can figure it out, they say you are like your grandfather! My, I knew him all my life! Stubborn as they come! But kind-hearted. Always helping somebody."

Maxine was sewing busily on the blue dress. Occasionally, her large violet eyes lifted to meet Sarah's in a deliberately expressionless look. Once she winked, and Sarah almost broke up. The woman was so very blunt!

"I remember when your father was a little fellow. He went out and did something, can't remember just now what it was. Old Adam was so mad! Wanted to punish

him, but couldn't bear to spank him. Finally come to
me to spank his boy, figured I was so little it wouldn't
hurt him. But your dad, he was heart-broke. Real
insulted that his paw wouldn't spank him, come to me
and cried and cried. I told Old Adam he would have to
do his own spanking. Guess he settled for putting the
boy in his bedroom for a couple hours for punishment.
Wonder the boy didn't grow up wild, with no mother.
Your grandmother, she died when Old Adam was
away, he never forgive himself for being away."

"Oh, I didn't know that. I knew she died when my
father was three years old—"

That set old Mrs. Hunsberger off on another series of
reminiscences, all about the grandmother, and her
pretty embroidery, and the way she could bake custard.
"I learned that recipe from her, the custard I brought
you," she said, proudly. "It's a special caramel custard.
You come around when you're feeling better, and I'll
show you some of your grandmother's recipes. She give
me a lot, as generous as Old Adam about everything,
she was. Don't know if Old Adam kept them. She had
them in two books bound with red, you look about and
see if you can find them. She was a real fine cook."

It seemed that Old Adam had been fond of racing
horses, and had ridden about the countryside. It was
during one of these jaunts that the grandmother had
taken sick, and died. No one knew what had ailed her.
Mrs. Hunsberger had taken in young Adam, and cared
for him until Old Adam had returned the following
week.

"When he found out his wife was dead, and he
away—oh, my, that was a cruel blow," said Mrs.
Hunsberger, tears in her eyes. She blinked them away,
and wiped them daintily with a white-edged handker-
chief. "He was like a dazed man for a time. Couldn't
settle down at nothing. Didn't want to farm, hated his
horses. Finally he started working at a tavern where
they took in overnight guests."

"That was when he decided to start an inn," said Maxine, innocently, cutting her thread.

Mrs. Hunsberger gave her a severe look. "I was just going to tell that, Mrs. Gibson," she said, very strongly.

"Oh, I beg your pardon," said Maxine, flushing guiltily.

Sarah stifled a giggle. The woman could not be turned off. But she did say such interesting things, at least they were fascinating to Sarah. Maxine probably thought they were rather dull and dry, old stuff to her.

"So—Old Adam noticed how the folks, even the well-bred ones, were being treated pretty rough, sleeping on benches and the floor, and such like. And the food! Oh, terrible, just beans and pork and cornbread, stale as likely as not. He opened an inn in a small house, and it went so well that he soon began to build this one, and he named it for the Golden Goose, because it seemed to lay golden eggs for him. He couldn't keep up with the guests sometimes. Every room full. I remember when the inn would be so full, he'd come around and ask if I could put up a nice lady and her husband just for the night. Of course, I always did whenever I didn't have company myself."

And the food, she said, with a sigh of remembrance. Always the best foods, the best cooks. Custards, pies, meats done to perfection, the best vegetables from the country. And wines, specially brought in on the stage. Though she didn't approve of wines in general, she did take a sip now and then, she said.

Joel stopped in for the third time about the time Mrs. Hunsberger was elaborating on the kinds and varieties of wines which Old Adam served. He looked at Sarah's drooping eyelids, the way she moved uncomfortably in bed, and ended the visit. He was very polite, but very firm.

"She isn't very well. I know she enjoys your visit, you must come again, Mrs. Hunsberger. Let me show you out through the kitchen, you wanted to see Justina's herb bottles." And he had her out ot there in three minutes.

"And I should go home too," said Maxine, folding up the sewing. "I really did stay to protect you from being talked to death, Sarah! Isn't she a character? If she ever lays her tongue on the wrong side of you, watch out! She's the worst gossip ever."

"I was interested—in what she said," said Sarah, a little faintly. Her head was throbbing uncomfortably, and she rubbed her forehead. Joel returned as Maxine was preparing to leave.

"Just what I was going to suggest," he said grimly. "This isn't my idea of resting, Sarah!"

"They are—very kind—Joel," she said, weakly. But she was glad he was firm, and saw Maxine out, and shut the door on all of them. He sat down in the living room, with a book, she thought. And she drifted off into a hazy sleep.

She slept for more than an hour. Then Justina brought her some lunch. The boiled beef was chopped in small bite-sized pieces, as tender as could be. The baked potato had been cut from its shell, whipped with butter and salt and pepper, returned to the crisp shell, and baked a few more minutes to a light yellowy brown. The lettuce was from the garden, fresh picked, cut with some red tomatoes and some yellow small tomatoes. And the custard was a caramel custard, the gift of Mrs. Hunsberger. And as good as she had bragged it would be.

Sarah sat back in bed, sighed. "I am going to get fat," she said, without sorrow.

"They mean to feed you good, so you'll stay," said Joel bluntly. Justina looked at him sideways, a smile curving her mouth.

"She going to stay, I see it in the cards," she said happily. "I read the cards last night. Bad troubles, but Miss Sarah, she going to stay, she going to be all right.

Saw something else too," and she giggled, happily. "Won't tell you that right now."

Joel raised his eyebrows at Sarah, and she shook her head. Whether she stayed or not was not going to depend on Justina's cards, or her good food either. She would think about it, and decide in a sensible manner.

Justina seemed happy, whatever her cards had told her had made her happy. She hummed as she plumped up Sarah's pillows, straightened the bed clothes, took the tray away.

Presently Hugo Forrester came back. Joel opened the door for him, and looked at the couple with him.

"She had visitors all morning," said Joel, his mouth a tight line as he turned toward Sarah questioningly.

"We won't stay long," said the gentleman pleasantly. "I just wanted to make Miss Overmiller's acquaintance, and tell her a little about the state of her grandfather's financial affairs."

Joel shrugged in resignation, folded his arms, as Hugo Forrester brought the couple into the bedroom.

"Sarah, this is Mr. and Mrs. George Crawford. He owns the bank," said Hugo. "I thought you should meet soon. It might affect your decisions." He looked at her significantly.

The banker and his wife were plump, in their forties, comfortable, but a little pompous, Sarah thought.

Mrs. Crawford was an echo of her husband, and he did most of the talking. He settled himself on a straight chair, looked longingly at the rocker where his wife reposed, and then began.

"Your grandfather was quite well off, Miss Overmiller," he said. "I brought bank statements with me, and will attempt to explain them." He put the statements in her hands, and went over them briskly and patiently with her.

The totals were unexpectedly large. She questioned some of them.

"Well, there are probably some outstanding bills.

Have you gone through his desk, yet? No? You should do that as soon as you feel better. Even so, I feel sure that your grandfather left you quite well off, Miss Sarah. And that has nothing to do with the gold, of course."

Everyone in the room stiffened. He spoke so casually of the gold.

"Did you know about the gold, Mr. Crawford?" asked Sarah, quietly, feeling tension come over her.

"He spoke of it. He was rather uneasy about it. Let me see, that was a couple years ago. I urged him strongly to bring it into the bank, and let us handle it. I could send it to a large city bank, or keep it under lock here. He wouldn't agree. We quarreled over it," he added, with a laugh creasing his plump cheeks. "But that wasn't for the first time! We talked of it several times, but managed to quarrel each time. He would make insulting remarks about the lack of safety of banks. Well, that's beside the point. He finally came in one day, and said the gold was safe, no one would find it. He seemed quite pleased with himself. I do hope you can figure out what he did with it!"

"That means—there really is gold around. It isn't just an idle rumor," said Hugo Forrester, looking both excited and worried. He looked down at Sarah. "You really must find it, Miss Sarah, and put it in the bank before someone steals it."

She felt rather impatient. Everyone seemed to expect her to close her eyes and think where her grandfather had put it, as though it could be that simple. She had never talked with her grandfather, she didn't know how he thought, how he would figure, what kind of plans he might contrive. How could she be expected to find the gold so easily?

The Crawfords stayed about half an hour, then left with Hugo Forrester. Maxine came soon after they left, with her sewing. Sarah's head was aching, but she could not insult Maxine. Maxine settled down to the sewing and chatting.

She was full of talk this afternoon, of the town, of the past. "It's so nice to have a girl my own age here, Sarah," she finally said impulsively, her violet eyes glowing. "I told Dad what a difference it makes to have you here—so friendly, and so sweet. Why, we hit it off right away, didn't we?"

Sarah smiled at her. "Yes. I never did—have a good girl friend," she confided shyly. "When I was young, I was housekeeper for my father and brother. Then the war came—and I worked as a nurse. There was no time for fun."

"No—that war. Oh, it ruined so many things," sighed Maxine, and tears trembled on her golden lashes. She brushed them away before they could fall on the blue fabric. But the thought seemed to depress her. She soon folded up the material, and went away, saying she would leave Sarah to sleep. Gloom seemed to have settled down on her once more.

Joel came back, and settled himself in the living room with a couple of books. She thought they might be account books, he seemed to be writing in them, and adding and figuring, with a frown on his face. He scarcely looked in her direction, but she knew he was as intensely aware of her, as she was of him.

Something seemed to flow between them, some consciousness—messages without words. Sometimes she seemed to know what he was thinking, even though he didn't say a word. And he seemed to know when she was disturbed or in pain, or when she wanted to sleep.

It was odd, she had never felt this way with anyone before. She had never felt so in tune with a person, so that she felt as though a thin strong line was stretched between them, and when he pulled on it slightly she would react, and when she wanted him she could pull on that line also. And he had made her laugh.

She had thought at first that Joel was not a serious person, that he was frivolous. Laughter seemed to come easily to him, and he enjoyed teasing and fun. Underneath, she had discovered, was an intensely serious determined person, a strong man, one a girl could lean upon and not worry about falling.

She was thinking about him, and looking at him, when suddenly he looked up. Their eyes met across the two rooms, and she felt that like a shock. She caught her breath, wanted to close her eyes, but could not. They looked at each other, staring, studying. She could not move or speak.

"Go to sleep, Sarah," he said finally. And his cheek creased in a little odd smile. It was tender—or gentle—or a little mocking—she couldn't quite decide.

She slowly closed her eyes. But she felt him continuing to look at her. She opened her eyes again, and he was. The dark gray eyes were intense and cloudy, not angry, but strange. As though he were thinking deeply. As though someone troubled his mind, as though he had thoughts he had not considered before.

"Joel," she said, "you ought to get some sleep tonight."

He considered her face, her eyes. "I will," he said. "Right in that rocker."

"Not again tonight," she said firmly. "I will be perfectly all right. Now, Joel, I mean it—"

"So do I," he said. "And I'm stronger than you. And I know how to protect my own."

She didn't know how to answer that. He was saying to her, *you belong to me.* And she did not, she did not!

She closed her eyes, rebelliously wondering how to send him away that night. But sleep was drifting over her again, and she thought once about dinner and getting hungry, and then about Joel—and then— nothing.

When she wakened again, she saw it was dark. She could not remember what time of day it was, or what day. But Joel was sitting in the front room, before the rose-painted lamp, studying a book intently, and she finally remembered.

She stirred in bed, and he got up and came to the

door. "Awake, Sarah? Ready for dinner? Justina is cooking up a storm."

"I am hungry," she said, lazily moving in the bed, and stretching her arms in a big yawn. Then she saw him looking down at her, and blushed, and put her arms under the covers again.

"Yes, you are very pretty," he said. "Don't be vain," and he grinned, and went away.

She lay there, blushing, How had she become accustomed to him so quickly? She had stretched and moved on the bed, as though—as though he were not there—No. As though he was there, and *belonged* there.

She had moved and shifted on the bed, and stretched out her arms unself-consciously, as though—as though they were married.

As though they were married. As though Joel were her husband, and had the right to be there. And more than that, she thought, getting very warm under the covers. She had stretched, and moved, and the covers had fallen down from her throat, and she had wanted him to see her—

As though they were married. As though she loved him, and wanted him to see her, and know she was pretty, and—and desire her—maybe—

"Sarah Overmiller, stop thinking this instant!" she told herself, but could not stop.

Joel had guessed her thoughts. That was the worst!

How had he known, when she had not known herself? How had he known she wanted to be pretty for him, that she wanted him to desire her, that he was being invited to look at her and want—

"Oh, stop thinking!"

But she could not stop thinking. She knew now that she was in love with Joel Walden. She loved him, as directly and passionately as a girl could love, as a woman could desire.

She thought she was crazy, but she felt so happy she

didn't care. She stretched out her arms again, this time when he was not there. She felt so strange, so happy, so joyful and amazed.

She was in love!

She loved Joel Walden. He was so strong, and so tender, and he looked at her, and said she belonged to him, and now she wanted to believe that.

She *wanted* to belong to him.

She wanted to trust him, and lean on him, and ask him what to do. She wanted to go to him, and let him hold her in his arms, and kiss her any way he wanted to.

She closed her eyes at the thought of Joel kissing her. She remembered the feel of his hard arms, the passionate heat of his kisses, the pressure of his body against hers. The rough touch of his hand on her forehead, stroking back the hair, the hand that was so soothing and so gentle. And his voice murmuring about the springtime, and the blossoms—

Oh, she felt crazy. She felt light and happy and crazy and in love. She was in love. She loved him.

And—she came back to earth with a little bump. And someone wanted to kill her. *Someone hated her enough to kill.*

Oh, why had she discovered love at a moment like this? She thought, and sighed, and stretched on the bed, and thought about Joel, and thought about being murdered, and lying in the waters in the basement, and waiting for the killer to return—

She shuddered, and pulled up the covers again. She must not get giddy, she admonished herself sternly. She was not safe yet. She was not safe. She must not dream away, and get careless.

Someone wanted to kill her. She must find out who it was—before she could be free to love.

Chapter 10

~~~~~~

Joel spent the night in Sarah's room again, sitting in the rocker, half-awake, intensely alert. Sarah could not persuade him to leave. He was like a rock.

Finally she settled down and slept, and she admitted she was happier for his being there. But this could not continue, she thought.

The next morning, when Justina came in, she told the woman, "I am going to get up today. I am quite all right." And she said it so firmly that Justina gave in at once.

The woman helped her bathe and dress in her light blue wool dress. Then Sarah went downstairs with her to the kitchen.

Joel got up with a scowl. "You're not well enough to get up, Sarah!" he said, advancing on her.

"Yes, I am," she said, and sat down hastily on a chair. She thought it would be more difficult for him to move her. She glared up at him defiantly, "And I am so hungry!"

"I'll have your breakfast fixed in a few minutes, honeylamb," said Justina, immensely pleased, humming as she went about her cooking.

Sarah had not attempted to braid her hair. Just brushing the long golden-brown curls had been enough to tire her, though she would never admit it aloud. She had brushed it a little, then swept it back, and wrapped a childish blue ribbon around it to fasten at the back of her neck. The curls hung almost to her waist.

Joel stepped behind her, and put his hands gently on her head. "Hold still," he said, when she would have moved. She held very still, wincing a little as he carefully touched the wound. "It's healing. I'll put a bit more ointment on it."

By the time he had put salve on the wound, and stepped back from her, Justina had brought her breakfast. Sarah ate hungrily, her appetite increased by the marvelous odor of the fresh-cooked slice of ham, the fried eggs, and hot biscuits and melting butter and dripping honey.

"Well, you are better," said Joel, with a grin, as he devoured another biscuit. "That's your fourth biscuit, Sarah. Good for you."

She made an impish face at him. "Stop counting my biscuits," she ordered, "or I'll start counting yours!"

Justina chuckled at their teasing each other. "Yessum, Miss Sarah is muchly better," she said, happily, making it a song. "Yessum, she's muchly better, she better, all right."

Billy Dexter came in the back door, hesitated when he saw Sarah. "Well, good morning, Miss Sarah," he said, in surprise, his face splitting in a huge grin. "You are better, then. That's good!"

He came over to the table, and sat down. Justina brought him a huge platter of ham and eggs, and he fell to with great appetite. Sarah looked at him thoughtfully as she lingered over her third cup of hot tea.

She had waked early this morning, and the thoughts had been there in her mind waiting for her to turn them over and over. She had heard a great deal about her grandfather, and now she was ready to piece things together. He had been a strong man, an obstinate man, a man of many friends and many enemies, of willful courage, and devotion to causes.

A strong man, a man who knew horses, who had raced horses. A man who knew horses thoroughly, who had worked with them, and made money on them. Who kept his own stable.

Yet he had ridden in a carriage, and the horse had shied, and the carriage had overturned into a ditch, and Old Adam had died of a broken neck.

Strange. Very strange. Sarah had lain in bed, and thought and thought, putting the little jigsaw pieces together carefully.

Old Adam had made lasting friends, people remembered him fondly. Others were reserved with her, darkness in their eyes, remembering their enmity. He was a strong man, and strong men made strong enemies.

He was a man of conviction. He believed that the slaves should be free, and he had smuggled them away from the South, helped them up through Ohio on the underground railroad, helped them get to Canada. He had hidden them in his own inn, paid men to hide them on their farms. He had taken messages to save them, sent Joel to rescue them, fought all his life against slavery and the slave-holders. When slaves had been discovered, and taken in chains back down South, his fury had been tremendous and devastating.

Mad as fire, Clarence Gibson had said. *Old Adam would get mad as fire.*

And probably had not spared his enemies the lash of his tongue in his fury. He would not be one to forget or forgive someone who had treated him like that. Nor would they forgive him. Someone had hated enough to kill Roscoe—

Roscoe. The small quiet dark man, with the wooly white hair, staring at her somberly in the dimness of her room, that first night.

Roscoe had stared at her, recognized her from her portrait, had known she was Old Adam's granddaughter—and had spoken. In fear, in terror, but he had spoken.

What had he said?

She had been so weary that night, so longing to sleep—

He had said something like—*that horse don't never shy.* That horse— What horse? *Don't never shy—* It had meant nothing to her then. She had thought her grandfather had fallen ill and had died.

Then later she had found he had died in an accident. An accident involving a horse and carriage.

What horse? *That horse don't never shy.* Was that the one Old Adam had hitched to a carriage, and had ridden out, never to return alive?

"Billy," said Sarah, and when they all stared at her she realized she had been quiet for a long time. "You are familiar with my grandfather's stables, aren't you?"

"Yes, ma'am. He always let me put up my horses and the stagecoach in them." Billy wiped his mouth with his huge brown hand, staring at her questioningly.

"That is fine. I hope you can continue to do this, whether—whether I remain or not. You know, I have not yet decided." Sarah was not sure why she added this, perhaps in defiance to Joel, who had leaned back in his chair and was frankly studying her.

Justina's face shadowed, and she turned back to the fireplace.

"Yes, ma'am," said Billy Dexter. "Sure do hope you decide to stay, ma'am."

"I'm still considering the matter. However, the stables—they are one area I haven't looked at. I wonder if you would take me over to the stables and show me around this morning."

There was a little silence in the kitchen. Joel was still staring at her. Justina was silent, seemingly holding her breath. Zeke, in the corner, looked up from his work.

"Well—now—ma'am," said Billy slowly, and then took a big sip of hot coffee. "Ah—I'll be happy to do that, ma'am. You should know that it's mighty muddy and wet over there. Zeke has been cleaning it out, but it sure is muddy."

"I don't mind that. I would like to look at the stables this morning," she said very firmly.

"Yes, ma'am." He finally added, "You still looking for Old Adam's gold, ma'am?" He grinned as he said it, but he looked at her in a very odd questioning way.

"Of course," she said, and added, rather sarcastically and sharply, "I have to find it, everyone expects me to pull it out of my hat!"

"Reckon you'll find it all right. You just think like Old Adam, and you'll find it right enough," said Billy Dexter, but he sounded as though his mind was on other matters. Joel finally got up.

"If you're going around with Billy Dexter this morning, Sarah, you'll be all right. I'm going over to the stage office and work. Now, don't you go around by yourself! Promise?" He looked down worriedly at her.

"I promise," she said meekly. "Perhaps Billy will escort me back here and turn me over to Justina," she added, with a spark of defiance. "That way, no one can get after me."

Joel did not look amused. He scowled down at her. "No more adventuring by yourself, or I'll get mad!"

She shuddered. "No, I don't want any more adventures," she said. "Don't worry, Joel, I won't go off by myself."

"I'll look after her, Joel, don't you nevermind," said Billy Dexter, reassuringly. He finished his last bite of ham, swallowed the rest of his coffee and got up. "Reckon you'll want some heavy shoes or some boots, ma'am, it's *that* muddy."

"I'll go up and change," said Sarah. Joel followed her up the stairs. She was not surprised. He waited in the pretty living room while she changed to her heavier shoes, and got her heavy green cloak.

"Now, you be careful, Sarah," he said, soberly, looking down at her. He reached out, put one hand gently on a lock of her golden-brown hair, hanging down her back. "Promise?"

"I promise, Joel," she said, and glanced at his face

quickly, then away again. The expression on his face was so tender and so anxious, she wanted to reach out and touch his cheek. One of these days, she thought, she would not be able to stop herself, she would reach out and touch him— And then what?

Would he pull her into his arms, and kiss her again, the way he had before, so possessively and so hard? A little thrill ran down her spine, and she pulled the cloak about herself warmly.

Joel followed her down the narrow winding stairs to the kitchen. The door to Roscoe's old room was shut. She thought again of the old man, all that blood soaking the rug under him, and shivered. He had died—why? Because he had told her about the horse that had never shied?

Joel walked part way down the street with them. The muddy street was thick and gluey. She found it hard walking. The sky was a dark gray, with ominous clouds rolling in the west.

"By golly, you'd think we had enough rain," said Billy. "Don't know when we're going to get out of Paintsville, at this rate. Never knew it to rain so long and so hard."

"I remember it did a few times when I was a boy," said Joel, as though his mind was not on that at all. "I remember a couple times in October, when it rained, seems like, from time school started 'til Christmas. Bridges were always out, and Old Adam used to get mad as fire 'cause no men turned out to fix them until he had nagged at them long enough."

"Mad as fire." It was the expression they always used to describe Adam's anger. Had he made many enemies that way?

Joel left them at the hardware shop, and watched them as they walked on down the thick mud of the main street toward the stable area. Billy Dexter took her arm awkwardly, and helped her as her feet stuck again and again.

"Reckon your pretty shoes will be ruint," he said, anxiously.

"Oh, these are old ones. I used to wear them—" Then she stopped abruptly. She had not thought for a week about the war, the heartbreaking tours out on the battlefields. She had not had nightmares about the bloody surgical rooms, the men moaning and screaming with pain. Her exhaustion was gone, the heart-weary exhaustion of the long anxious years of nursing, the pain of her loss of brother and father.

She felt alive again, vigorous and happy, in spite of all that had happened to her. Why? she wondered, then thought of Joel. Was it that? Had falling in love with Joel made her feel alive and happy again? She was suddenly light-hearted, in spite of the dark skies, the drizzling rain, the thick glue of the mud, the worries over the situation here in Paintsville. Wondering if she might be murdered.

She might be killed— And now she felt more alive than she had ever felt in her life. The shell of wariness which she had built about herself to shelter herself from pain and grief had been cracked, and now she was open and vulnerable to the world once more. And it felt good, she thought. It was good, to be alive and eager, and vulnerable, and wanting, full of desire and hope—

They entered the dark stables. There was only the stamping of the horses as Billy came in, and talked slowly to the animals. One whuffed at him, and whinnied as though he was talking to Billy.

"Yes, old man, yes, sir, I know how you feel, all penned up like that," said Billy, in a low caressing tone, stroking the long handsome nose of the dark gray horse. The horse pushed at Billy's hat, cocking it sideways, whuffing at his neck.

"Now, don't you knock off my hat, Prince," he said, affectionately, and patted the long nose again and again. "This has been my lead horse for three years now, ma'am," he said, as though introducing the animal to her.

Sarah put her hand up timidly, let the animal whuff at her, and then dared to stroke her hand slowly over the long soft nose. The animal stamped his feet, whinnied, and hung his head over the edge of the stable, watching them wistfully as they moved on down the line.

The stable was huge, holding about two dozen stalls. Billy explained that it was large, to accommodate the horses of the guests at the inn, as well as Adam's horses, and the stage horses. Someone came out of the shadows at the back, an elderly colored man, who shook with palsy and looked up oddly at Sarah.

He had worked for old Adam for years, said Billy. The man watched them as they looked at the horses, the two carriages and the stagecoach at the back of the stables. There were dark shadows all around, she thought, and felt a little prickling of warning at the back of her neck. Up in the hay ricks, a man could hide, and never be seen, she thought, looking up at them.

"I don't reckon Old Adam hid the gold up there," said Billy, looking where she looked. "That hay gets cleaned out regular. These horses eat their weight in hay."

"I don't suppose he would," said Sarah, who had not been thinking of the gold. She moved on back to the carriages. "Which one did my grandfather drive?" she asked, looking at them. One carriage had a long gash in its side, and the paint was new on the wheels.

"Why, both of them," said Billy, "they both belonged to him."

The old stable hand came up to them. "He was a-riding that one to his death," he said, in a low tone, pointing to the one nearest Sarah. "See that gash, that's where it turned over. Broke the wheels off. Had to mend them."

They were all silent, looking at the carriage.

Finally Sarah asked the stable hand, "How did it happen? Were you nearby?"

"No, oh, no, ma'am, I warn't nearby," he said hastily, fearfully, backing up a little. "I just work here, cleaning out the stables and looking after the horses. I feeds them, and waters them—"

"How did it happen?" she asked again.

The old man looked around and around, helplessly, from Sarah to Billy, to the shadows of the stables. Finally he said, in a low tone, "Why, Old Adam, he hitched up, and went out, in this carriage. He went to the edge of town, on some errand, and the horse shied, and he tipped over into a ditch—"

The horse shied.

Sarah asked sharply, "Wasn't he out in the country?"

"Oh, no, ma'am, it was just at the edge of town, it was. The horse shied, and the ditch, it was right there—"

"Which horse was he driving?" asked Sarah.

Billy Dexter was listening intently, a frown of concentration on his heavy face. Now he turned with them, and went to the near stall, where a large brown horse waited with its nose hung over the stall, watching them with big brown eyes, so patiently, Sarah thought.

"That's the one, ma'am. That one there. Ain't nobody drive him since," said the stable hand. "He's mighty fresh. Stamping all the time."

Billy Dexter studied the animal, put out his hand, stroked the long brown nose carefully. The animal seemed to shudder in surprise, back away, then push closer to the friendly hand.

"Ain't nobody touched him since," said the stable hand.

"He seems mild enough," said Billy. "Wonder why he shied."

The stable hand looked at him, away again, shuffled his feet. He grabbed a rake, said, "Guess I gotta work. Excuse me, ma'am." He went busily down the center of the stables, doing very little work that Sarah could see.

Sarah watched in silence as Billy Dexter petted the animal, talked softly to it, looked inside the stall and studied the mane and sides.

"Looks all right. Don't seem jittery, that is, for not being out in so long," said Billy. "Wonder why he shied?"

Sarah said, softly, "So do I wonder. Billy—I want to tell you something."

He turned around to face her. She did trust him, she did, she thought to herself. He was as honest and trustworthy as one of his big sturdy horses.

"Roscoe said something to me—that first night in the inn," she said, quietly. "You know, he was in the hallway. Joel called him in, and he was with me alone in the room for a minute. He said, Billy, I swear this was what he said, though I was tired, and worn out, and didn't understand—" She paused, looking at him desperately. Would he understand, would he help?

"What was it, ma'am? What did he say?" Billy was still petting the long brown nose of the large horse. His shrewd, small dark eyes were very dark in his tanned face as he stared down at Sarah.

"He said something about the horse that never shied. That horse never did shy, he said. I think he meant—this one, Billy."

Billy stared down at her for a long silent moment. Then he turned, and studied the horse for a long time. They were silent, both thinking. Finally Billy gave a last pat to the horse.

"I'll take you back to the inn, ma'am," he said. "Reckon you better go back now."

He took her arm in his big hand, as though she needed protection, and walked her down the long shadowy center of the stables to the front, and out into the air again. She drew a long trembling breath. Somehow she had been frightened back in there, in the dark shadows, as though there was something there that might harm her.

She was glad to be out in the street, though it was muddy, and the drizzling rain had come on harder. Billy was intensely silent as he walked her back to the inn, and in the back door to the kitchen. Justina greeted her in relief.

"Lord have mercy, child, you been gone long enough! Scared me to death, you did. And look at your shoes, and the hem of your dress. You come right upstairs and change."

Sarah let her scold and pamper her. She took her muddy shoes off, and gave them to Zeke to clean. Justina took off the worst of the mud from the hem of the dress, then escorted her upstairs to change.

Sarah changed to a gray wool, fastened back her hair with a red ribbon, and put on her mother's cameo pin. Joel might come back for lunch, she thought, and blushed at herself. She was really having a hard case of it, she decided with some resignation. All she could think about was Joel, Joel, Joel.

She went back with Justina to the kitchen, put her feet up comfortably near the fire, and tried to think. The horse had seemed so gentle. Surely it could not be—the horse might have been frightened at something on the road. Any horse would shy at—what? a piece of paper blowing in the wind, a branch crashing in front of it—

She sat on, absorbed in her thoughts. Justina looked at her now and then, thoughtfully, then turned back to her cooking. Sarah struggled with the ideas she had, trying to find her way through the maze of them. Her head throbbed a little, but it did not ache as it had yesterday. There was an answer to the questions she had, but she could not seem to find it.

Finally she put up her hand, ruffled her hair, and sighed. She stirred in the chair.

Justina said, "You sit there thinking, just like Old Adam used to do. Just like him, you are. I been thinking day after day, how much you like Old Adam."

Sarah looked up at her, smiled, was about to answer when the back door crashed open. Sarah jumped up, Justina dropped a kettle with a loud bang.

Zeke backed in with care. He was holding something—a door? On it lay—the huge form of a man, his arm hanging limply down over the edge of the makeshift stretcher.

"Oh—no—no—" Sarah for a moment was back in

the world of the war, seeing a man brought in to surgery, head bloody, body limp. She put her hand to her face, hid her eyes, then forced herself to look again.

Joel was carrying the other end, and they laid it down on the bench. "Hot water, Justina. Bandages. Salve," he said curtly.

Sarah forced herself to walk across the floor to the bench. She looked down at the still form of the unconscious man. Billy Dexter, lying limp, his arm broken, his forehead bloody, his face a mask of blood.

"What—happened—" she said, tonelessly.

"Took out the carriage and horse that your grandfather did," said Zeke, briefly. "The horse shied. Went into the ditch, just the way Old Adam—"

"My—fault—" she whispered. Zeke looked at her with his big gentle questioning eyes.

Joel came back, started to push her away. "Wait, you can help," he said curtly. "Know anything about broken bones?"

She nodded, and forced herself to forget her own problems for the moment. Between them, they managed to set the broken arm, bandage it, strap it to his body. Justina was bathing his face, gently revealing the several cuts and gashes. When they had finished with the arm, Justina stood aside for Sarah to examine the gashes.

"They aren't very deep, Joel, but bad enough. He must have been knocked out."

"Yes. Lucky he wasn't killed. The horse was too fresh, I guess," said Joel, frowning.

So that answered that. The horse did shy, thought Sarah, unhappily. Billy Dexter must have gone right back to the stable, hitched up the horse and carriage, and tried it. It was a hard way to prove a point, and he had proved it with his injuries. Now she could forget that her grandfather might have been murdered, she thought. It was an accidental death. The horse *had* shied, he simply was not dependable.

While Sarah was smoothing ointment on the cuts,

Billy Dexter came to himself. He lay blinking up at her, while she worked, not even wincing. He was a sturdy man, used to being knocked about, she thought.

"I'm so sorry, Billy," she whispered once.

He just looked at her. "Tell you later," he said, in a low growl.

Joel and Zeke got him up to a room, and settled in bed. Sarah, in a passion of remorse, volunteered to nurse him. She saw him settled, put blankets about him in case of shock, and settled down in a chair near the bed.

Joel and Zeke went out for a time. Billy Dexter beckoned painfully to Sarah. "Come—closer—to the bed—so won't be heard," he growled, in what he must have thought was a whisper.

She got up, went to the bed, leaned down.

He looked at her, his brows set in a scowl of pain. "Listen, Miss Sarah, you be damn careful, awful damn careful. That horse—it don't shy. Somebody—set something—got to see—that horse had something under the harness—got away from me, ran—scared. Listen—you get it? Wasn't no accident."

She stared down at him, scared cold. Chills went up and down her spine under her wool dress. "Oh—Billy—" she whispered. "No—accident?"

"I know—horses," he said painfully, and closed his eyes. "That horse—gentle as I ever seen. Might have shied at something—but don't think so. Had something—under the harness—wouldn't be surprised—Old Adam too—"

He sighed, and seemed to move down into the blankets. Justina had given him something for the pain, and it was making him sleepy.

Sarah set the blankets more closely under his chin, looking down at him soberly. Billy Dexter was not a man with a lively imagination. He was sober, sturdy, a man of facts. If he said there was something wrong with the harness, that the horse had been forced into an accident, then he meant it, and it was true.

It had been no accident.

And perhaps the accident to Old Adam had been no accident.

She went back to her chair, and waited until Billy Dexter was sound asleep. She was thinking, thinking, thinking, so hard that her head ached all over again. And she was frightened.

Someone must have been hiding in the stables, listening to their conversation, observing them. Someone who hated, someone who hated enough to kill. The chills down her spine had not been a vivid imagination on her part. There had been danger lurking in the shadows.

"Sarah?" The whisper brought her up from the chair. With relief, she saw Joel in the doorway.

She went to him. He drew her gently out into the hallway.

"He's sleeping? Good. Hadn't you better get some rest? I'll come back and watch over him for a time."

"No, I can stay—"

His will was stronger than hers. He led her back to her rooms, watched as she unlocked the door. Inside, she looked at him. She had been thinking about him a great deal, pondering about him, thinking how she loved him. Now she was before him, and she was blushing and silent as a schoolgirl.

"Where did you learn to nurse like that?" he asked. "I know you worked in the hospital, but I thought you just patted pillows, or something."

She managed a smile. "No—I was a nurse," she said. She frowned a little as memories began coming back. "Four years," she added, absently. Four nightmare years.

He took her elbow, and guided her to a comfortable chair. "Talk about it, Sarah, get it out," he said, gently. "It's been under your skin too long. Get it out."

He sat down opposite her, the door closed and bolted. She felt comfortable, safe. She leaned back, and began to talk. At first awkwardly, in a few words, then in a rush of sentences, she told him about the war years for her.

She had gone first to the hospital because the brother of a friend of hers had been injured. She had stayed because others needed her. At first, she had sat beside their beds, "patted pillows," she said, with a wry smile. Then she began to help with changing bandages, especially of the burn victims, who had such painful sores.

"They were so patient, so good, they tried not to scream," she said, shivering a little in remembrance. "They didn't want to frighten me. But sometimes, they just couldn't help it. The pain was so great."

He listened, encouraged her to talk, his sympathy a tangible thing between them. She realized he knew what she was saying, because he had endured also, the pain, the suffering, the dying of his friends and his comrades.

"Later on—there was such a need of nurses—and they asked me to help in surgery. I thought I could not, could not endure it. But they needed me—and I went—and tried to help. But oh, Joel—the agony they went through—with little to ease the pain—oh the agony—" She closed her eyes, and tightened her mouth to hold back the tears as she remembered.

Telling it did help, she found. The tension eased, she could relax finally, and stop talking, and lean her head back against the soft back of the chair.

She opened her eyes, and saw his face, so grave, his eyes so hurt, and she realized he had been remembering too.

"Oh, Joel, I'm sorry—it was so much worse for you. You were—out there—in the battles—"

He looked at her, and smiled, and their eyes met in understanding. "It was the same, we were both fighting," he said, gently. "Pretty soon, it didn't seem to have any meaning, just to stay alive. But I thought, someday it will matter again. So I kept trying to stay alive."

"Yes. Yes, I thought so also." She reached out her hand, impulsively, and he clasped it strongly.

Finally he stood up to leave, and he was still holding her hand. He drew her up with him, and the way he looked at her, she knew he was going to kiss her. She felt paralyzed, not wanting to pull away, knowing he was going to embrace her, and not wanting to stop him.

He drew her close to him, in to his hard body, pulling her close, his hand at the small of her back, his other hand going behind her head, up under the long curls, holding her neck. He bent his head. Through half-closed eyes, she saw his mouth coming closer to hers. Then it came over hers, and pressed, and took hers completely.

His mouth was tender, but it was hard also, holding hers for a long moment. She felt as though he pulled her so tightly that she was melting against him, heat running through her body, molding her to his body. She could not breathe. She didn't want to breathe. She wanted to stay pressed to him, feeling him, knowing him, responding to the lips on hers, moving her lips as he moved his, and half-fainting with the pleasure of it.

His hand on her back pulled her more tightly in to him, and he bent her backward, holding her so fiercely that her blood ran hot. Their lips parted, clasped again, and she gasped, and turned her head to get her breath. His lips slid down over her chin, down to her throat, to the collar, hotly learning her soft skin.

They were alone in that enclosed room. Alone. And he was kissing her and bending her to himself, as though he wanted—

She pressed her arms against his chest, and protested. "No—Joel—no, Joel—please—"

He finally heard her, and lifted up, staring down at her in a daze. She wondered if her face glowed as his did, his eyes blazing down into hers.

His lips moved, but no words came. He finally set her free, his hands lingering as he moved them over her, to release her. He went to the door, unlocked it, went out into the hall. Finally he smiled back at her, a little ruefully.

"Sorry, Sarah. I forgot we weren't married—yet," he said, his eyes flashing with wicked humor. He grinned down at her, touched her cheek. "Now, lock the door after me. Go on, close the door and bolt it."

She was looking up at him, not really thinking about anything or anyone but him. His smile, the way his eyes sparkled, the words he had said—

She closed and bolted the door, the smile lingering on her own mouth. He was so—so brazen, yet so—so sweet—

Then she knew. Behind him, far down the hall, had been a slight movement. Over his shoulder, she had seen a movement. A flash of something light, white, perhaps.

Someone had been in the hallway, listening, watching them, observing them. *Someone—there—watching—again—*

Chapter 11

~~~~~~

Sarah did not want to remain in her room. She felt restless, confused, too many thoughts crowding for place in her brain. Heated over the encounter with Joel, chilled with the knowledge that someone had been in that dark hallway, listening, watching—

She went down to the kitchen. It seemed the one safe warm lighted place in the inn. Justina was ironing sheets, humming over them. She gave Sarah a warm smile.

"Mr. Billy, he's all right, okay now?" she asked.

"Yes, he is sleeping now," said Sarah. She walked around the room, looked at the spice shelf, touched the pile of warm sheets. She sighed to herself. Justina watched her with wise dark eyes, smiling a little. She had seen Joel come down, thought Sarah.

"The inn be ready for company when the rains let up," said Justina presently. "Miss Maxine, she working on the chairs again. Pearl helped her all this morning."

That reminded Sarah that she hadn't seen Maxine that morning. "I believe I'll go look for Maxine. Where is she working?"

Justina looked at Zeke, as he sat at his tool bench, mending harness. "She working in the far front parlor, Miss Sarah. Pearl helping her."

"I'll go talk to her," said Sarah, starting for the door.

Justina nodded to Zeke, who promptly got up and followed her. Sarah was going to protest, when she remembered that shadowed light figure in the hallway, moving beyond Joel's shoulder. She let him come. He was so nice and big and safe, she thought, as the large boy followed her.

She heard voices as they came to the front of the inn. She started toward the far parlor, then hesitated. A man's voice was speaking, a firm voice, a gentleman's voice. Hugo Forrester. She paused, turned back indecisively.

"You see, Miss Maxine," said Hugo, "when I came West, my family objected, but they didn't cut me off. I could go back anytime I wanted. On the other hand, I like it out here, and my practice has built up very quickly—"

Hum, thought Sarah, in some surprise. He sounded like a man who was working up to propose to a girl. She hadn't thought he was that fond of Maxine, but the woman was a very attractive one, with her beautiful blonde hair, her large violet eyes, her pretty figure, her dainty ways. And she was too lively and wonderful a girl for gloomy Leonard. Maybe that would be a match.

Zeke was watching Sarah alertly, to see what she wanted to do. She hesitated, turning about. She had only just begun an inventory of the china.

She went over to the registration desk, and took out the inventory book. It was just where she had left it. "I believe I'll count china, Zeke. Miss Maxine is busy just now," she said.

"Yes, ma'am." He watched to see where she would start, then followed her eagerly to help. She went first to the case that held her favorite china, with the blue sprigs on it. She counted the cups, and was pleased that they were in good condition, not a crack or chip on them.

Zeke helped her, holding up items as she wanted, lifting out the heavy platters and bowls. She listed each item carefully, checked the condition.

It was light enough that afternoon to work without a lamp there in the front room near the reception desk. She could see now how pleasant the inn was, with its roomy parlors, the comfortable chairs and couches and tables. She could picture how it was on a busy day, with ladies and gentlemen roaming about, the servants scurrying to make rooms ready. She became quite eager, thinking about taking care of the inn. She and Joel could do it, she thought, absently. Joel was good with people, and strong and firm. He could—

She stopped her thoughts abruptly, and blushed hotly. She was taking too much for granted, just like Joel! He had not asked her to marry him. He had offered to buy the inn, not help her in running it.

Still—it would be so nice, she thought. Between them, they could run the place. She could manage the servants, and the foods, and bedding, and supplies. She could do the accounts. Joel would manage the people, and be firm with them, and collect the accounts, and manage any drunken persons, and order the wine, and—

Oh, dear, she thought, as she counted a set of dishes for the third time. Zeke would think her mind was gone completely.

She went over to another cupboard and started in there. She could hear Hugo's voice going on and on, with a little charming encouragement from Maxine.

"So I came West, and started my practice here. As I said, it has gone well—am I holding the fabric tight enough, Miss Maxine?"

"Just a little tighter, Hugo. Please. There. Pearl, stitch that over and over, that's right."

"Of course, I don't have any great fortune, and I probably never will have. Still, a lawyer does have a steady living, and his wife would never want for anything."

"And one is so respected," said Maxine, prettily. "Your wife could hold up her head in any company, I'm sure."

Sarah smiled a little guiltily, realizing she was eavesdropping. It was too interesting to move away, and besides she did have to count the china in this cupboard. It was a good set, she thought, with white ivory finish, a gold border, a formal look to it. She wondered if Old Adam had used it for the best company, as when the governor came.

Hugo was going on and on. She had never heard him talk so much about himself. He sounded quite eager and anxious. She wondered if he were on the verge of proposing to Maxine. Of course, he would not propose in front of Pearl.

"I have several cases pending in Cincinnati. After that, I am free until Christmas. I thought I might come back here, to Paintsville, and rest up. It is exhausting to travel about so much. One wants a home, doesn't one? And there is no home without a fine woman in it, don't you agree?"

Sarah raised her eyebrows. He was going a bit far, she thought.

"Oh, I do agree," said Maxine, softly, so softly that Sarah could scarcely hear her words. "No place like home, and no home without a fine woman—I do agree. My, you do have a gift with words, Hugo. No wonder you're such a fine lawyer!"

"Thank you. You are a very kind woman. You know, it is rather unusual—forgive me, I don't mean to offend—when a beautiful woman like you makes fast friends with another woman like Miss Sarah. Often, I find a type of jealousy builds up. I think it is beautiful when two women can be such friends."

"Oh, I am so pleased that we are friends," said Maxine. "I wish she had come years ago! I never met anybody I liked so much, right away. And of course she is so much like Old Adam, who was our dearest friend!"

"Yes, I think she is very much like Adam, trustworthy, strong, firm, intelligent," said Hugo.

Sarah blushed, and moved away hastily from the

cupboard without finishing her count. It was nice to hear such compliments about oneself, but a little embarrassing also.

Sarah counted some of the glassware in another cupboard, until she thought it was safe to return to the other one with the white formal china. Zeke followed her patiently about, lifting out items, holding the inventory book for her, filling her pen from the ink stand. She wondered if he heard and understood the conversation they were overhearing, or if it all went beyond him.

To her surprise, Hugo was going on about a case he had handled. It was not like him to brag, she thought. He must really want to impress Maxine.

Maxine murmured her charming encouragement at intervals, and he went on and on.

"You see, it was so difficult because we could find no witnesses against the man. He was a well-liked person, and no one could believe he would do such a crime. I remained in the town for several weeks, just trying to find someone who had seen something, anything—"

"You have such patience—" murmured Maxine.

Sarah shook her head, finished the third cupboard, and she and Zeke went back to the kitchen. Justina had some tea ready, with some hot biscuits, and she decided she could not wait until dinner.

Justina set the hot tea before her, with the pretty blue sprigged china glowing on the rude table, in front of the fireplace.

"How comfortable this is," sighed Sarah, settling down, reaching for a hot biscuit. She spread it lavishly with butter, then with the golden honey. "You spoil me, Justina, you know you do."

"Yes, ma'am. I means to spoil you, Miss Sarah," said Justina, giggling a little. "Mr. Joel, he right. We-all want you to be so happy here, you stay forever."

Presently Sarah heard a quick light step in the passageway, and Maxine came in from the front of the inn. Sarah looked up at her, and stared.

The woman was glowing with beauty, her cheeks pink, her eyes sparkling with violet fire. She had never looked so lovely. Her trim figure seemed to vibrate with life. She smiled at Sarah, her face so open and so happy that Sarah was happy for her.

"Oh—tea," she said, as though someone had offered nectar and ambrosia. "Oh, biscuits and honey—"

"Sit right down, Miss Maxine," said Justina, bustling about. "You be hungry from all your work."

"Oh, I am," she said, but as though in a daze. She sat down opposite Sarah. "Pearl helped me—and Hugo," she added, her voice softening. "Hugo went out to the stables to see to a horse. What happened to Billy Dexter?" she added.

"He was trying out a horse and carriage, and took a bad tumble," said Sarah. It was the story they had agreed on.

"Oh, that's too bad. We just heard about it," said Maxine. Her cheeks were glowing. "Hugo said—he said he would go see what had happened. My, he is such a dependable person, isn't he? And so intelligent."

"Yes, he certainly is. And very kind-hearted," said Sarah. "When I was coming to Paintsville, no one could have been more courteous. And to a perfect stranger. Why, I can imagine how he would be to his wife, or to his own family. He would treat her like a queen," she added, her eyes on the biscuit she was buttering industriously.

"Oh, yes, he would," sighed Maxine, letting her biscuit lie on her plate. Her eyes were dreamy. "My, he is attractive, too. You don't often find a man so intelligent—and attractive— Of course, my Tim was the handsomest man you ever want to see."

"He was a beautiful man," said Justina, bringing a hot jug of fresh tea to Maxine's side. "A very beautiful man. A very good man. He'd want you to be happy, Miss Maxine. He was that kind a man."

Maxine's face puckered up, and for a moment Sarah

thought she was going to cry. But she straightened up, and drew a deep breath. "Yes, he would want me to be happy," she said. "Tim was like that. He thought about other people more than himself. He was very kind— like Hugo," she added, thoughtfully, and took a bite of biscuit.

"Mr. Hugo, he coming for supper tonight, Miss Sarah," said Justina, then. "I thought I could fix some steaks, and corn on the cob, and bread pudding—"

"Whatever you want to, Justina. You know better than I what the men like. Joel is coming also," she added, trying not to blush. She couldn't help thinking how nice it would be, some distant future time, when Maxine and Hugo might be married and coming for dinner with Sarah and Joel—Sarah and Joel Walden. How nice that sounded, she thought. Sarah and Joel Walden. Sarah Walden. Married to Joel. Joel would treat her like—like a woman, a flesh and blood woman, she thought, and tried to stop her riotous thoughts. They were running away with her.

"Yes, ma'am. I'll fix corn on the cob, and bread pudding with raisins, and green beans—and plums for dessert with cake." And Justina bustled back happily to her favorite occupation, planning and cooking meals.

"I think I'll go home and change my dress," said Maxine, rather absently, looking down at the lavender cotton.

"Oh, that is quite pretty, Maxine," said Sarah, mischievously.

"But I've had it on all day," said Maxine. She jumped up, said goodbye and was out the back door into the rain, as though she did not even notice it.

Maxine returned within an hour, wearing a bright blue silk that set off her pretty peaches and cream complexion and her large violet eyes. Her blonde hair was unbound, brushed out, and tied back with a blue ribbon, as Sarah's was. She came up to Sarah's rooms, tapped, was admitted.

She was radiantly beautiful, and Sarah said so. "My,

you are just lovely tonight, Maxine. Hugo won't be able to take his eyes off you."

Maxine blushed vividly. "Oh, Sarah, is it so obvious? Don't you think he likes me?" she demanded eagerly. She whirled about the room, making her skirts flare up. "Oh, I am so happy," she said, half under her breath. "Isn't he a wonderful man? He is so attractive. Do you think he likes me?"

"I think he likes you very much," said Sarah, remembering the conversation she had overheard. "And he is very intelligent. I think he probably will have a brilliant future. Lawyers are much in demand out here. Some of them go into politics," she added.

"Politics!" Maxine stood still in the middle of the room, her violet eyes glowing. "Politics! Oh, Sarah! Imagine. The wife of a congressman! Or a governor! Oh, my, the entertaining! The parties. Everyone around me—oh, and clothes, and jewels—"

Sarah began to laugh. "Slow down, Maxine! He isn't elected yet!"

"I'll bet he could be, in a minute! People will like him, they do already. And they trust him! Oh, imagine!" And Maxine flung herself into a chair, with the due regard for the brilliant blue silk of her dress, and the little train that flirted with her small blue-shod feet. "Oh, imagine," she sighed, her eyes glowing.

Sarah smiled down at her affectionately. She was pleased with the match. Gloomy Leonard could just go by the board, she thought. He wasn't good enough for pretty vivacious Maxine.

She brushed out her long golden-brown hair, thinking about Joel. They would not have such a spectacular marriage, she did not expect Joel would go out for election to an office. But he would be liked, and respected. And they could make the inn a good place to be, a popular place for the guests, a home for themselves. Her own cheeks glowed as she thought of the rosy future—if Joel did love her. If he was not just teasing or playing with her. If Joel did love her—

Maxine was going on breathlessly. "I really have

mourned Tim a terribly long time, Sarah, I really have.
I didn't even want to go out with Leonard, anyone can
tell you that. Dad insisted I should have some fun. But
I missed Tim, I really missed my Tim. I mourned him
more than two years."

"I know you have, my dear," said Sarah, gently.

Maxine did not seem to hear her. Her eyes were
half-closed, contemplating the toes of her blue shoes.
"Tim would want me to be happy," she murmured. "It
isn't as though I had rushed into anything. And of
course Hugo has not declared himself. I think he is a
very fine gentleman, don't you, Sarah?"

"Very fine." Sarah finished brushing back her hair,
and tied the red ribbon about it again. It set off the grey
dress, and made her costume brighter. She repinned
the cameo, and wondered if Joel would think she was
pretty, especially next to the bright radiant beauty of
Maxine, so blonde, in her brilliant blue silk. Should she
have changed to the new dress, the rose silk? But no,
she must save that for some special occasion.

And Joel was not one to pay that much attention to
dress, she thought. He had known Maxine all his life,
and had not tried to propose to her. He had turned to
Sarah, as soon as they had met. He had been sort of
courting her all week, she thought, and met her own
blue eyes in the mirror half-shyly. Only a week, she
thought, and she was deeply in love already. How did
Joel really feel about her? Had he kissed her on
impulse? Or did he mean that he loved her?

"And we wouldn't have to live in Paintsville," added
Maxine, suddenly. "We could live anywhere. Why, we
could live in Columbus, or Cincinnati! He travels so
much, he wants a home someplace, but it wouldn't
have to be here! Would it? We could go to some
glamorous city, and have a brilliant social life! Oh, how
marvelous that would be— It would be worth everything, all the sorrow and troubles—"

"Of course it would," said Sarah, soberly. She felt a
little unhappy that Maxine was already thinking about

leaving town! She had thought of the two couples, being friends for a long time, visiting each other, helping each other. But already Maxine was thinking of going to gayer places.

"I asked Tim to take me to Cincinnati, but he wouldn't leave Dad," said Maxine dreamily. "Of course—there is the store. And Dad will be leaving the store to me. Still I could have someone run it for me—oh, dear, such plans we will have to make," and she laughed, a pretty bubble of laughter. "Dear me, I'm thinking about leaving town, and Hugo has never even proposed to me! What am I thinking about?" Her changeable face crinkled up with her laughter, and she looked up appealingly at Sarah. "Oh, dear Sarah, am I really mad?"

Sarah relaxed, and laughed back. "Oh, we all dream on, I guess," she said. "But when it comes right down to planning, and carrying out the plans, that is always a different story, isn't it? I expect things will work out for both of us, eventually."

"Yes, they will," said Maxine, firmly, her eyes narrowing at some distant thought. "I know they will."

Joel tapped on the door, and called to them. "Are you ladies ready for dinner? I'm starving!"

Sarah opened the door for him, and he looked down at her, and his eyes were smiling at her, and her heart was light as air, bouncing around in an alarming fashion inside her.

"Hello, there," he said, and she thought that was the most important thing she had heard in hours.

Chapter 12

~~~~~~

Dinner turned into a large affair. Hugo Forrester came, and sat across from Maxine, at Sarah's right hand. Joel was there, and took the seat at the foot of the table, near the fireplace. Leonard Ensley had come in, and been invited. And Clarence Gibson came also, and was invited by Sarah.

It was very pleasant, there in the huge warm kitchen, so cosy and firelit, with the rain pouring down outside. Yet Sarah had a funny uneasy feeling which grew as the dinner went on and on.

Clarence Gibson was sitting at her left. She would have given him place of honor at her right, but Hugo had already been seated when Clarence had come in the back door. She wondered if he had followed Leonard. Clarence had given Maxine such a long keen look, then a look at Leonard.

What was going on? Sarah wondered. Leonard grew more and more cross, as Maxine addressed most of her remarks to Hugo. Maxine was so radiantly lovely, her cheeks pink with excitement, her violet eyes shining up at Hugo. She paid little attention to Clarence on her one hand and Leonard on her other.

Leonard kept looking at Maxine sideways, then down at his plate. His dark brown curly hair and dark brown eyes were not lightened by the black suit he wore. He looked like a store clerk, which was what he was, thought Sarah, and wondered why she didn't like him. Maybe it was his gloomy air, his pessimistic attitude, so different from Joel Walden's.

Joel, she thought, had had enough troubles to make him the most gloomy person in the world. But instead his gray eyes sparkled with humor and mischief, his face lightened in mirth more often than not. He loved to tease, and he could get even Leonard to laugh at times. Not tonight, though.

Sarah's eyes kept meeting Joel's. She kept feeling drawn to him, remembering his kisses, the way he had held her so tightly, so possessively to him. When she looked at him, she knew he was thinking about her also, about holding her. Somehow she knew that he was remembering vividly, and wanting to do it again. She could feel the warm color coming into her cheeks, and her blood racing. It was odd, the way she *knew* what he was thinking about. It was as though they were so close that they could read each other's minds.

Maxine had been asking Hugo Forrester about his law experiences, and for once the usually silent courteous lawyer was talking eagerly, monopolizing the conversation. He kept looking across at Maxine, then turning to Sarah and looking down at her as he elaborated a point. Sarah nodded again, again, absently, scarcely hearing him.

"There are several cases pending," he was saying, when she started listening again. "Some of them involve the legality of claims to the land. You know, the Indians have not given up all claim to the land here in Ohio. By the Treaty of Greeneville—"

Her mind wandered again. Maxine was gazing at him, forgetting to eat, spellbound, her eyes glistening. Leonard was staring down at his plate, scowling. And Clarence looked at Hugo, at Maxine, at Leonard, and was frowning thoughtfully. Was anyone really hearing what Hugo said? Sarah wondered. There were some

strong undercurrents here that she did not comprehend. She wondered if Joel knew. He was listening
alertly, his gray eyes half-closed at times, as though he
heard more than words.

His gaze at Maxine was sadly compassionate, she
thought. He had known Tim and Maxine all their lives.
She felt he did not care much for Leonard. Did he also
hope that Maxine would find a happy marriage with
Hugo?

Justina had served the thick juicy steaks, the corn on
the cob, which was so tender it must have come just
from the garden. The green beans were crisp and
flavored with ham broth. The bread pudding was
melting with raisins and custard.

Justina cleared away their plates, with a sigh of
satisfaction at how much had been eaten. Little Pearl
was carefully cutting a yellow cake, and spooning plums
and syrup into dishes.

"Miss Sarah, you surely live well here," said Hugo
Forrester, turning to her, and gazing down at her again.
His brown eyes were twinkling. "I don't think I am
mistaken in saying that Justina is trying to make a good
impression on you!"

Maxine laughed prettily. "Oh, we all are, Hugo!"
She said his name, with a special shy emphasis which
brought Leonard's scowling gaze to her face again.
"We do want Sarah to stay here! Why, I haven't had a
best friend like Sarah—in all my life!"

Clarence stirred and cleared his throat carefully.
"Someone isn't as fond of Sarah as all that, from the
attempts on her life, I would say." His dry dispassion-
ate tone sent a chill through Sarah.

"Oh, it must be a bum," said Maxine, a shadow
falling on her face. "It has to be someone—crazy, don't
you think, Leonard?"

"Sure. Has to be," said Leonard, glumly. "Wish the
sheriff would come back and catch the fellow. Menace
to all of us."

"Any sign of the gold, Sarah?" asked Clarence
Gibson, picking up a spoon to dish up a bit of plum.

"Not yet. I really haven't had time to look." She felt again the exasperation that came over her when people took so for granted that she could locate it easily.

"I'd drop everything to look if I were you. The inventory can wait," said Clarence.

She started visibly, and looked down the long table to Joel. He gazed back at her steadily. How had Clarence known she was working on the china inventory this afternoon? Did everyone know what she did, by some silent communication? Or had Clarence Gibson been watching over her activities? Had he been the silent figure in the back of the hallway, watching her and Joel?

A chill went through and through her. She lost all taste for the cake. Only Justina's eager gaze watching her made her pick up her fork and break off a bite. It was delicious, so light and tender, full of butter and cream.

"I expect it will turn up somewhere," she said finally. "In the meantime, the banker called on me. Evidently grandfather left plenty in the bank to take care of bills. I don't need to worry about expenses for a time. And when the rains let up, we should have guests once more."

"That's right. Soon as the rains let up, and the bridges get fixed up," chimed in Justina eagerly. "The inn be bright and full of company once more." And she beamed at the thought.

"I was thinking today," said Sarah, determined to change the topic from the gold and the attacks on her, "that the inn must be very lovely and exciting when it is full of guests. I hope to do as well as grandfather in running the inn, in time. Of course, it will take practice."

"And you should have a man to help you," said Hugo Forrester, firmly. "Have you thought of hiring someone?"

"Not yet," she said, blushing at her own thoughts. She had thought that she and Joel—that Joel might be interested—that he just might propose—If he did, and if they got married, that would solve *that* problem. Joel would help her, he would always help her.

Maxine's quick gaze went from Hugo to Sarah and back, speculatively. "You must have been talking about the inn," she said. "Are you really thinking about staying, Sarah? Could you face the managing of the inn alone? What did Hugo advise?"

"Oh, he advised me to stay on. It is a good investment," said Sarah.

For some reason, Maxine's face shadowed. She laid down her fork, and pushed the plate of cake away from her like a petulant child. "Oh, business, business," she muttered, as though she were tired of it. "I'll bet—you'll be so busy with the inn that you won't have time for fun, Sarah."

"I've never had much time for fun," she said, quietly, not knowing why she should feel a little hurt at the words. Maxine seemed to imply that Sarah was a dull girl, with no time or inclination for partying. Indeed, she had enjoyed parties as a child. But when her mother had died, she had had to stop being a child very rapidly. There was always work to be done at the house, supervising the servants, doing some cleaning and marketing. Later there had been the nursing.

Hugo laid his hand lightly on hers. "You are thinking about the war again, Miss Sarah. You must forget it," he said, in a low tone. "That is over. You ought to take time for fun. You deserve it."

She smiled back at him, his brown eyes were so gentle and so thoughtful. "Thank you. There will be time—later, I'm sure. And yes, the war is over, thank God." She glanced up, drawn by Joel's gaze. He was looking at hers and Hugo's hands together on the table. She flushed, and drew her hand gently away to pick up the fork again..

"The war is over, but it won't be finished with, not for another hundred years," said Clarence Gibson, unexpectedly. "No, the bitterness will linger for a long time."

Sarah jumped, and turned to stare at him. He was

frowning, his handsome blue eyes flicked at her face, then down again. He was very good-looking she thought. And they said Tim Gibson had been even better. Was this what he meant, she wondered, when he thought about his son, his lost hopes, his only child dead? Would he never forgive or forget?

"Oh, I hope not, I hope the bitterness will not linger. Oh, I could not bear it if the war went on and on in the hearts of people," she said, with unexpected violence. "The wards were full of the wounded and dying. There was so much pain—I saw so much of—of man's inhumanity to man, of the cruelty and pain and death—Oh, that must not continue! If only we might never have another war. No more murder and killing—never again!"

Joel stirred, and got up to get a pot of coffee from the fire. He said, his back to them, "It would not continue—if people could forgive. War begins first in people's hearts. It spreads to their hands, and to actions which can never be taken back." He turned back to the table, the heavy coffee pot in his hands. He looked down at the table of companions in a strangely compassionate concerned fashion. "If we can forget and forgive—there is hope for the human race, isn't there? It begins with us, with each person, in his heart."

There was a long, somehow strained silence. Justina held the coffee cups while Joel poured out the coffee and gave some to each person. Maxine and Leonard and Clarence were staring at the cups, as though seeing fortunes in them, bitter fortunes. Hugo looked from one to the other, slightly frowning, detached, his face a study in concentration. Joel was looking only at the coffee pot, holding the pot steady in his hands.

They could not forget, thought Sarah. Even though they all liked and loved Old Adam, they could not forget that he had encouraged Tim Gibson to go to war. They could not forget that he had rescued slaves, sent them on to Canada, fought against his own townspeople to help the slaves. The town had been violently divided, and Old Adam had been part of the divisions. Yet in the inn, they had said, there was no war.

Sarah said, finally, quietly, yet with such feeling that they all looked to her, "I hope, if I do manage the inn, that I can manage it as grandfather did. You said— some of you—that there was no war in the inn. All could come and be welcome, whatever his politics or beliefs. I want it to be that way again. A place where all men and women can come and be at home for a time. A place of peace."

Joel smiled down straight at her, his eyes suddenly glowing. "That sounds wonderful, a place of peace," he said.

"Yet it wasn't like that, Miss Sarah," said Justina, suddenly in the conversation again. She put her hands on her ample hips, her brown face worried. "Miss Sarah—your grandfather welcomed people, he surely did. But he was fighting his own war, he was. He fought against people who was going to slave us. He fought against dividing the nation and letting the South go. I heard him many a time, telling how he would go to war hisself, so the country would be together. And I saw him myself with his shotgun in his hands, just dassing somebody to take us away."

Clarence Gibson's mouth twisted in a smile at her remarks. A pained rueful smile. "Yes, and the shotgun was pointed at me once," he said, roughly. "My own best friend—pointing a gun at me. Do you still think, Miss Sarah, that you can make the inn a place of peace? Old Adam couldn't. He talked it up big, yes, but when the people came, he fought them stubbornly. He was a hard man. And I think you have something of Old Adam in you."

Her hands twisted together, and she was aware that they were all looking at her, studying her, rather impersonally, judging her. Her fingers straightened, and she put them flat on the table before her.

"You are right, Mr. Gibson," she said, firmly. "I do hope I have something of my grandfather in me, his courage, his willingness to fight for his beliefs. I want peace, yes, but not compromise with evil. I too would fight for what I believe. I have in the past, I will again. I cannot sit back, and let evil overcome me. I will not be a coward!"

Clarence Gibson grinned a little, a twisted grin. She did not like to see it. "That's what I thought. So—join the battle, my dear! You are Old Adam come to life again—as I had hoped—and feared." He pushed back his chair abruptly, suddenly looking older and a little bowed as he got up rudely.

"I must go back to the store. I haven't locked up yet," he said. "Coming, Leonard? You didn't finish the rolls of new fabric. We want them on the shelves by the time the rains let up."

Leonard pushed back his chair, looked down at Maxine. "Might as well go," he said, and followed Clarence out the back door. Neither had thanked Sarah for the meal, or expressed any courtesy. She felt the lack keenly, as both were gentlemen in their manners. Both must have been deeply disturbed by the conversation, she thought, to have acted so.

Joel sat down at his place, and drank his hot coffee slowly. Maxine was sitting looking at Hugo, her violet eyes troubled. Sarah turned to Hugo.

"Forgive us, Hugo, for dragging the troubles into the conversation. They need not concern you," she said, gently. "I am afraid it will be a long time before the war is forgotten in Paintsville. Perhaps I am wrong to stay here."

"Don't let this upset you," he said. "Time will heal all the wounds, I feel certain."

Maxine sipped at her coffee daintily, saying little as they finished their meal. Justina had forgotten the talk, it seemed, and was humming over the dishes. Sarah felt strangely disturbed and upset over the talking. There had been such a strong undercurrent, and she did not understand it all. Did Clarence Gibson hate her because of her grandfather? Did he think of her in the same terms as Old Adam? Did he expect to fight with her over the issues of slavery and union? She felt very weary and discouraged at the thought. The Gibsons, Clarence and Maxine, were some of her closest friends in this town, her first friends. If they could not forgive and forget, what hope was there in remaining?

"Maxine, I'll walk you home. The rain has let up," said Joel, finally. "Why don't we walk down the street and back? I bet you haven't been outdoors all day."

"No—just in and out," she said, her tone depressed.

"You need some fresh air," he said, and held her chair back for her. He grinned down at Sarah and Hugo. "You finish your coffee in peace, no more war talk for you. Talk about the inn, how you'll fix it up, Sarah, because you are going to stay, you know! You're too ornery to give up and go away!"

She smiled at his cheerful teasing, her heart lightened a little. But she didn't like it that he was walking Maxine home. What was he? She had felt for a little while that Joel belonged to her. Was he doing it as an old friend, did he sense that Maxine was hurt and disturbed? Or did he like her very much, and want to take her away from Hugo's presence? She didn't know how Hugo felt, but she herself felt very jealous and upset.

Sarah had thought there was nothing between Joel and Maxine. Perhaps there was more underneath than she had realized. Perhaps Joel was only waiting until Maxine's period of mourning was over, and then he might marry her.

She toyed with the fork, sipped at her cooling coffee, looking down at the polished wood table. Hugo was sitting silently with her. Justina finished up all the dishes but their coffee cups, then went to her rooms with Pearl and Zeke. They would eat their supper in there, and finish the dishes later, as was their habit.

Sarah and Hugo sat in front of the fire, silently, yet in some communion. Joel did not return. He usually came back to see Sarah safely to her room, she thought. It must mean either that he had forgotten her, or that he found Maxine's company very interesting.

She felt a little painful unusual stab in her chest. Didn't Joel mean it when he kissed a girl? Or did he just like to tease and play with a girl's vulnerable heart?

Hugo finally broke the long silence. "I should take advantage of this opportunity to see you alone," he said, quietly. "I feel dumb. It is unusual for me. I usually have a facility for words, you know."

His words scarcely penetrated. But she must be courteous. She glanced up at him, tried to think what he was saying. She met his concerned intelligent brown eyes.

"Yes, you do have a—facility for words. You are probably an excellent lawyer," she said, and wondered if she sounded like Maxine.

"I have more ability to plead other men's causes than my own," he said, and she thought she did not imagine a flush high on his cheekbones. The fire was dying down a little, the light in the kitchen was dimming.

"I would imagine—you are able to do either," she said, thinking of his words to Maxine that day.

"I hope you are not seriously thinking of leaving Paintsville and returning to the East—though that would not necessarily stop my plans," he said, seriously, and reached out to touch her hand gently. "Sarah, I feel that you—are not indifferent to me. Forgive my unseemly haste in saying these words to you. I deeply honor you. I have admired you since the first minutes we met. I wondered to myself why I was so concerned over your safety on the miserable journey to Paintsville. It is only in the past two days that I have begun to realize what is wrong with me—I mean, what has happened to me."

She was so startled she could not stop him. She gazed up at him, wide-eyed. He could not be proposing. He liked Maxine, he had been saying all those things to Maxine about his prospects, his family, his future—

"I deeply honor and respect you, Sarah," he was

saying, his hand closing warmly over her fingers. "I have only just begun to realize that I have—forgive me—fallen in love with you. You are so honest and so fine, such a pure good woman—"

My goodness, she thought. She had never thought she would ever be proposed to in such solid old-fashioned manner— Propose! The thought shocked her awake. She was not dreaming. Hugo Forrester was sitting there, earnestly proposing to her.

"You are very much like your grandfather, as they have said. He was a good man, of solid virtues. Your family is a fine one, I know this. My own family would be delighted to meet you, to come to know you, to welcome you into our midst. I have a sister and two brothers. My parents are still living, thank God. If you decide not to remain here, I could escort you back East, with a suitable female traveling companion, if you wish. I would like you to come to my family in Philadelphia, meet them, come to know them. I hope by this time you would come to love me and consent to be my wife—"

She must stop this flow of traveling plans! "Hugo, I am not—not planning anything—I have not decided yet—" she managed to gasp. Her hand was limp, she felt numb, she could not pull her hand from his, she seemed to have no strength in her at all.

"Of course. You must have time to decide. But I wanted you to know that whatever you decide will be excellent with me. I love the West, I love Ohio, I had planned to live here all my days. If you decide to make your home here, I will be delighted, my dear. I shall set up my office here, we can hire such help as you need to assist you in running the inn, if you wish to do that. If you want to sell out, and return East, then I shall do that. My future is in your hands, whatever you decide, I shall be well-pleased. I have found at last that it is not where one is that matters, it is the person who is one's life companion—"

She finally managed to pull her hand away, and sit back in her chair. She was too stunned to get up. She could not think of the words to reject him. She could not say she loved another man, she was not yet sure of her feelings for Joel, or his for her. (And where was he, anyway? He and Maxine had been gone more than an hour!)

"Hugo, please. I am flattered over your proposal— but I am so—surprised—I cannot really—"

"I know. This is very precipitous of me," he said, but firmly, not apologetically. "But when I learned to know my own heart, I could not wait to inform you, to place some claim on you. You are a very lovely and fine woman. One does not find a person like you every day, and I cannot hope that I am the only one with eyes to see your quality! I am putting in my claim first, and I can only hope that one day, perhaps soon, you will come to realize that you can love me as I love you. When that day comes, I shall be the happiest man in the world—"

She stopped his rush of words. He had really found his tongue, she thought ruefully. "Please, Hugo, please, don't! I am surprised, yes, but it is very early—I mean late—I mean the day is late, and I am tired—I mean, it is very soon after meeting you to know my own feelings—You are so extremely kind to me, and I am grateful—but I do not know—"

He smiled, and his smile was very attractive and affectionate. She thought, involuntarily, that if her heart was not already being pulled to Joel's with thick strings of love, she would be tempted to accept Hugo's offer. He was such an intelligent fine man. He would respect her, love her, take care of her always. And like Maxine, she found the thought of his high position very tempting!

Hugo was a fine lawyer, in a state where lawyers were scarce. He might become quite famous, maybe become a congressman or a governor. Surely, he would have a fine beautiful home, and his wife would share the respect of important people. They would entertain and—

Oh, what was she thinking, she gasped to herself. She would not marry a man for that! No, but she added, it would be very nice to be in such a position. To be treated like a queen! To be the wife of Hugo Forrester would be a fine thing. If she loved him.

"I do not mean to throw you into confusion, my dear," he said, very gently. "I shall not press you. I only wanted to express my deep affection and respect, to tell you of my love, and hope that someday you might come to return the feeling. I wanted also to inform you that the decision on the inn, whether to remain or to return East, is up to you alone. I shall be most happy to follow you in this. Yours shall be the decision as to where we shall live."

"Thank you, Hugo, you are very kind, but I cannot make this decision—"

She stopped abruptly. Maxine and Joel were walking into the kitchen from the hallway in the front of the inn. They had heard the last words, she knew instinctively. Maxine's face was crumpled up with such hurt that Sarah's feelings went out to her instinctively and at once. She could not hide her thoughts any more than a small child. She stared at both of them.

"S-Sarah?" she stammered. "We—we had a walk— we—it is so nice—out—" But she couldn't keep it up. She gave a funny little sob, a choking sound, and dashed out the back door.

Joel followed her slowly, closed and locked the door after her, first peering into the darkness to make sure she had made it next door. Then he came back in, and sat down at the end of the table again.

"Wonder if the coffee is still hot?" he said, into the embarrassed silence. He sat down there solidly, scowling, not like his usual self. And Sarah knew he had heard and misunderstood their last words.

Hugo frowned at him, with dignity. But he had said

his piece, and was somewhat satisfied over the results, thought Sarah. She had not refused him, not said no. There had been insufficient time to word her refusal. And she had not thought of the right kind words to tell him she would not, could not marry him, because she was more than half in love with another man.

"More coffee?" said Joel, finally. "It is still hot. Anybody want more cake?"

"I believe I do. It is delicious." Hugo sat there and let Joel wait on him. Sarah felt more embarrassed than ever as Joel limped about the kitchen, cutting cake, pouring coffee. He brought her a cup, unasked. She added cream and sugar, stirred and stirred it.

She had a lump in her throat. She wasn't sure if the coffee could get around it. She hated it that Maxine and Joel had overheard Hugo's proposal, and her words. Maxine would be so terribly hurt. She would think that Sarah had deceived her, Hugo as well. She had dressed up for Hugo that evening, she had talked about marrying him. Maxine would be so angry and upset when she finally took in the shock, that Hugo had been talking to her, rehearsing what he would say to Sarah! Perhaps hoping that she would repeat to Sarah about his prospects. Thinking of them as close friends.

Not any more, not for a while, thought Sarah, ruefully. Maxine would be too hurt to be friends for a while. Oh, dear, why did life have to be so mixed up? She had been enjoying so much the friendship of lovely Maxine. And Maxine had been sewing for her, helping her. And she had been the means of hurting Maxine badly. She hated that.

What about Joel? She stirred and stirred the coffee. Hugo was eating his cake with fresh appetite, as though he had come unscathed through an ordeal. Maybe he did think of it that way. Proposing was probably hard work, she thought.

Finally she ventured to peep under her lashes at Joel. He was looking down at his coffee. In spite of saying he wanted it, he had scarcely touched it.

As she gazed at him, his lashes came up, his head turned slightly, and he was looking directly at her.

The dark gray eyes were cold, he was glaring silently and reproachfully. Oh, dear, he was hurt also.

And that mattered, terribly much. She thought of his hurt, and was hurt for him. And wished she could jump up from the table, and go to him and hold his head against her breast, and say, never mind, it didn't mean anything, I am going to turn down Hugo as soon as I can find the words, I don't love him, I love you, Joel, don't mind about words, we don't need words, we understand each other without words—

Please, Joel, she thought, we understand each other without words—don't we? But he went on glaring at her, until her eyes half-closed to shut out the hurt from his.

Chapter 13

~~~~~~

Sarah spent a very uncomfortable wakeful night, tossing and turning on the comfortable soft bed, pushing back the covers, pulling them up again as she turned colder.

Joel had escorted her up to her room, searched it after she unlocked it, waited for her to bolt it after him. He had been gallant, but silent, protecting her without words. She wanted to say something, but she could not speak.

Why not? she wondered in the dark hours of early morning. Why couldn't she turn to Joel and tell him quite simply that she did not mean to marry Hugo, that she had been groping for words to refuse him?

Joel had said nothing to her, maybe her imagination was working overtime. Maybe he didn't really love her. Maybe she was jumping to conclusions.

She punched her pillows again, and turned over on her back. She stared up into the dimness as the early gray dawn crept in the windows, lighting up the mantelpiece, the lovely furniture, the bright colors of the afghan on her bed. She felt so odd, she thought. She felt restless, wondering, impatient, muddleheaded. She couldn't think straight. She kept thinking about Joel, rehearsing words to say to him.

If this was love, she thought, then love was a most uncomfortable feeling, a strange yearning, a cross-happy laughing-crying feeling that made her all mixed up.

She turned her hot cheek into the warm pillow, and dozed a little, half-asleep, half-dreaming deliberately. Maybe Joel would give her a chance today to speak to him. Or maybe she should make that chance, tell him bluntly, frankly, that she did not mean to accept Hugo.

Then what? What if it really meant nothing to Joel, except that he felt sorry for his life-long friend, Maxine?

"Oh, dear!" she whispered, and sat up. She might as well get up, though it was so early.

She padded to the door, listened, cautiously unbolted the door. She heard someone stirring even as she opened the door. The bedroom door opposite her suite was open. She saw Joel sitting up in the bed, and staring at her.

"Oh!" She felt suddenly blank, frightened, pleased. Was this where Joel slept, did he do this to guard her through the night? "Joel—good morning."

"You're awake early. I'll yell down for Zeke to fetch hot water," he said, and swung his long bare legs out of bed. Blushing, she closed her door.

"Well," she gasped, leaning limply against her bolted door. No wonder Zeke knew just when to guard her, when to bring hot water. Joel must have been sleeping there all week, instead of in his own room at the stagecoach office. Guarding her.

She felt a little dizzy pleasure, and found herself smiling, dreaming into the distance. Joel. How nice he was. How thoughtful.

Someone tapped briskly at her door. "Miss Sarah?" said Zeke's cautiously raised voice. "Your hot water, Miss Sarah."

She opened the door, smiled and thanked him, and accepted the hot kettle. Across from her, the door was closed. Joel must be getting up also.

She would speak to him today, she thought. She would clear up the misunderstanding between them, no matter how he reacted. Maybe he didn't really care about her. She couldn't take the chance of not being honest and open.

She put on her most becoming blue wool dress, brushed her light golden-brown curly hair again and again, until it was crackling and crispy about her shoulders. She tied it back, found a blue ribbon to fasten it, and finished it with a bow. She looked about ten years old, she thought, with her cheeks so pink and her eyes so shining. What would Joel think?

She hurried with her dressing, then, and opened the door cautiously. She started as she saw Joel leaning against the wall, waiting patiently for her. He was wearing a dark gray sweater and dark gray trousers, and his eyes were very dark. He looked down at her thoughtfully. She couldn't help smiling up at him, and he finally relaxed and smiled back, the laugh lines crinkling at the corners of his mouth and deeply into his thin cheeks.

"Joel, I didn't know you were sleeping nearby. You're taking an awful chance with your door open."

"I'm a light sleeper," he said, briefly. He motioned for her to go ahead of him down the stairs to the kitchen. She remembered what she wanted to say, and turned around, halfway down.

"Joel? I want to talk to you—sometime today, if you can make the time." She looked up at him anxiously.

He paused behind her, gazed down at her. "Sure, Sarah. Whenever you want. It's a nice day for a change. Want to go for a walk outdoors?"

"Yes, please." Then she remembered that he had gone for a walk with Maxine last night, and she wondered what he had said to Maxine.

She had so much she wanted to say to him, so much she wanted to ask, like blurting, "Do you love me? Can I count on you? Will you let me love you?" Oh, she must be mad, she thought, and continued to gaze up at him, and he was staring down at her, for quite a long minute.

She flushed finally, guiltily, turned-around and went on down to the kitchen. The fire was lit, and Justina was stirring up fresh biscuits. Sarah went to help with the coffee, and then the eggs.

Joel went to the back door, unlocked and opened it. "It's a nice day," he said, surprise in his voice. "Looks like the rain has let up."

"That's good," said Justina. "All of us feel better if we get some sunshine on our bones."

There was a cool wind blowing into the kitchen from the open door. Joel gazed outdoors for a minute, then closed the door again and swung back to the table. "I'll go up and see how Billy Dexter is doing. Is he awake?"

"Awake these two hours," said Justina. "Reckon he's in a bit of pain. I fed him some breakfast and he's a-sleeping again."

Sarah was stricken with remorse. She had forgotten all about Billy in brooding over her own problems. "I'll go up after breakfast and see how he is," she said. "I do wish a doctor was around here."

"Your grandfather was hoping to get a young man to move here, nothing come of it after he died," said Justina.

Joel nodded, and sat down at the end of the table. It seemed natural to have him there, thought Sarah. Maybe, someday, it would be his own place. If they married—if he and she were married—and ran the inn together— And days like this, all sunshine and cool wind and beauty, would be theirs to share together. Getting up early, talking, planning, how sweet it would be! She thought, working with Joel, talking to Joel, planning with Joel—sleeping with Joel—

"You feverish?" asked Justina, critically, and put her hand on Sarah's cheek for a moment. "You look all warm. Did you catch a chill?"

"No, no, I don't think, I don't believe I have. I just didn't sleep much last night."

"Hum, hum," said Justina, looking at her closely. Then she smiled, and turned back to her ham sizzling over the fire. Sarah set the coffee cups on the table, then went back to the heavy hot coffee pot. She had not heard Joel move behind her, but suddenly he was there, very close.

"I'll lift that, Sarah. It's heavy," he said. And his big sure hands were lifting the coffee pot and carrying it to the table. He poured out coffee for them both. Since her cup and saucer was near his, she sat down at his side instead of moving to the head of the table.

"What kept you awake? Did you hear anything?" asked Joel, looking searchingly at her flushed face as she seated herself next to him.

"No—no—just thinking." She looked up shyly, met his gray eyes at close range, and looked down again. It was crazy to feel all shaky and happy and trembling just because his hand was near hers on the table, and she could feel his warmth near her, and his voice was sort of rumbly when he spoke low and leaned to her.

"We'll talk to Billy Dexter, then go for that walk," he said softly.

She nodded. Justina brought huge plates of ham and eggs to the table, then went back for the biscuits. Sarah had felt hungry, now suddenly she could scarcely eat a bite. She cut a piece of ham, put it in her mouth, chewed it slowly. What in the world ailed her? Of course, she was hungry. She was crazy too. Feeling all fluttery in her stomach, just because Joel was so close to her.

"How about some honey, Sarah?" asked Joel. She started, reached for the golden pot, and handed it to him. Their fingers touched, and she almost dropped the pot. He looked at her again.

She would, must get control of herself. She couldn't keep on shaking like this, everyone would think she was sick.

She braced herself, looked down at her plate, concentrated on the ham, and the fluffy eggs, and the hot biscuit which she split and buttered and covered with honey. She drank a swallow of coffee. It was boiling hot, and she sputtered.

"You know that coffee is hot," rebuked Joel, and reached over and took the large cup from her and set it down on the saucer. "Have to look after you like a child." The affectionate teasing note was back in his voice, and she was suddenly radiantly happy.

"She's no child," said Justina, beaming down at them both. "Just 'cause her hair is long and has a bow in it, that's no reason to think she's a child, is it, Miss Sarah?"

"Of course not," she said, with some dignity. "If that's how you feel, I'll go upstairs and put my hair up again."

"Don't move," said Joel, though she had not moved to carry out her threat. He put his hand on her slim wrist, and held it prisoned while he laughed down at her. "Don't change a thing. I like children."

"I *will* put my hair up again," she threatened, a little silly with pleasure. He was looking at her hair as though he liked it very much.

"Then I'll yank it down again," he said, simply, and she knew he meant what he said. She flushed, tried to pull her wrist away from his hard grip. He finally let her go.

There was a long silence between them as they ate. Justina brought fresh biscuits, hot and delicate. It was not an unfriendly silence, just a little awkward one, full of unsaid remarks and thoughts that seemed to reach out for each other, as though their minds were trying to meet, a little timidly.

They were finally finished, though Sarah lingered over her coffee. She wanted to be alone with him, she wanted to talk to him, but she was afraid also. Afraid of herself, of betraying herself, of saying too much. What if he was just teasing her? What if he didn't really love her?

Well, she would tell him the truth anyway. That

would do no harm, and it might do some good. She would tell him about her and Hugo, and let him make what he wanted of her explanation.

"Let's go up and see Billy," said Joel. He had been watching her, and as soon as she set down her empty coffee cup, he pushed back his chair briskly. "Justina, we'll go out for a walk after. Going to look around."

"You take care of Miss Sarah," she said, a little anxiously, frowning. Her dark brown eyes were soft and concerned.

"I sure will," he said, his voice soft, but there was steel behind it. He caught hold of Sarah's arm as she would have gone ahead of him. He held it as they went up the stairs together.

At the top of the stairs, in the dark hallway, he said, "Do you know what Billy was up to yesterday?"

She gazed up at him. "Yes, I think so," she said. "We'll—ask him together. If he is awake."

"Okay." They went on down the hall. She was very aware of his closeness behind her. They paused at the door to Billy's room and listened. "Billy?" said Joel, his voice raised. "Awake now, Billy? It's Joel and Sarah."

"Sure. Come in." Joel opened the door. Then she gasped and stared. Billy was sitting propped up against pillows, with a flowery comforter over him, his broken arm in white bandages, just as she had fixed it. But beside his good arm lay an immense shotgun, pointed in the direction of the bedroom door!

He gazed back at her steadily, his usually cheerful genial face rather grim. "Just a precaution, Miss Sarah," he said, and patted the shotgun. "I don't like accidents much."

She sat down limply on the nearest bedroom chair. Joel put his hand on her shoulder reassuringly, and kept it there. He had closed the door after him.

"We came to ask you about your—accident," said Joel, his hand warm and steadying on Sarah's shoulder. "What happened? How did a good driver like you come to get upset?"

"Wasn't no accident," said Billy tersely. "Miss Sarah and I was looking at the horse her grandfather was driving. Seemed to me he was a mild and gentle one, not one to go shying and bucking around. Decided to try him out."

"So?" asked Joel, gazing down at Billy thoughtfully. "And you used the same carriage?"

"Right. I hitched up, petted the horse. He was fresh, all right. Hadn't been driv for a time, I figure. He was eager to get out, went sniffing at the air like he was all happy and calm. You know, not really calm, but okay? I've handled much worse horses. Remember that Thunderer, when he was racing for your granddad, Joel? I was just a tyke, but I could handle him. Well, I hitched up, made friends with this here horse, and started him out." He paused, shook his head.

"So what happened?" asked Sarah, impatiently, sitting forward on the chair.

"I driv him out to the edge of town. He was fine, prancing a bit, but taking hold all right, and drawing steady and easy. Old Adam had good horses. He never kept a mean one, said he didn't like mean horses and mean people, wouldn't have them about him."

They looked at him thoughtfully, the experienced driver drawling out his story. He was frowning, thinking.

"So we started back toward the stables. There's a dark patch of alley nearby, you know it, Joel, near the Smithson house, old Smithson who died a couple years back, and nobody's lived there. Kept his stable behind the house. I thought I'd drive through the alley and get on back, it was coming on to rain harder. I saw the ditch, but thought I was yards away. Then—" He frowned again, picking at the flowery coverlet so incongruous under his deeply tanned hand.

They just listened while he thought.

"Then—seems like I saw something out of the corner of my eyes. Something dark, moving, like a shadow. Maybe a cat, only bigger. No, wasn't a cat," he mused.

"I've been thinking and thinking, what it could be. Anyway, it shot at the horse, and that fool horse reared up and went crazy. I was trying to hold it, and half standing up in the carriage. We tipped over into the ditch, and I knocked my head and went plumb out."

Sarah took a deep unsteady breath. Joel's hand tightened painfully on her shoulder, then slowly loosened.

"That cat, or something bigger," said Joel, slowly. "What did it look like? Think, Billy."

The man crinkled up his face painfully, trying to think. He finally shook his head, slowly, his face screwing against the pain in it. "I don't know, Joel. Seems like it was like a cat, only thinner, longer. I can't tell you, Joel, boy. Wish I could. It was longer, though."

"Maybe like a snake? A blacksnake, or a rattler?"

Billy stared at Joel, Joel stared back.

"Well—it could have been. But durn it, don't put ideas into my head," he said, a little irritably. "Don't know if it was a snake or not. Could have been. But damn it—who'd do a thing like that? I was just trying out the horse. Sure, it might have spooked though—especially if it hated snakes."

"Right. It might have spooked, even a horse that doesn't usually shy. I've known horses to go right out of their minds when a rattler sounds." Joel relaxed his hold on Sarah's shoulder, and patted it gently. "Okay, Sarah, let's go for a walk. We've got some talking to do."

Billy was leaning back, the pain lines deeper. He managed to lift his good arm in a salute.

"Take care of Miss Sarah," said Billy.

"I aim to," said Joel. "Don't know why everybody thinks he has to tell me to!"

Billy grinned, looking from Joel to Sarah keenly, his shrewd small dark eyes noticing. Sarah felt a blush rising to her cheeks again.

"You take care of yourself, Billy," said Sarah gently.

She felt bitterly that it was her fault he was injured, that he might have been killed, trying out her theory. "Do you want me to send up Zeke?"

"Nope. Me and my friend here," he patted the shotgun, "we'll make out fine. Something about a shotgun kinda puts off folks that think about trouble." He grinned tightly.

Joel drew her out the door, and down the hall to her rooms. "You'll need a cloak. It's chilly outside."

"And you'll need a coat, Joel."

"You looking after me now?" He grinned down at her, the wicked teasing twinkle in his eyes.

She unlocked her door, was not surprised when he followed her inside. He lifted down her thick dark plaid cloak, and set it around her shoulders. With one hand, he lifted her soft hair under the ribbon, and set the cloak more closely about her. His fingers lingered on the back of her neck, fussing more than necessary to get the cloak and the hair in place.

"Will I need a scarf?" She didn't care, she just wanted to say something to break the sweet scary spell of his hand on her neck.

"Nope. Not that cold. Come along. I'll get another sweater for me." They went across to his room opposite hers. She lingered in the doorway shyly as he got another thick gray sweater and put his arms into it. He buttoned the buttons, and shrugged himself into it more closely. "Seems sometimes I can't ever be warm enough," he said, half to himself. "I got so durn cold sometimes in the Army, sleeping on the ground. I'd wake up wet and shivering after a rain, and start thinking about home. Seemed like it was never going to be over."

She shuddered with him, as the memory of the war years returned like a red bloody wave of horror. She tucked her hand into his arm, surprising herself. She wanted to touch him, to make sure he was really there.

"We'll go down the front way," he said. He patted her hand reassuringly. "It is over, Sarah. The war is really over. We don't have to have nightmares anymore. Sorry I brought it up."

He read her so accurately, she thought. He knew just what she was thinking.

They went down the front stairs, down into the wide beautiful sweep of the front lobby, down the shining staircase and the polished bannister and the beautiful rugs.

"It is so beautiful here, Joel," she said, and drew a deep happy breath. "Oh, I do want to stay, and make a pleasant inn here again. I think grandfather would have wanted me to do that."

"He wanted you to come," said Joel. "Specially after he got that portrait of you. Said you were an Overmiller, and you belonged here. Said he was going to send for you after the war was over."

"Did he really?" she asked happily, still clinging to his arm. She turned her head. A curtain had lifted at the store next door, just as she and Joel had gone out on the wide veranda. Maxine? She wondered, pityingly, and was reminded of last night.

Joel and she started off down the street. She glanced back, but the curtain was in place once more, only stirring a little as though someone was behind it.

"Joel—about last night, that conversation," she blurted out before she lost her nerve. "I wanted to explain—"

His arm tightened under her hand, as though the steel under the flesh had hardened. "Yes?" he said, curtly.

She let the words come out in a rush, embarrassed. "Hugo Forrester—did propose to me. I was so surprised—I wasn't expecting it, really. And I was so shocked, I couldn't think of how to say no, and not hurt him too much."

"How to say no?" repeated Joel slowly.

She dared not look up at him. "Yes. I was going to turn him down, but the words wouldn't come, then you and Maxine came back—and heard him—and me—"

He was silent. She could not look at him. She walked along blindly, letting Joel lead her. She didn't know or care where they were walking.

Finally the arm under her hand relaxed a little. "Why were you going to say no? Just going to think it over?"

She shook her head so hard the ribbon bumped on her hair. "No! I don't love him. I mean—I know I don't, and I wasn't going to keep him dangling—I mean—" She couldn't think of anything more to say.

"You don't love him," said Joel slowly. "Why? He's a fine fellow, going to be rich someday. Fine family."

She stiffened. "That doesn't matter," she said coldly. "I'm no fortune hunter!"

"And besides you have your own gold. All you have to do is find it," said Joel.

She stopped and whirled about, and glared up at him. But he was laughing down at her, his wicked dark eyes twinkling and showing her he was deliberately rousing her temper.

"Oh—you—you're a devil," she said, and never knew her voice could be so soft and tantalizing and sensuous. "I don't know why I bother to explain anything!"

"Don't you know?" They stood looking at each other on the wide-open street of Paintsville, and everything else seemed to drift away into nothingness. Just his eyes looking down into hers, and hers seeking the truth in his, and his hand reaching out and taking hers in a tight grip.

"Hey, Joel, how's Billy Dexter?" A cheerful voice from behind them hailed them, made them turn about, shocked to find other people in the same world.

"Coming along fine, broken arm," said Joel briefly.

"Too bad. Thought he was too good a driver to let that happen." The man in the white apron laughed cheerfully, and swept with his broom at the front of the store.

"Yes, he is," said Joel, in a low tone. "Much too good. So was your grandfather."

Sarah looked at him, the thought sweeping away romantic ideas abruptly, like a chill wind sweeping through a flower garden, scattering the petals of roses. "Joel—do you think—could it have been—was my grandfather—killed?"

He was frowning, holding her hand tightly, for comfort now. "Hold on, Sarah, let's not go jumping up to conclusions. Let's think about it, and look around."

"Where was it, actually? Where did it happen? My grandfather's—accident," she finally asked.

"I'll show you. Come on, we'll walk that way. Good a way as any today. Watch the mud there." He half-lifted her around a muddy patch, his arm easily swinging her up and down again.

They were silent now as they walked down the street. She drew closer to Joel as they walked, so his shoulder brushed against her as he half-turned to point out a way. She wanted the closeness of him for comfort, to drive away the coldness of fear.

They walked down the main street, turned off to the right, almost at once came to the end of town and into the countryside. There was a wide field of corn, desolate now, lying fallow in dark ground. A few corn shocks still stood, but most had been cleared away. Along the edge of the field ran a wide deep ditch.

"The river comes near here," said Joel. The ditch was full of water, running deep and muddy. "This is to catch the overflow, so the field won't flood and mildew the corn, or rot the roots. Your grandfather was probably driving back from one of the fields he had half-ownership of. Up that way." He pointed along the field to a distant road.

She followed his pointing, trying to picture the scene. "And it was dark?"

"No, it must have been midday, we figure. We just didn't find him till dark. He must have been driving along, and the horse spooked at something." Joel paused, frowned. "But—if a snake was there—he would have driven around. And if someone threw the snake at the horse—why, Old Adam would have seen the man, maybe talked to him. That means—maybe he had pulled up to talk, or was pulling up the horse—and knew the man. Then the snake was thrown—if that was what happened, the horse spooked, and the carriage overturned, and Old Adam went into the ditch. It was dry then, just about. Just a little mud on the bottom."

"And hit his head—"

Joel scowled, and turned his head away. "No. Wasn't nothing to hit his head on," he said gruffly. "Not unless he hit his head on the carriage, or it overturned onto him. And it didn't come over on him. It wasn't on him when we found him dead."

A chill went through her, and she shivered convulsively. "Joel—what if—"

"Come on, let's go back. That wind is fierce." He took her arm gently, and began to lead her back toward town. "We'll talk later," he said. "Got some thinking to do, some new thoughts. Wonder why I didn't think of them before."

They paced along, their heads down, thinking. He was holding her arm comfortingly.

"That alley—" she said, noticing it. "Is that where Billy was starting back?"

"Yes, that's the Smithson house. We figure he was going back into the alley toward the stable—"

"Let's walk through there, see if we can see something," she suggested eagerly.

He hesitated, then agreed. "I've been wanting to see how that ditch runs. It seems like a wide-enough alley, dark though. Maybe something fell on the horse and spooked him, and Billy didn't realize the ditch was so close."

They turned into the dark alley. It was overgrown with thick trees and bushes, hardly a path at all, just wide enough for a carriage. A wide ditch ran along from the house to the stable at the back, and it was all decrepit and forlorn. The house and stables were gray and black, grimy with dirt, hanging with cobwebs.

Snakes might live there, she thought, and grimaced, and regretted she had suggested coming.

"Grandfather didn't come this—" she was beginning to say. Something hurtled at her back, and she went down, with no breath to scream.

She went sprawling in the dust of the alley, knocked out of her senses. She half-turned, stunned, staring up. And saw Joel struggling with a man, who was in the shadows.

The two figures swayed back and forth. Afterwards, she berated herself for not getting up. But she could not. She was dizzy, scared, half-knocked out.

She struggled to her elbow in the dirt, staring, fascinated. She kept trying to see the face of Joel's enemy. The two men struggled, swayed, evenly matched, she thought, in an agony for Joel. She got up to sitting position—reached out her hand—helplessly—

"Joel—Joel—" she was screaming, as soon as she got her breath.

The antagonist was half-turned toward her. Why couldn't she make out his face? He wore a hat pulled way down, firmly. His clothes were dark and dusty. And there was a scarf over his face, covering all but the eyes.

The eyes gleamed at her in the darkness of the hat brim. Fierce, hating eyes.

She stared back, trying to recognize him, trying to know—

Joel punched viciously. The other man countered with a gleaming knife, slicing upward toward Joel's vital parts. Sarah screamed piercingly.

Joel kicked and punched, and managed to get in a hard right to the stomach of the other man. He bent over, gagged, then ducked out from under, and went running.

Joel staggered, tried to catch his breath, start after him.

"No—Joel—no! Don't go—Joel—" Sarah cried at him, in an agony of apprehension. The man had a knife, and he was headed for the darkness of the stables.

Joel staggered right into the thick trunk of a tree, tried to catch his balance, went down into a sitting position under the tree. He was open-mouthed, gasping for breath. He stared at Sarah, she stared back at him, wavering to her feet. She went over to him, half-fell down beside him.

"Oh—Joel—oh, Joel—" was all she could say. He lifted a limp arm, and she crouched down into its shelter.

They might have died. They might both have died, she thought, even as his arm tightened. He leaned back against the tree, his breathing rasping.

Chapter 14

〰〰〰〰〰〰〰〰〰〰〰〰〰〰〰〰〰〰〰〰〰〰

It was a time before either Joel or Sarah wanted to move. They had to catch their breath, get over the shock, look about in a dazed manner. It had been so sudden, so violent.

Finally Joel shook himself, got to his knees, then carefully up to his feet. He stretched himself, looked ruefully at his clothes covered with dust, the trousers ripped. He reached down and lifted Sarah up with hands under her shoulders, holding her tenderly.

"All right, Sarah? You weren't hurt?"

She clung to his arms with her shaking hands. She shuddered again and again before she could speak. "I'm—all—right, I think—oh, Joel. It must have been—"

"Let's get back to the inn. And Sarah—we'll sneak in. I don't want folks to know about this attack. Let me dust you off a bit."

She looked at his grim face as he dusted at her cloak and dress efficiently. "Why—why not tell folks—" she began.

"We'll talk later. At the inn. Will you brush off my back?" He turned his back to her, and she brushed the thick dust and cobwebs from his sweater and neck.

They walked back slowly, the long way around,

avoiding Smithson's stable. She kept looking about her. This peaceful friendly town hid a violent man, someone who wanted to kill them. That knife, so shining and wicked, had meant business.

She could scarcely believe it. But it was true, it had happened. She felt bruised in body and spirit.

Joel led her back into the front door of the inn, up the shining clear stairs to the second floor. The way they had come so cheerfully just a short time ago.

She went back to her room, washed, brushed her hair, tied the ribbon again. Joel tapped at her door as she finished.

She let him in. He bolted the door after himself, and they sat down on opposite sides of the small work table with the rose-covered lamp. He had changed to another pair of trousers, and a blue sweater. His face was grim and hard, no laugh lines on it. His dark eyes were almost black.

She looked at him, waiting for him to start.

"Well, Sarah," he said, rather gently. "It looks like your grandfather was murdered. It must have been deliberate. And someone is after you, as we thought. Not a bum, not a vagrant. Someone wants to kill. Now, let's sit and figure out why, and who it is."

It was both horrible and cleansing to hear the words spoken aloud, so deliberately and coldly.

"It could be the gold," said Joel, after waiting for her to speak.

"Somehow it doesn't feel like that, Joel. It could be—but why kill for the gold? *They* know that I don't know where it is. Why not just search for it, as before? Why kill?"

"Yes, and why kill Old Adam? No, I think you are right. It's more than that. Of course, he made many an enemy. But who hated enough to kill?"

Sarah took a deep breath. "I think—we shall have to name names," she said, and looked at him anxiously. After all, these people had been his friends for years. "It is probably not Billy Dexter. He would not cause an accident to himself. It is probably not Hugo Forrester, he was not here, I believe. And he is detached from affairs here."

"Yes, I think we can eliminate those two safely," said Joel, frowning a little. He reached for a note on the table. "May I write on this?" At her nod, he wrote down Billy Dexter's name, and Hugo's, then crossed lightly through them. "Who else?"

"Well—Maxine. She is a woman. She liked grandfather. But he did send her husband off to fight, and she adored Tim."

She watched in silence as Joel wrote down "Maxine Gibson" in slow careful letters, as though he was thinking deeply as he did.

He did not cross off her name. "Who else? Leonard?"

"Yes," said Sarah. "He is so gloomy and quiet, I never know what he is really thinking. And I don't think he liked grandfather. Still, what reason would he have? Grandfather never hurt him. And he adores Maxine. The fact that Tim Gibson died cleared the way for Leonard to court Maxine."

He wrote down Leonard. And he stared at the little list for a time.

"Then," said Joel, very slowly, very quietly, "there is Justina, and Zeke. And Pearl. We think they loved him. But they lived here, they had the opportunity. And who knows what insults they might have felt, however he did not mean to say them? I have heard him call them niggers, and tease them."

He wrote down their names. Sarah wanted to wince. She did not want to believe that. Joel's pencil tapped lightly on the paper for a time.

"Clarence Gibson," said Sarah, finally, when he said nothing else. "He fought with Adam. He said so. He didn't want me to stay. He wanted to buy the inn."

Joel wrote down Clarence Gibson's name, and moved the pencil slowly over it. "And his son was Tim—and Tim was his only son."

"Yes. And he loved him very much. You can see how fond he is of Maxine, how he tries to protect her for Tim's sake. And the fighting about Copperheads and Unionists—all through the years. He hated the slaves, fought for states' rights."

"But he's a good solid man, Sarah. He wouldn't do that. He respected Adam. They were enemies, yes, but they respected each other." Joel lifted his head, his gray eyes troubled. "I just can't see Clarence—"

"I can't see anybody killing, Joel. But someone did. I am convinced of that now," she said, quietly. "Someone killed my grandfather, and someone killed Roscoe who tried to tell me about the horse that did not shy—"

His eyes blinked, and she realized she had not told him about that. She wanted to trust him, to tell him everything. So she told him about Roscoe, and the words in the dark room, and the shadows in the hallway, and the feeling that someone was back there. And finding Roscoe in the morning, the attack on her.

"It could have been Clarence Gibson," she said. "He is not old yet. He is very strong. And his feelings run deep."

"Yes, yes," said Joel. "Wish I had known about old Roscoe. It would have made sense to me. Why didn't you tell me, Sarah?"

"Well—" she met his eyes, then looked down. "I guess—I didn't know whom to trust at first, Joel—" She wanted to say that she trusted him and loved him now. But she could not. No modest lady proclaims to a man that she loves him deeply and would trust him with her life. She ended lamely, "I didn't really know anybody here."

"That's right, I guess," he said slowly. There was hurt in his face, then he seemed to close it up against her. She looked at the careful blankness of his face, and felt hurt for him. Oh, why, why did ladies have to be so polite?

"But now I do," she added, shyly. "And I do—trust you, Joel. Really."

"Thank you," he said, very politely, not looking up

from the note. She felt he did not believe her, and was exasperated, with herself and with him.

A tap on the door startled them both so they jerked. Joel shrugged with embarrassment at his own taut feelings, and went to the door. He called, "Who is it?"

"It's me, Justina. I brung you-all some tea."

He unbolted and unlocked the door and swung it open. "I thought I heard you folks come back. I guessed you like some tea. It's chilly outdoors. About two hours till lunch," she said cheerfully, and set the large tray on the table. It looked and smelled delicious.

She looked at their faces, beaming, then her smile began slowly to fade. "What's wrong? What happened to you?" she asked, her soft voice almost sharp.

She looked from one to the other.

"We—we're trying to figure out some things, Justina," said Sarah finally. "Please sit down." She got up, pulled over a chair for Justina, closed and bolted the door again. "Justina, please—" Justina looked at the chair, looked at them, finally sat stiffly uneasily on the edge.

"What are you figuring at?" she asked. "I don't know nothing about finances."

"It isn't that. Justina—we believe that grandfather was murdered as well as Roscoe."

Sarah watched the round brown face alertly. The eyes blinked, then the woman slowly nodded, "Yes, yessum, I figure that too," she said simply.

"You do?" asked Joel, sharply. "Why didn't you say so?"

"Didn't know who to turn to. Didn't think anybody strike again. Your poor grandfather, Miss Sarah," said Justina, tears welling into her eyes. "He was loved and he was hated. Strong man, a man who gets loved or hated. And he had his enemies, he shorely did."

"What enemies, Justina?" asked Sarah, softly. "Please—please talk to us. We have to know. You see—I think someone is trying to kill me also."

"I know, ma'am, I know." Justina nodded slowly and finally. "Yes, I know. But we going to protect you, we are. Won't let it happen again. You just do what we say, we protect you," she said firmly.

Sarah took a deep breath. She must not get exasperated and shout. "We have to find out who did it, Justina. I won't be safe until we do. Now, you have lived here with Old Adam for many years. Who do you think murdered him?"

Justina looked at her with troubled soft brown eyes. "I don't know, ma'am, and that's God's truth."

Joel interrupted, his voice slow and deliberately careful. "We have been making a little list of the folks who might have done it. We crossed off Billy Dexter and Hugo Forrester—"

"Oh, Lawdy, Lawdy, not that dear Billy. And Mr. Forrester, he's a right kind man."

"And there is Maxine Gibson. Her husband Tim was killed in the war, and Old Adam encouraged him to go."

To their surprise, Justina nodded. "Yes, yes, and he went on trips for Old Adam too. I don't know what he did, but they were close. But that little Maxine, she loved Old Adam. Always putting her arms around his neck and kissing him and tell him he's gooder to her than her own daddy. Reckon he was, too. Her own daddy, he didn't have the money to spend on her. Old Adam would laugh, and tell her to buy a pretty new dress, or a bonnet, and she would, and charge it to him."

"And Leonard Ensley," said Joel, after her voice paused, and she was smiling with gentle pleasure at the past.

"Oh, that Leonard. I'd believe anything of him. Silent as the grave, he is," said Justina. "Such a *dark* man. Always sees the bad sides, he can't be any good."

Sarah looked at Joel helplessly. Justina wasn't doing much good. She was frankly prejudiced by her own likes and dislikes.

Joel shook his head slightly, and looked at his list again. "And Clarence Gibson," he said.

They both stared at Justina as she frowned, and was silent, picking nervously at her voluminous dress folds.

"Justina—what about Clarence Gibson?" Joel prompted.

"Well—that man, I do be mad at him sometimes," she said, slowly. "Reckon I ain't the one to ask, seeing as he did us so dirty, me and my Zeke and Pearl."

"What did he do?" asked Sarah softly.

Justina didn't seem to want to talk. Her brown eyes were hurt and distant, her mouth folded in tight unusual lines, compressed by fear and her memories.

"Come on, Justina, we must know, or we can't judge," said Joel. "Don't you realize this is important to Miss Sarah? Someone might try again to kill her."

"Oh, Lawdy, Lawdy," moaned Justina. "I didn't want to 'member ever again. I put it away, and told the Lawd my gratitude for saving us, and I tell Him I forgive and forget. Lawdy, Lawdy, I don't want to bring it up again."

"Not even to save Miss Sarah?" Joel prodded relentlessly.

Justina looked over shyly to Sarah, and smiled at her. "Miss Sarah, she just like Old Adam," she said. "I seen it at first, right the first day. Just like him, so strong and good and fine. Never let nobody down ever."

"And what about Clarence Gibson?"

The expressive brown eyes, so liquid and earnest, shadowed again. She spread out her large capable brown hands, the pink palms uppermost, as though she appealed to the heavens.

"I tells you. All right. Old Adam, he brought us North, and we got up to the farm, and then he said we wasn't safe, and he would pertect us, and he brung us here. To the Inn. And he puts us down in the cellar behind the wall. It's tight and warm, but it's safe."

She paused, and picked at her dress nervously. Joel and Sarah waited, without prompting her. She was living now in a dark terrible past.

"And that same night," she continued, low. "That

same night, the slave-catchers, they come, and start poking around. But we know Old Adam won't let us be ketched. He a good man, you see that right away. He bind up my Zeke's feet with his own two hands. Then—then they find the wall, and open it, and Old Adam—he be mad as fire, and my Pearl fainted dead away, and my Zeke fighting them like crazy." She closed her eyes, and tears trickled down slowly over her smooth brown cheeks.

Sarah held her breath. "They—they betrayed—"

"*He* did. Clarence Gibson. They be nine of us in the wall. And he sicked them on us. And they take us back down South. My Zeke, he got beaten something terrible. One of the old men, he died—on the way, he died with the cold. I nurse him, when they let me, but he die. They don't even bury him, they leave him out on the cold hard ground, like a dog."

Joel muttered something, his face hard and stonelike. The list was crumpled in his hand.

"We stay together, thank the Lawd," said Justina, her voice cracking. "Me and Zeke and Pearl. They take us back to our old master and he beat us good. He looked at Pearl—he want her, he say, you come to me, gal."

"He got Pearl?" whispered Sarah, sick at heart. That poor frightened child with the big eyes. No wonder she was so silent, and so afraid.

"No," said Justina, smiling grimly. "I know some tricks. I give my Pearl something. When he try to take her, she get awfully sick at her stomach, throw up all over his suit. My, he get mad. He throw her back to me, he say, take care of that bitch-gal. I hide her away from him."

"Then you escaped again," said Joel finally, as she was silent, her brooding eyes on the distance.

"No. No, not escape. Old Adam, he sent Tim Gibson down there. They don't know him. He buy us," she said simply, proudly. "He buy us and bring us North. Old Clarence Gibson, he about popped his buttons!" She giggled, like a girl. "When he find out Old Adam sent his Tim South and buy us back—and Tim take all that trouble, and tell his daddy how 'shamed he was of being his son—"

Joel cut in sharply. "Clarence and Tim fought over that? Tim said he was ashamed of being his son?"

Justina nodded. "Right in the kitchen, it was. We was a-sitting there and resting after the trip, and Tim drinking some coffee, and so tired. Old Clarence, he come in, and started raging, and we all hear him. Tim say, I did it 'cause I'm so 'shamed of you. I did it to make up for you, what you did, that was so mean."

"But Tim—he must have been quite young," said Joel. "You've been here—"

"He only sixteen, but he a big handsome boy, look older. He dress up, put a little gray in his hair. A smart boy, that Tim, and Old Adam, he coached him how to do it and what to say."

They were all silent then, thinking about it, their minds filled with the past. Justina finally stirred and got up, rather shyly.

"Got to get back to the kitchen and fix dinner," she said, simply. "You want something, you call, all right?"

Joel let her out, bolted the door and came back. Sarah leaned forward to pour out the hot tea. Joel lifted the napkin from the biscuit plate, and they ate and drank in silence.

Sarah was thinking and thinking, trying to piece fragments of information together. It was not just in recent years, then, that Old Adam had influenced Tim Gibson. The boy had been only sixteen when he had bought back some slaves for Old Adam, at a considerable risk to his life. He had gone South, disguised, boldly entered the enemy camp, bought slaves, brought them back to Old Adam. And Clarence Gibson had been shamed in front of them all, by his own son.

No wonder that bitterness and fury mingled in him when he spoke of Old Adam. His own son had been turned hard against him, had defied him, had risked his life, had finally died, in beliefs that were opposite to those of his father.

They sat in the quiet peaceful room, filled with watery sunshine, the lovely wood furniture glowing, the rugs cheerful and the drapes gay with color. It seemed another world, the world of which Justina had spoken. An old slave dying of cold, watched in callous indifference by the slave-catchers. A young boy daring to disguise himself as an older man, and go into the deep South to buy back some slaves, his own soul burning with the shame of the deed his father had done. A family in despair to be delivered again into the hands of the cruel master who wanted the girl, a small timid girl, no more than a child.

This was what it had been about, thought Sarah, stirring her tea absently. The cruel terrible war, father against son, brother against brother, cousin opposed to cousin, family ties broken beyond repair, homes uprooted, homes burned, the horrors of war turned loose.

The wards full of the injured and dying, the surgery rooms covered and spattered with blood, the surgeons operating when their arms were limp with fatigue, the nurses crying silently from weariness and despair as the men died about them, some crying out, some biting their lips and turning their faces to the wall.

Tears filled her eyes and began to run down her cheeks. She was crying into the tea, her hands shaking as she thought and remembered.

Joel set down his cup and saucer with a little clatter. He got up and came over to her, and stood behind her.

"Sarah, Sarah, don't do that. I can't stand it." He put his arms around her shoulders and drew her back to his hard body. "Stop that, or I'll—I'll—"

She turned her face against his blue sweater, and wept silently. He rubbed her hair and her face with his big hands, bent down to her, crooning to her.

"Sarah—don't cry—it's all over. It's the past, you must not go on like this—Sarah, don't—it makes me feel like going out and wringing someone's neck—"

"I was numb," she muttered, finally, wearily. "I was numb. I couldn't feel for a long time. Now I'm coming alive again, and it hurts, it hurts."

"I know, I know." He rubbed the back of her neck soothingly, moved his hand caressingly over her long hair, held her against his body, kissed her hair. "It hurts to be alive, to feel and love and be moved by someone's troubles. But it's the only way, Sarah. You have to live. You don't want to walk around half alive, now, do you?"

She shook her head. "But—it—hurts—"

"Yes, I know. It hurts me too," he said, and held her closely. She could hear the heavy thumping of his heart against her ear. His hands came over her shoulders, lifting her towards him. She caught her breath.

"Sarah," he whispered tenderly.

He drew her up from the chair, and into his arms. She wanted to be comforted, but this was more than that. He pulled her fiercely close, and lifted her head with his hand at the back of her neck. His other hand had moved to swing her round.

She let him hold her, no longer thinking of comfort, uneasy at the flickering flame that began to burn up in her. She rested against him, his kisses on her wet cheeks, on her eyelids. He was muttering soft love words.

"Sarah—my dearest—my little love—Sarah—my dove, my pretty—Sarah—don't cry—I can't stand it—Sarah—let me kiss you—Sarah—" His lips found hers, time stood abruptly still, and the flames in her were burning out all the tears and sorrow. She could not think, she could only feel—feel—feel—

He gave her comfort, then forgetfulness, then—love. He wanted her.

She tried to move her head, to break away, but he held her all the tighter, and she knew the steel in his arms. She tried to say his name, to protest. His mouth came to hers again, taking her lips into her possession. She was limp, weak.

He lifted up. He glared down at her, frowning. "You're not answering me," he accused, amazingly. "What is it? Sarah, you love me, I know you love me!"

She opened her eyes slowly, in a daze, staring up at him. She saw the hard taut lines of his face, the blazing dark eyes.

"You don't trust me either!" he accused. "You love me, but you don't trust me! I can feel it in your body. You're holding back!"

"Joel—" She pushed him back, and tried to sit up. She was weak with the unaccustomed emotions. She wanted to laugh at his accusations, she wanted to cry. She had never in her life felt such a storm inside her. "We must—not—this is insane—"

He stood up, glaring down at her bitterly. "You don't trust me. The only reason I'm not on the list is because I wrote the list! You think I'm after the gold! My God, Sarah, do you think I would kill for that? I adore you—but you drive me crazy!"

She shook her head, trying to shake out the cobwebs. Too much had happened this morning, she thought. She couldn't even think. She could only feel. And how she felt! Every inch of her body was ablaze.

"I'm going. I can't stay here and not want to make love to you. You're a cold woman, Sarah. No wonder you rejected Hugo! You don't love him, or anybody!" He stormed over to the door, wrenched it open, went out, and slammed the door shut after him.

It opened again immediately, and he yelled at her.

"And bolt this after me! You want to get killed?" And he slammed the door shut again.

She managed to stagger to the door, and shoot the bolt home. Then she leaned against the door, hoping her head would clear soon.

Finally she got back to the chair, and sat down limply. She picked up the cup and saucer, and drank a swallow of tea, though it was cold now. Joel, she thought, you crazy insane marvelous man!

A slow smile curled her lips, a dreamy smile. He would recover from his anger, and then—then he would try again. Dear Joel. Did he think she could learn to kiss and respond and love a man passionately, all in one week? She had never kissed any man except her father and brother in her life. She touched her lips with one trembling hand, felt the soft crushed bruised lips Joel had claimed so eagerly.

She wanted to kiss him, she just didn't know how yet. He would teach her—when he recovered from his anger.

Could she really learn to love a man in one week? Oh, dear, she sighed to herself. She could, she had, she did. She loved Joel, only she didn't know yet how to express that love.

Dear Joel. His dark gray eyes, so calm and laughing, so fiercely darkly stormy, so thoughtful, so gentle, so angry— And his face, so lean and hard, and those laugh lines—she wanted to put her finger inside the creases and trace them slowly down to his mouth—

Maybe the next time Joel kissed her, she would get the courage to touch his face with her finger, and touch his mouth with hers.

She sat there for a time, until the trembling stopped. She cleared up the dishes, and set them on the tea tray. She had another hour until dinner. She wanted to think, but she hardly dared to, her brain was so confused.

She took out one of the older account books from the bookcase, and leafed idly through it. She wanted to come closer to her grandfather. If only he had kept a diary, she thought. She reached for another book, and her finger struck an envelope.

She frowned, she had not thought to look behind all that row of books. She crouched down on her knees, and pulled out enough of the books so that she could get behind them.

She found three thick envelopes, fastened with cord.

A little excited, she got them out, and put them on the table, and cut the cord. The knots were too tight to untie.

She opened the first one. She was disappointed at first. All the envelope contained seemed to be receipts. She leafed through them, frowning a little. Why hadn't Adam kept a diary?

Most of the receipts were for items like sets of china, sets of glass. Then she came across an odd one. She read it, read it again.

Across the side it had two names she did not recognize, and after the names it said, "Negro Brokers." She turned the receipt the long way and read it:

Atlanta, Ga., July 14, 1857

Received of *James Hobbs forty dollars*, being in full for the purchase of 1 Negro slave named *Timmy* the right and title of said slave *Timmy* warrant and defend against the claims of all persons whatsoever, and likewise warrant *Timmy* sound and healthy. As Witness *my* Hand and Seal.

At the bottom was a signature and a stamp.

It was a slave receipt. She turned it over, studied it with fascination. There were other receipts. The others said James Hobbs had bought slaves, a few said Tim Gibson. The writing was the same!

Tim Gibson had made many such trips South. She sat back and thought about it, stunned. Tim had gone again and again, on trips for Old Adam. He would never have had the money to buy slaves for himself. Old Adam had sent him on buying trips, to buy slaves, bring them North, and set them free!

She went over more of the receipts. She found a few curious ones, made out to Adam Overmiller, acknowledging receipt of sums of money. Some were to various persons she did not know. Had he loaned money, or given it away?

Then she came to Leonard Ensley's name. Nine receipts, made out to amounts from one hundred to three hundred dollars. Over a period of five years.

How curious. She looked at them, and looked and studied, but could not figure it out. Did Leonard owe her grandfather money, or had the debts been paid long ago, and the receipts never destroyed?

Puzzle added to puzzle. She thought that if she could only understand these receipts, she might have a valuable clue to her grandfather's death. But they made no sense to her.

Finally with a sigh she put them all away again, fastened them with fresh cord, restored them to their hiding place behind the account books. Perhaps she would show them to Joel. He might guess or understand what had happened.

Dear Joel. As she washed, and brushed her hair for lunch, she saw a smile sweetening the corners of her mouth, in the mirror. Would he kiss her again—and how soon?

Chapter 15

Sarah went down to lunch, feeling rather shy and yet eager to see Joel again. She wondered if she really wanted to be in love, it was such a mixture of feelings, such crazy funny feelings, she was high in the heavens one moment, and down deeper than earth the next.

It was not a very comfortable way to live, she decided.

Justina was alone in the kitchen when she came in. She turned around quickly. "Miss Sarah, did you come down alone?" she said sharply, a worried frown on her face.

"Yes. I forgot," she said, guiltily.

Justina shook her head at her. "Now, don't you start forgetting, or we is all in trouble," she said ominously, turning back to the thick pot of stew. Sarah went over to the fire, and sniffed at it hungrily.

Hugo Forrester came into the kitchen from somewhere in the inn. He smiled happily at her, and she thought, I have to tell him soon, oh, dear, how can I hurt him, but I must.

Zeke came from upstairs, padding softly over to his mother. "Billy Dexter, he wake and hungry, mama," he said.

Sarah overheard. "Let me fix his tray, Justina," she

said, and got the heavy tray from the side table. She arranged a cloth, a napkin and silver. Justina spooned up a huge bowl of the stew, added a plate of hot cornbread and butter, a little jug of maple syrup, put a napkin over the cornbread, and sent Zeke upstairs with it.

"Nothing fancy today," said Justina, rather apologetically. Sarah laughed a little.

"Nothing fancy—only the best smelling food—oh, Justina, are you going to teach me to cook?"

Justina smiled, well-pleased, but made light of it. "This is just leftover meat and vegetables, honey, and some ol' cornbread. Why, anybody mixes that up."

Sarah waited a little, fearing Joel would not come. Maxine came in shyly from outdoors, by the back door. She looked oddly at Sarah and Hugo, finally said, "May I join you? Dad is so cross today, and Leonard hasn't had a good word for anybody."

"Of course—please do come, Maxine," said Sarah, quickly. She hoped to heal the rift soon. When Maxine heard that Hugo was not going to marry Sarah, that ought to help, though her feelings would still be hurt.

Maxine hesitated, then finally sat down opposite Hugo, her violet eyes downcast. Sarah took her usual place, still waiting uneasily for Joel. Would he come, or would he still be angry at her?

When Joel walked in from the inn, she went limp with relief. He looked at her, hesitated, then half-smiled. She smiled back, and said, "Hello, Joel," and hoped her voice was natural.

"Hello, Sarah." He went to his place at the end of the table. As Justina started to serve them, he added, "I went to look at the bridges. They aren't so bad, Hugo. Guess we could get started working on them today."

"Billy Dexter says more rain," said Hugo, his mouth curving downward.

There was a chorus of protest. "Oh, no, no," said Sarah.

"Oh, it can't rain—it just can't keep on," wailed Maxine.

"We done had enough rain," said Justina firmly.

The two men laughed, more naturally than they had for a while. "Tell the Lawd, Justina," teased Joel. "Have Him turn it off. Tell Him he sent enough."

"I *have* told Him," said Justina.

Justina put her hands on her hips, and shook her head. She had forgotten the maple syrup for them, in her interest in the weather. Sarah got up quietly and went to get the jug. She hesitated, then as everyone was listening with amusement to Justina, she paused beside Joel. She leaned over and set the jug beside his plate, and managed to touch his hand with her fingers for a moment.

Joel looked up quickly at her. She knew she was blushing. She had done that deliberately, touching his hand. "Thank you," he said, very softly, just to her.

She went back to her plate. Justina, remembering her hungry folks, began to spoon up the fragrant beef stew. Joel and Hugo began to discuss how to repair the bridges, and what men could be talked into helping.

"What are you going to do this afternoon, Sarah?" asked Maxine. "I have to help in the store. Leonard has accounts to finish."

"Well—I thought I might go through the inn with Justina, and see what needs cleaning," said Sarah, thoughtfully. "If the rains ever do let up—I am sure they have to eventually—then we might have guests. Some of the front rooms need cleaning."

"That's a good idea, Miss Sarah," said Justina eagerly. She brought a fresh plate of cornbread, steaming hot, yellow with corn, and set the butter plate near Sarah's hand. "I get Pearl to help, and that Zeke too."

Sarah looked directly at Joel. "Joel, do you need Zeke on the bridges?"

Joel looked at her, and she seemed to be sinking deeply into his dark gray eyes. She could not look away. She wondered if the pause was obvious to everyone at the table as he looked at her, and she looked at him. "Well—yes, I'd like to have Zeke. He's clever with tools. But if you need him—"

"There's no rush about the rooms. Justina and Pearl and I can manage," said Sarah, and finally managed to look away, and down at her plate. She felt out of breath, as though she had been running. Her heart beat in an odd fashion, with a skipping motion.

They finished the meal more cheerfully than they had started. Hugo and Joel ate heartily of the dessert, huge helpings of pumpkin pie with thick cream melting on the hot pie. Sarah and Maxine had filled up on cornbread and maple syrup, and could not face much more. Maxine left to mind the store. Sarah helped clear off the dishes, then the three women began a little tour of the bedrooms.

"I'd like to get the front ones ready first, they are the prettiest," said Sarah, finally. "We'll get brooms and scrub brushes. Let's do the blue one first, then the rose one. I don't think they are very dirty, but I want them fresh and nice for company."

"Yes, Miss Sarah. But you don't do the heavy work. You ain't used to it," said Justina. "Pearl and me will do that. Why don't you do the windows, and get them all sparkly, the way they used to be?"

They divided the labor like that, and the hours sped past. It felt good to be doing work like this, Sarah thought, something practical and useful, with the results quickly visible in clean woodwork, fresh linens, smoothly polished furniture, sparkling glass windows.

Justina and Pearl talked little as they worked. Pearl scarcely spoke a word, and her big eyes seemed as scared as ever, which puzzled Sarah deeply. Surely, even though she had had such bad experiences in the past, the years at the inn had been peaceful ones, except for Roscoe's murder. Had that brought back all her fears again?

By the darkening of the afternoon, they had accomplished much. The first six rooms were spanking clean and ready for guests. Sarah resolved to work on more rooms the next day. If the rains would kindly stay off, and the bridges were fixed, the inn might be full soon. At least, she must be ready. She would talk to Justina about putting in more supplies. She ought to go to the pantry and count food supplies also. And the smokehouse in the back of the inn—she ought to check there also, and see what was needed for the winter.

Her head was full of such housewifely thoughts, and she started back to the front of the rooms to close the windows she had left open to the wind. They ought to be good and dry now, even the woodwork, she thought.

She went back to the blue room, and was closing the windows there when she noticed the sign of the Golden Goose and its Golden Egg. It hung from a strong triangle of wood, and she reached out curiously to see how it worked. At her touch, the goose and its egg swung back toward her, so she could touch it. That was how it was painted, she thought.

Curious. For a piece of wood it was very heavy, thought Sarah. Very very heavy. She stared at the tarnished gold of the goose and its egg. Tarnish. In an odd pattern. Not like streaks of rain or rust.

She leaned forward carefully and gazed out into the street. She saw no one there. Justina and Pearl were in one of the bedrooms farther back. She took a small brush and scrubbed at the tarnish. It did not start to fade.

It was on hard.

Finally she took a fingernail, and scraped. She caught her breath. The tarnish was coming off—like paint. And underneath, under the tarnish—was pure gold.

Not the other way around. There was no wood under the tarnish. The tarnish covered the gold. It had been cleverly painted on.

Oh, God, thought Sarah. Old Adam, I found the

gold. What a clever man you were. She felt lightheaded and weak, as she carefully swung the Golden Goose and its Golden Egg back into place, to stand majestically outside the window on its perch, proclaiming to all the curious that this was the Inn of the Sign of the Golden Goose.

She had to sit down for a minute, staring at her fingernail. It was covered with tarnish. She wiped it off carefully. She was shaking. The Goose and its Egg were huge. And they were composed of pure gold, melted and formed into shape. She looked out again, looking at the little smile on the beak of the Goose. A grin of triumph, she thought. Hiding all that gold.

All that gold. A fortune in gold. Enough to last her all her life, and longer. She would never have to work again, if she didn't want to.

Or she could put some of the money into the inn and the stagecoach office, make it less bare and plain, fix it up for her and Joel. They could run both—they could—

Oh, glory, she thought. Dizzy. Glory. *The gold.* All that gold.

She finally got up, looked again at the Goose, then made her way back to Justina and Pearl. Justina was chatting away about the bedding. "There you be, Miss Sarah. I was wondering if you was finished. I think I best go down and start supper. The men folks will be right starved after their work," she said cheerfully.

"I'll come and help you," said Sarah, quickly. She had to work, she could not stop and think, she was so scared and so happy, and so thrilled, all at once. If only her face did not give her away!

"No, Miss Sarah, you need some rest," and Justina was firm. She escorted Sarah back to her rooms, after a brief pause to see how Billy Dexter and his shotgun were faring. They were both resting peacefully on the bed.

Sarah lay down on her comfortable bed, and pulled the colorful afghan over her. But she could not sleep, her brain was whirling. How she could use this knowledge—how she could use it to trap the killer—how could she?

She could, she felt sure. If only she could figure out how—

The killer would not kill her if he thought she had the gold, and only she knew where it was!

Her eyes opened wide, and she gazed unseeingly at the picture over the mantel. The lovely horse in the field, the barn—

How could she figure it? What could she do?

By the time, finally, that she had risen from bed, bathed and made herself ready for supper, she knew what she was going to do. It was a terrible chance, but she had to do it.

She wanted to stay alive, and she wanted to trap the killer of her grandfather and Roscoe. She could do it—if she was very very careful.

Zeke came for her, to escort her down to supper. She felt restless, anxious. Maxine came in early, and that was an omen to Sarah.

She took Maxine by the arm, and led her over to the side of the room. "Come and see the pies, Maxine. Do you think this is enough if we have a party tomorrow?"

Maxine looked at her as though she had gone mad. "A party?" she said, pulling back, stiffly.

Her face was closed and dark to Sarah. She still had not forgiven her that deception over Hugo.

"Hush—listen," said Sarah rapidly, in a low tone. "Maxine, I have to tell you. You must think—tell me whom to trust. I have found the gold!"

Maxine stopped pulling away. Her violet eyes opened wide as she stared at Sarah. Sarah looked at her, then back over her shoulder toward the fireplace. Zeke and Justina were drawing huge pans from the fire on their cranes, they were absorbed.

"You—found—" Maxine gasped. "Where?"

"I can't tell you—yet. Listen, the bank is closed. It won't be open until Monday. I can't tell anyone yet.

But you must help me, please, Maxine. Tell me whom I can trust here in town! The gold is immense—a huge pile—I'll need help in getting it to the bank safely. And can I trust the banker?"

Maxine was staring, her color flushing into her pink and white cheeks until her face was crimson with excitement.

"Gold—huge pile—oh, Sarah, is it true?"

Sarah nodded, glancing about as though fearful. She was afraid of being overheard, that was true enough. "Keep it to yourself. We'll talk tomorrow morning— you will help me, won't you? I don't know who else to trust!"

"Of course—of course—I'll help, Sarah. You can count on me."

"I don't dare tell people—" Sarah whispered. "It is so much—a fortune in gold— Oh, here comes Hugo. Don't tell him! I'm not going to marry him—you know that—I don't love him. I thought he liked you," she ended rapidly, then turned to Hugo with a smile.

"Good evening, ladies," he said, advancing toward them with a smile. His eyes lingered, first on one and then on the other. Maxine stood there in a state of some shock, and it took all Sarah's wits to cover up for her.

They finally went to sit down at the table. Hugo showed them his bruised and work-worn hands, cheerfully, begging them for some sympathy in amusing tones. "You will take pity on a man who isn't accustomed to this type of work? I have been laughed at all afternoon."

"Oooh, what a shame," cooed Maxine, almost normally. "That wicked Joel, I can just hear him. You must let me help you after dinner, we can soak your poor dear hands in water and herbs—"

"You are very kind," said Hugo, looking toward Sarah hopefully. Sarah only smiled vaguely in their general direction, and looked toward the door as Joel came in.

He looked tired, but satisfied. "Got one of the bridges fixed completely," he said triumphantly. "We'll do the worst one tomorrow, if it doesn't come on to rain."

Hugo groaned, and held up his hands obviously. "At the risk of incurring the wrath of everyone here, I warn you, I am going to pray for rain tonight!"

Everyone laughed. Joel said drily, "Fortunately, we don't know your prayer record. It isn't all that good, is it?"

"Now that is mean, Joel!" said Maxine, spiritedly, laughing up at him. Her violet eyes flashed, she had recovered her high spirits evidently. "Don't listen to him, Hugo!"

"I would much rather listen to you, Miss Maxine. Your voice is so much more beautiful and soothing than Joel's."

Joel only grinned, and sat down at his place. He looked quite satisfied, for some reason. Perhaps it was the bridge, thought Sarah, and peeped at him over her water glass, only to find him just taking a quick look at her. She flushed red.

To her surprise, Clarence Gibson and Leonard came in before they were well started. Sarah greeted them cordially. This fit into her plans, and her heart beat harder as she thought how it might work out. She set places for them.

"I'm so happy you came. And Justina has fixed ham in my favorite way, with green beans and potatoes. And we have such a lot of pumpkin pie—" She smiled at them both, feeling like a cheat. But one can't be fair to murderers, she thought.

She chatted nervously, quite unlike herself. She caught Joel looking at her curiously again and again. But she could not stop talking.

"I must take inventory at the smokehouse tomorrow. I haven't the least idea how many hams and steaks we have. Is there a record book, Justina? And the pantry shelves, they must be getting bare. I wonder if I can get the vegetable man who came to grandfather. Surely the rains will let up soon, and we will have guests again."

Clarence Gibson was listening, gravely, with rather shattering attention to her words and her voice. He kept glancing down the table at her, past Maxine, his dark blue eyes unreadable.

Leonard was his gloomy self, and frowning because he had been doing accounts, as Maxine said impishly, and he hated figures. "But you'll have to learn accounts, Leonard!" she added. "You know Dad wants you to learn all aspects of the business."

"I'll learn—somehow," said Leonard, scowling. "You could help me more if you wanted to, Maxine! You know figures."

She tossed her blond hair and laughed. The teasing note reached the men, and Sarah. They all looked at her. She was radiant tonight. Was it the excitement about the gold, Sarah wondered, or was it the news about Hugo?

They ate hungrily at the pumpkin pies, and drank gallons of rich coffee with thick cream in the coffee and on the pies. The men were genuinely starving from their hard outdoor work. Sarah ate automatically, tasting, yet not knowing what she ate. Her mind was busy, busy, busy.

After dinner, Maxine brought a bowl of hot water and some herbs, and some ointment and cloth, to bathe Hugo's hands. She reproached Joel as she did so. "You ought to know he isn't hard, like you, Joel. You should have given him some of the easier things to do."

"There weren't any easy parts, Maxine," said Joel, drily, pushing back on his chair. He watched them with a funny smile on his lips. Leonard scowled at them jealously, and finally left, saying he didn't need medical help, he needed bookkeeping help.

Sarah went over to Clarence Gibson as he was about to follow. "Oh, Mr. Gibson, perhaps you would look at the pantry—I wanted to ask you—"

Joel scowled at them as Sarah and Clarence went

over to the pantry door. But he could see their backs, and that seemed to satisfy him. Sarah felt very nervous with Clarence. He was such a clever man, seeing much more than one might think at first.

They were out of hearing of the rest of the group, and no one was paying much attention to them except Joel. Sarah whispered to Clarence, pointing at the shelves as though she were speaking about them, "Mr. Gibson, I need your help."

"What is it?" he whispered back, frowning heavily, his shrewd blue eyes gazing down at her.

"I have—found—the gold. And there is such a frightful amount of it. It is—terribly—heavy," she quavered, and was suddenly coldly afraid. If she found it, Clarence Gibson could find it. Once he was sure there was gold, could he not murder her, and make off with it?

"My God, girl. Get it to the bank," he said brusquely. "You don't want it about! You're asking for trouble."

"I can't. The bank is closed, until Monday."

He bit his lips. "I'll get the banker. He'll open it up. For this, he would. You're taking a horrible chance, Sarah. Where is it?"

"I can—can't tell you now. But it is so heavy, and I need help. It will take several men probably to move it—"

He frowned down at her again, his dark blue eyes glittering. "It's that much? A big fortune, the way he spent money? I could not believe he was saving—"

"It is all melted down, into several huge chunks. So much I can't even lift it," she whispered. She must make the bait thick and juicy. "Please—please think about it—how you can help me. I'll talk to you tomorrow—we could move it on Monday—"

"Right. Though I think we ought to move it tonight—"

"Not, not tonight. I don't want—if anything goes wrong, and we can't get it into the bank—"

"That may be correct." He raised his voice, and she saw Maxine coming toward them. "I'd advise you to fill the pantry, Miss Sarah. As you say, you can't tell when you'll have guests. I recall one time a company of thirty came to dinner without warning, a congressman and his party. Old Adam came out splendidly, but it wiped his pantry clean, I can tell you! But he was never unprepared."

"We must go home, Daddy," said Maxine, putting her arm affectionately into her father-in-law's. "Goodnight, Sarah. Thank you for being so kind and letting us come so often." She smiled as sweetly at Sarah as she ever had, her cheeks still glowing with pretty color, her violet eyes shining.

"It is my pleasure. Come tomorrow, do, Maxine," said Sarah, cordially. She accompanied them to the back door.

She went back to the table, shaking a little. She felt like a gambler, betting on very high stakes, her own life.

She sat down at her place again, and lifted her coffee cup. Joel came with the huge pot and filled her cup again. "That was cold, Sarah. Here's fresh."

His tone was warm and affectionate again. Hugo looked alertly from one of them to the other. His hands were thoroughly bandaged. Zeke came out from the inn.

"Mr. Joel, that leak ain't really fixed, I reckon," he said. "There's water coming in on the desk in the stage office."

Joel muttered to himself. "All right. Come along, Zeke. Bring the tools. Hugo, you staying here with Sarah? Don't leave her alone."

"My pleasure," said Hugo, smiling at Sarah. Joel scowled at them, hesitated, then finally went off with Zeke.

"I have been wanting to talk to you," said Sarah, rapidly, as soon as Joel was gone. "Two things. I must tell you before they return."

"Of course. But as I said, you must not make up your mind in a hurry, my dear—" Hugo leaned forward, his elbows on the table, looking at her earnestly.

"That—is one of the things I must tell you, Hugo. While I like and admire you immensely, I am—not ready—I mean—I don't feel I shall marry yet. And I am not—in love—with you. I cannot marry you, Hugo. I am sorry. I meant to tell you last evening, but I was so surprised—"

"Surprised? That I admire and love you so soon?" He smiled at her gently, not at all upset. "I am surprised at myself. It is not like me, I must confess, to be bowled over so soon! But I am, and I have patience to wait until you too can come to know me, and understand my deep feelings for you."

"Please—Hugo—no more," she said, feeling like a wretched tricky woman. She could not go on with her plans if he made her feel so awful. "Don't say any more about that—please!"

"If it distresses you, I shall not."

He was watching her face with gentle loving kindness. She could scarcely continue. "The other thing—" She lowered her tone to a bare whisper. "Hugo, I have found the gold. I found it. And it is immense—a huge amount, heavy. And the bank is not open again until Monday morning."

"My God," he said, blankly. He stared at her. "You found the gold—it really exists—"

"Exists! It is so much—Hugo, I would never need to work again. I shall, of course, I shall keep up the inn, and enjoy it. But there is so much money—it is a fortune—"

She heard Joel and Zeke coming back along the hallway, talking. She touched Hugo's bandaged right hand, and whispered, "No more now. I'll talk to you tomorrow—how to get it to the bank—"

"Right." He leaned back. He still looked shocked and dazed, and his eyes glittered with excitement.

Oh, that gold, she thought sadly. How much trouble it has caused, and will cause, before this matter is ended.

Joel came back, cussing a little, and earning Justina's displeasure. "Oh, why not cuss," said Joel. "That blankety-blank drip is ruining my counter. I got two buckets full already, and that cussed roof is still leaking. Damned if I'm going up on the roof tonight and patch it, either!"

"It gonna rain tomorrow," said Zeke. "Billy Dexter, he say so."

"Then I'll stick Billy Dexter into the roof and use him for a patch," said Joel, crossly. Zeke exploded with laughter, slapping his thigh until his mother looked at him sternly.

Joel sat down at the table, and got some more hot coffee. He looked tired and scowly. She thought he was probably very tired, and she regretted the necessity of tricking him also. But she had made up her mind, and she would go through with it.

Joel looked like he was going to sit there forever, and Hugo must have felt he was being outlasted. So Hugo excused himself and went up to his room, looking at Sarah significantly as he said, "I'll hope to see you tomorrow, then, Miss Sarah!"

"Yes, of course, Hugo. Goodnight."

He left the room. Justina and Zeke and Pearl went to eat comfortably at the table in their rooms. Joel and Sarah sat there a few minutes longer.

Sarah finally said, "Joel, will you escort me to my rooms? I feel rather tired."

"Right." He got to his feet, and went after her to the stairs. "You've had a big day. Say anything to anybody about this morning?" he added, as though casually.

This morning—the attempt at murder—she had almost forgotten it. "No, I haven't, Joel."

"Good. We'll talk about it tomorrow," he said. He followed her up the stairs.

She unlocked her room, he looked about as usual, and reported that all was well. Then he stepped up closer to her, and said,

"Sarah, about this afternoon, I'm sorry. It was unreasonable of me. You need time—"

She looked directly into his eyes, then down again. She could not look at him and deceive him. "Joel, I don't know how to kiss," she said softly. "I don't know—how to respond. Give me time."

His face lightened, and he reached for her. She let him kiss her mouth, holding her closely, and found that somehow she had been learning something about kissing, because she had no trouble in moving her mouth under his and answering his kiss.

"That wasn't so bad," said Joel, and ducked down for another one. That went even better, and she almost forgot her mission.

Then she pushed his face a little away, not forgetting her decision to put her finger into the laugh crease beside his mouth. That almost wrecked the whole matter. He bent down again.

"No—Joel—no more. I want to tell you something," she said breathlessly. She would rather go on kissing, and learning all about that interesting art, but she had other things on her mind.

He paused very reluctantly. She glanced outside the door, and he watched her, frowning a little. She came back, and whispered, "Joel—I found the gold today."

"You found—oh, God. More trouble," he said simply. "Where is it?"

She hesitated. He knew her so well, he could practically read her mind. "I don't want—to tell you until Monday," she whispered. "We can't move it until then. And we'll have to get several men we can trust to help move it. It's horribly heavy. There is quite a lot."

He nodded, his face suddenly more serious, a little sad. "Okay, Sarah. We'll take care of it on Monday. Want to take it to the bank?"

She nodded. "There is—so much it scares me," she said. That was true enough.

"Going to be a rich woman, huh? Well, dream about it, Sarah," he said, and smiled a little odd smile, reached out and touched her face gently with his hand. Then he walked to the door. She stared after him.

Weren't there going to be any more kissing lessons tonight? Evidently not.

"Lock and bolt the door, Sarah," he ordered. "Goodnight."

"Goodnight, Joel," she said. She closed and bolted the door, and abruptly wanted to cry.

The gold changed everybody. It wasn't very nice, what it did to people.

Chapter 16

~~~~~~

Sarah was tired of thinking and worrying. She went to bed early, tossed for a while, finally fell into a restless sleep. She wakened at times, her mind fretting between sleep and waking, mulling over her dangerous plot.

It must work, it had to work.

She got up early in the morning, and Zeke brought her hot water. She dressed, brushed out her hair thoroughly, and finally wound it up in braids coiled on top of her head. She didn't feel young and eager and childish this morning. She was afraid.

It was Sunday morning. There were no church bells, the pastor was out of town, but there was a Sunday hush in the small town. No pounding of hammers, no cheerful calling.

When she went downstairs, she found out why it was so quiet.

"Good morning, Miss Sarah, did the rain wake you up last night?" asked Justina, stirring the thick rashers of bacon in the skillet.

"Rain? Oh, not more rain, Justina!"

"Sure enough. The skies done opened up and we got a flood, ma'am. Worse than ever. Zeke, he went down early to the bridge they fixed yesterday, and you know? It's out again. The water done swept away more supports. Zeke, he say that Mr. Joel is gonna cuss more than ever when he hear dat!"

"He sure will," sighed Sarah, her spirits drooping. She went to the back door, opened it a crack, then gasped. The wind was sweeping across the back yard, the rain was in gray sheets of darkness. The yard was flooded, the water running inches deep.

"When Mr. Joel start cussing, you better put your hands over your ears and pray," said Justina, chuckling. "That man, he did learn some choice words in that Army!"

Sarah smiled a little, but she didn't feel one bit happy. The fresh fierce storm was very depressing. She felt so uneasy over the gold, and the killer, and now this—She closed the door finally, and turned back into the warmth of the room. She held her chilled hands to the fire, looking down thoughtfully as though she might read her fortune in the flames.

"Whyfore you don't wear your pretty bright dress and a pretty ribbon?" demanded Justina, looking over at her. "Why your hair all up and tight, and you wearing a dark dress today?"

"Oh—I didn't—think about it," she said, absently.

"Men, they always like bright colors," said Justina wisely.

Sarah knew she was blushing. She met Justina's wise dark eyes for a moment, then turned away.

"That Mr. Joel," said Justina, after a pause, "he a right good man. He don't got money, but I figure that don't matter so much, 'cause he got a good heart. Course, that Mr. Hugo, he a good man too, but not like Mr. Joel."

"You have a special place in your heart for Mr. Joel, I think, Justina," Sarah teased her. She felt a little lighter. She too had a special place in her heart for Joel; depressed as she felt this morning she looked forward to seeing him. She didn't want the money to make that much difference to him. Why should it? He knew she had inherited the inn, and some money. Why should it make a difference to him, when the money turned out to be a fortune?

But it would. She had a bad feeling that it would matter.

"Here he come now, clap your hands over your ears, Miss Sarah," Justina advised.

Sarah heard Joel at the same time Justina did. The cheerful husky voice was giving out some really fine words. "That——, ————water, washing out that——bridge, we gotta do all that work over again. Oh cuss, I'm gonna give up on that darn—"

Justina shook her head vigorously. "Oh, my, oh, my, how that man do go on!" She said it between sighing and chuckling.

"Yes, suh, yes, suh," Zeke was chuckling, ambling along behind him as the two came through the inn. Zeke was grinning as he followed his idol into the kitchen. Joel was scowling heavily. He paused as he saw Sarah, his eyes a little startled.

Then he came on. His raincoat was streaming with water, his hair was plastered to his head. Justina handed him a towel and he went over to the fire and rubbed his head vigorously, shaking himself at the same time. Justina took the wet raincoat from him. Underneath, his sweater and pants seemed almost as soaked. He seemed tired, dispirited.

"Is it bad, Joel?" asked Sarah, in her soft voice, when he seemed a little more dry.

He nodded. "Worse than before. Fresh rains swelled the creeks, now they're flooding the river, and spilling over the banks. Reckon we'll be trapped in town another week, longer maybe. The bridge we fixed is out again. Other supports were weak."

He finally sat down at the end of the table, his head down, his arms on the table. She had never seen him so dejected. She wondered if it was just the rain. Or was it her news of last night also?

"It will let up eventually, Joel," she said, when he was so quiet, not looking up at her at all. "It isn't like you to give up. I'm sure you never gave up when you were fighting."

She said it slowly, deliberately. She wanted him to understand the double meaning behind her words. At first, she thought he did not get it. Then finally he lifted his head, and looked at her, his gray eyes puzzled. He stared at her. She looked back, though her cheeks were flushing pink, and she felt warm all over.

He leaned back in the chair, and finally his face relaxed. "Guess you're right, Sarah," he said, more cheerfully. "Can't stop fighting, can I? And rains do let up finally."

"Of course they do. All troubles end eventually." She smiled to thank Justina for her plate of ham and bacon and eggs. Justina often seemed to think Sarah had the appetite of a mule skinner, she thought, with humor. And she did! The food looked and smelled and tasted so good, there in the warm steamy kitchen. "You just have to keep—trying—and keep working at it," she ended, a smile trembling on her mouth.

"I'll do that, Sarah," he said, and now a laugh line creased his cheek. She wanted to put her finger on it again. It had felt good last night—to put her finger on his cheek, and touch the rough texture, and caress that little deep line—

Maxine and Leonard dashed in the back door, raincoats streaming. "Oh—my—oh—my!" gasped Maxine, shaking herself. "I'm sorry, Justina—all over your floor—but we can't get any food! Dad tried this morning—he can't get past the end of the street!"

"Don't you fret about a little water on the floor, Miss Maxine, honey," said Justina. "You come over near the fire and get yo'self good and dry. My, my, your pretty hair all wet. You-all come and get dry, and have some hot coffee."

Leonard said nothing, just scowled at them all as though they were somehow to blame for the situation. He wrenched off his coat, and huddled miserably at the fire, getting into Justina's way as she tried to get at the coffee pot. Joel got up, moved Leonard over quietly, and brought the pot to the table.

"Can't get past the end of the street, you said," said Joel, casually. "Found that myself. The water is so deep on Apple Street, that it's no use walking that way. Probably the grocer won't open up anyway, being it's Sunday, and he don't have to."

"Dad thought he would, for him, but he couldn't even get up that way. Oh, dear, Sarah, I hope we don't eat you out of house and home," Maxine ended childishly, patting Sarah's hand.

"I think there is plenty yet in the smokehouse. I mean to take inventory when the rain lets up. We shan't starve. I wonder how the other town folks are making out, though," Sarah added thoughtfully.

"They are pooling their supplies," said Joel. "Talked to some of them yesterday. Can't get out into the country and get more. We'll all make out."

Leonard sneezed, violently, three times. Maxine got up and went over to him. "Are you getting feverish again?" she asked anxiously, putting her hand to his forehead.

He nodded. "Shouldn't have come out," he said sullenly. "I'm not hungry anyway."

"You'll be better for some eggs and coffee," she soothed, gently, stroking his forehead before turning back. "Justina, maybe you'd fix him some of your herb tea."

"Shorely I will," said Justina, and went to the shelf of her herbs and spices. "Poor man, bet he feels miserable."

Leonard looked miserable, but he so often looked and sounded miserable, Sarah did not notice much difference. She berated herself for her unkind thoughts. The poor man probably had a chill and fever.

Hugo Forrester came in, and reported that Billy Dexter was awake and hungry. "And he was right about the rain storm," added Hugo ruefully. "It wasn't my doing, my prayers didn't do it."

"Prove it," said Maxine, and giggled, her violet eyes flashing up at him.

He smiled down at her, his gaze lingering on her pretty fair face and the light violet gown she wore. "How can I? Except, as Joel said, my prayer record isn't all that good."

"Just like a lawyer, throw your words back into your face," growled Joel, but he didn't sound mad.

That was about the last of cheerful words at the breakfast table. Maxine was visibly nervous and excited, Leonard looked and felt gloomy and grouchy. Hugo was thoughtful, and kept looking at Sarah speculatively, she thought.

Even Joel seemed affected, and was absent-minded, gazing off into the distance. Were they all thinking about the gold, she wondered, and felt certain that was it.

She wondered if Maxine had told Leonard. Probably she had. They were very close, in spite of Maxine's flirtatious ways with other men. She seemed to have affection for Leonard, and certainly he was crazy about her. And Clarence Gibson seemed to be grooming Leonard to take over the store, which he would not do unless he was going to marry Maxine.

She could feel the tension like a living thing in the room, a cloudy presence affecting them all. Her nerves in the back of her neck were so taut, that she felt a headache coming on. She longed to rub the back of her neck, but did not want to attract attention to herself.

They were all aware of her anyway, she thought. Whenever she glanced up, one of them was looking at her, then away again. They were thinking about the gold, about the fact that Sarah had found the gold, and there was a great deal of it, and she would be a wealthy woman.

If she lived.

Maxine found an opportunity to whisper to Sarah before she and Leonard left. She stood near her and said softly, "I'm thinking about it—you know. I'll come back later in the day, and talk to you. You'll be in your room, won't you?"

"Yes. You'll tell me—whom to trust—"

"Don't—trust—Hugo. Or Joel! They both want the money, I feel sure," whispered Maxine fiercely, her eyes sparkling with excitement. "They are men—and greedy—the money would set up Joel for life! And he never had any. The temptation would be too much."

The words sent a cold chill down Sarah's back. She swallowed hard. Maxine pressed her arm affectionately, whispered again, "And don't trust Dad! I love him—but he would do anything to get his hands on the gold. And I wonder sometimes—you know how he and Old Adam fought—oh, I must not say any more—" She frowned at herself, and went away.

Hugo said something to her, quietly, as she came back to the table for another cup of coffee. Joel was talking to Justina, standing near the fireplace.

"I'm considering what to do, Sarah. When can we talk about the matter? This afternoon?"

She would have a regular parade of visitors to her rooms, she thought ironically. All with advice to offer, some with greed and hate in their hearts. If only she could recognize soon enough which were which.

"Yes, fine. This afternoon."

"Don't go near the gold. Someone might suspect."

"I shan't go near it."

"Is it in the inn?"

She hesitated. "Don't ask me, Hugo," she whispered. "At any rate—the rain will prevent me going near it—"

"I see." He frowned, a little puzzled. "Well, at any event, be careful. Be sure to lock yourself in when you are in your rooms. Do you want me to remain with you?"

She shook her head. Joel had turned back from the fireplace, and was frowning at them suspiciously, his dark gray eyes angry again. Oh, dear, she thought. If only she could read their minds, and understand all their motives, how much simpler it would be! Hugo might be concerned for her safety, and the security of the gold—or planning to get it for himself. Maxine the same.

And everyone warning her against everyone else!

Hugo went up to see Billy Dexter. Joel came and sat at Hugo's place, with his own fresh cup of coffee.

"What are you up to, Sarah?" he asked quietly, looking at her keenly.

She started. "Up to?" she asked, her brain working frantically.

"You have told Hugo about the gold. I can see it on his face. He is all excited and upset. And Maxine, did you tell her also? She is mighty friendly all of a sudden."

She bit her lips, and finally lifted the coffee to them to keep from having to answer. He waited a moment, then went on gently.

"You're playing a dangerous game, Sarah. Your mind works like Old Adam's, I believe. You want to trap them, is that it? My God, girl, you are insane. Who else did you tell? Everyone on the list, plus me?"

She could not look at him, she bent her head unhappily.

"Did you tell Clarence Gibson?" he asked sharply.

She finally nodded.

"Oh, God," he groaned. "And we're all trapped here in this town, the creek and river all swollen. No way in and out. Why didn't you ask me first? You got to have your own stubborn way all the time, Sarah, girl?"

"I have to know, Joel. I can't go on and on, without knowing," she finally admitted. "I thought I could trap the killer this way. He won't kill me—unless I tell him where the gold is, and I won't do that. He'll want the gold, too, I think. I have a feeling about that."

"Bet you haven't even found the gold," said Joel, quietly. "It's a trick, isn't it?"

She shook her head firmly. "I found it. It's there. That isn't a trick. I'm sorry, Joel."

He was silent for a few minutes. She watched the fire

flaming up in the fireplace, watched Justina working about, humming happily, no hint of the explosive matters thickening in the kitchen.

"I'll stick around you, nearby, do my best," he finally said. "Wish you weren't doing it this way."

"No, you must not. I want to draw the killer out, Joel. You must not stay near me."

"And what are you going to do when he comes? Squeal?" he asked drily, his face lined and hard. "God, girl, you're up against a man who has killed twice. Think he'll draw the line at a third victim?"

She shuddered. He was looking down at her with hard angry eyes, his voice impatient and raw with emotion. She knew it was going to be difficult, but she didn't want to face the thoughts he was thrusting at her.

The fact that she might draw out the killer—and he would kill again.

Chapter 17

~~~~~~

Sarah went back to her rooms after breakfast. She took out the latest account book, and pretended to study it. She had a small sharp knife hidden in her skirt pocket, but she was not at all sure she could use it if necessary. She was cold and chilled and afraid.

But she had to go through with this. It was the only way she could think of to trap the killer of her grandfather and old Roscoe. The person who was trying to kill her.

She wondered what Joel would do. When she had left the kitchen, he had escorted her to her rooms, saying little, just scowling down with that frown that meant he was worried. He had gone back to the kitchen, at least his footsteps had gone down that way.

She sat in the rocker, moving slowly, then pausing, not soothed by the motions, she was so tense. She looked around the room, tensely aware of every movement, the curtains at the windows, the sounds in the hallway, Zeke's voice as he brought breakfast to Billy Dexter.

One hour passed, then another. What if the killer did not take the bait? She bit her lips until they stung. Her long sturdy hands were shaking sometimes as she tried to read the account book.

When a knock came at her door, she jumped with fear. It was then she realized fully what a chance she was taking.

She went to the door and called out, "Who is it?"

"Maxine—oh, Sarah, I need help!"

Sarah unbolted the door and let Maxine in. Maxine was wearing only a thin scarf over her hair. "What's the matter?"

"It's Leonard—he's so feverish, and out of his head. And Dad went away somewhere trying to get groceries, he doesn't want to keep taking from you. Oh, please come. You've been a nurse, haven't you?" The violet eyes were full of unshed tears, her slim hands were trembling. She reached out to grasp Sarah's arm, her grip intense. "Poor Leonard. I didn't know I was so fond of him until he got sick. He's so good and so patient with me—oh, Sarah, if anything happens to Leonard, I'll die!"

Sarah forgot for a minute about the gold and her own troubles. "You mustn't carry on so, Maxine. I'll come right away—I think some hot tea, and blankets, to keep the chill off—do you have plenty of blankets?"

"Yes, yes, plenty. But he is so hot! Should he have blankets on him? I thought sponging with alcohol—"

"No, never, he must not get a further chill—"

She paused to lock the door behind her, and follow Maxine down the long hall to the front of the inn. They passed Billy Dexter's closed door, she thought briefly of him. She had not gone to see how he was this morning. But Leonard's illness was more urgent.

They went down the long shining staircase to the side door, out to the store. "It's quickest this way, and we won't get rained on so long," Maxine panted, as they dashed across the short distance between the inn veranda and the porch to the store. They went inside, and Maxine stopped to take off her head scarf again. "He's upstairs, in his room. We'll just go right up. Should I make some more herb tea? Justina gave me the herbs."

"Let's see how he is first," suggested Sarah, and

Maxine led the way upstairs. Sarah looked about her curiously. The store was huge. Above it were the family quarters, just as large, even luxurious. Rooms opened out from the large hallway. She glimpsed a living room, with velvet sofas and chairs, in shining blue colors that made her believe Maxine had designed the room.

"He's in here," said Maxine, opening a door near the end of the long hall. She went in first, and Sarah followed her. She looked past Maxine toward the bed—to find it empty.

The door shut after her. She whirled around, and stared wide-eyed—at Leonard, dressed, his gloomy face more dark and frowning than ever, locking the door.

"Gag her," said Leonard, briefly. From behind her, Sarah felt the long swirling scarf covering her face, pulling brutally tight. She was pulled backward, knocked down across the bed by Maxine.

Oh, what a fool, she thought, dazed, as they tied her up efficiently. Right into the trap. That scene this morning, Leonard feverish, then Maxine's acting—

"Search her. Got any weapons?" asked Leonard. Maxine went quickly over her garments, patting. The violet eyes were hard, as Sarah peered at her over the thick gag cutting off her speech and half her breathing. Her face was hard also, older and cruel.

"A knife," said Maxine, pulling it out, and tossing it into the corner. Her beautiful red mouth curled with contempt. "Stupid idiot! What good did she think that would do?" She stared down at Sarah. "All right. When you're ready to talk, and tell us where the gold is, we'll untie the gag. But no tricks, or you won't last long."

Sarah was out of breath, and out of ideas. They had her right enough, tied up like a chicken ready to pluck. She could not believe it at first, Leonard and Maxine. But why, why, why? Did they just want the gold, were they greedy for the gold? Or were they really the killers also? She had to know that.

Leonard and Maxine were talking in low tones. "No,

he won't interfere, he won't come here," said Maxine. "No, he didn't see me, but it's Sunday, he won't expect me in the store."

Leonard muttered. Maxine shrugged impatiently, they talked a few more minutes then turned back to Sarah. They looked down at her with the cold curiosity of hardened kidnappers, she thought, in bewilderment.

"You ready to talk?" asked Leonard.

Sarah nodded slowly. Leonard leaned down to take off the gag.

"Wait a minute," said Maxine. She took a sharp small knife from her pocket, held it to Sarah's throat. "All right, take off the gag. If you so much as squeal, dear Sarah, you'll get this in your gullet. Understand? Right in. I have no feelings for you at all. The knife will go right into your throat."

Sarah nodded with a little shudder. Leonard took off the gag. She moved to sit up, in spite of the tying of her hands and feet.

Maxine said sharply, "Lie still. You can talk from there."

She lay back. Maxine looked even more deadly than Leonard.

"I want—to know—why," said Sarah, croaking a little. She felt still in her mouth the wooliness of the gag.

"Why? No talking except tell us where the gold is," said Leonard, impatiently. His hands were shaking, she noticed.

"Why should I just tell you?" asked Sarah, slowly, clearing her throat. "You mean to kill me when I tell you, don't you? You are both—practical people. You can't get the information about the gold, and then let me go, can you?"

Leonard looked at Maxine, his eyes fearful. Maxine's beautiful violet eyes stared down at Sarah's without expression.

"You're a smart girl, just not smart enough. You

found the gold, didn't you? Tell me that?" And Maxine pushed the knife against the other girl's throat hard enough to cause a pain, and she knew she had been cut.

"Hey, don't kill her yet, she ain't talked," said Leonard, putting out his hand, and holding Maxine's wrist back.

"I found—the gold—all right," said Sarah. "Now, I want to know—did you kill—grandfather? And how?"

"I don't like this fooling around," said Leonard uneasily.

"I'll tell her, fast, then she tells us about the gold," said Maxine. "Yes, we killed him. Damn him. He killed my Tim!"

"He died—in the war," said Sarah, moving a little. Her hands and feet were going numb from the tightness of the bonds. "That wasn't—grandfather's fault—"

"Lie still!" said Maxine, harshly. Her eyes glittered. Sarah got the distinct impression that Maxine was enjoying this much more than Leonard, who was uneasy at his girl friend's talking. "Sure it was his fault. He was the one who got Tim interested in those damn slaves! Sent him South again and again, getting him in trouble, buying up slaves. When the war came, he talked and talked to my Tim—talked him into enlisting. Dad would have found a way to keep him out—but no, Tim had to enlist. And they killed him, my handsome Tim!" Tears came to her eyes, but they seemed to burn in the hard glitter of the violet.

"He wasn't so great," muttered Leonard sullenly. "Just his good looks. What did he really have? Just the store. He wasn't no good in the store. Your Dad had to hire me—"

Maxine turned on him in a flash. "You shut up," she ordered, her voice ringing. "Don't you say one word against my Tim, or I'll slit your throat too! Don't know why I don't! I could say you and Sarah fought, that you were the killer!"

They faced each other, anger sparking between

them. Sarah held her breath. She did not doubt for a moment that Maxine would kill. Neither did Leonard doubt. He backed down.

"I don't mean nothing. He was fine, he was. Just young, hadn't been trained yet," he said, hastily. "Let's get this over, Maxine. Somebody's gonna come, if we don't hurry."

"Nobody's coming. They won't know where to look, if they do get suspicious. But come on, Sarah, tell us where the gold is. I want to know about that gold!" The knife approached Sarah's throat again. Maxine smiled gently, cruelly, as she pressed the point to Sarah's flesh.

"There are some things—I want to know yet. Call it—satisfaction—before I die—" said Sarah breathlessly, her eyes fixed warily on Maxine's face. "I want to know—how you killed grandfather. That horse—didn't shy—"

"Yes. He learned to," said Maxine, laughing a little, her pretty tinkling laugh that made Sarah shudder now. There was more than a touch of madness in that laugh. "I trained him! For three months, I took snakes down there, and trained that horse, until he knew if a snake came near him he was going to get hurt! I'd throw a snake at him, and then cut his neck or his leg. He learned, all right! We set it up—only Leonard got cold feet. After Old Adam was wrecked in the buggy, down in the ditch, Leonard couldn't touch him. I had to go into that ditch and hit him on the head, and hit him and hit in the same place until he died!"

Leonard was turning slightly green. Maxine watched his face, and laughed again, her soft tinkling teasing laugh. Her violet eyes glittered with madness at the recollection.

"I hated him, hated him. Old fool! Patting my hand and my head, and saying he was sorry about Tim. My beautiful Tim, my handsome Tim. Dead, and crushed, and they didn't even open the casket when he came. But I opened it. Didn't I, Leonard? I opened it, and looked at what they did to my Tim, and I vowed on his broken body I'd get them. Didn't I, Leonard?"

Leonard looked so sick, Sarah thought she could see him turning greener by the minute. Maxine laughed at him, and turned back to Sarah.

"Enough of this talk. I want to know where the gold is. Leonard and I are going away from this dead town, and start somewhere new, and have a fine time with beautiful clothes. And no work, no work in a deadly dull store, handling fish and pickles and catering to stupid women about the bonnets on their stupid heads— Come on, tell me, Sarah!"

The knife pricked painfully in Sarah's throat.

"Roscoe," she said, slowly, carefully. "I want to know—about Roscoe—why did you kill—"

Maxine shrugged, her voice shrill with impatience. "Oh, the old fool! He guessed, hinted. Then Leonard heard him the first night when you came. Leonard was hiding in the hallway, and heard him. He told me, and I said we'll have to fix Roscoe. So we both came back to the inn that night."

"What did—you do—" She wanted to keep them talking, talking. It was her only chance.

"Oh, we came back, and said we wanted to talk to him. The stupid old man, he came to the door and let us in. Leonard held him and tried to choke him, but the old man struggled. So I slit his throat. I always have to do it, don't I, Leonard? He's really a coward, Sarah," she said, and laughed again, sneering at her lover.

"There is something—else that puzzled me—I want to know—" said Sarah, carefully.

"Oh, stop it. Just tell us about the gold, my dearest Sarah!" said Maxine, coldly. "Look, I can slit your throat, and we'll find the gold ourselves." And she bent down closer, her eyes glittering, the wrist of her dainty white hand held in driving position.

"Why did Old Adam—pay Leonard—hundreds of dollars?" asked Sarah.

As she had hoped, the words jolted them both, and made Maxine pause in her deadly task. Maxine stood up, her hand away from Sarah, staring at Leonard.

"What are you talking about?" she said grimly, her mouth twisting.

"It's none of her business! Kill her! Kill her!" cried Leonard. "Go on, we can find the gold ourselves!"

"I want to know, Leonard, you tell me. What about the money? What did you do with the money?"

He only stared at her, stricken, guilt on his face. She stared at him coldly.

"Did he—take money—from Clarence Gibson?" asked Sarah. "Did Old Adam—find out, is that it?"

Maxine leaped at him like a panther, and stuck the knife at his throat. "Answer!" she hissed. "Did you take money from Dad? Those accounts—is that what happened? And you let me think it was my Tim? You thief!"

"No—no—never—stop it, Maxine—we're friends—I never—I put it back!" he cried out, catching her hand, trying to keep the deadly steel from him.

They stared at each other in enmity, doubt, fear. Maxine finally drew back. "You did do it. You stole from Dad, and you let me think my Tim did it. Oh, you liar! I'll fix you—but that later," she said, half to herself. "We'll fix her first! So Old Adam found out, and he paid you money to put the funds back. What did you do with that money, Leonard?"

"I put some back," he said sullenly. "But that's in the past. I don't juggle the books no more."

"No, not since I've been checking them," she said frigidly. "And you—you had the gall—you let me doubt my Tim! I could kill you for that!"

"We got to stick together, Maxine," he said, cunningly. "We got to go away together—after this." He nodded at Sarah, bound and tied on the bed.

"Yeah. After her. Well, Sarah, where is the money? Come on, where is the gold? We need it, we have to go away after we kill you. Someone might guess this time," said Maxine, with the crazed simplicity of the insane.

Sarah, staring up at her, thought, this girl is really insane. Tim's leaving her, and his death, had twisted her brain. Only an insane girl could have done what she did, open the casket, vow over her dead husband's body to have vengeance, plan carefully, murder twice. She must be crazy.

Maxine had had the help of Leonard, because Leonard was in fear of Old Adam. Old Adam knew he had embezzled funds from Clarence Gibson. He had put the blame on the dead Tim, and Maxine adored her Tim. Leonard had gone along with Maxine's planning, because he hated, and he feared.

"She won't talk this way," said Leonard, gazing down at Sarah. "She's just setting us against each other. We got to do more than talk to her, Maxine. You got the matches?"

"Yeah. I got them. Bring a candle," she said.

Sarah stiffened in fear. "But I still want to know—" she said, searching her mind frantically for something else to delay them.

"Gag her—when you're ready to really talk, you nod your head, Sarah dear," said Maxine, mockingly. "I think you'll really talk before long. There's nothing like a good warm fire to talk before, is there?"

They gagged her tightly, then Leonard, hurting her in his haste, pulled off her heavy shoes and her long stockings. They had to untie her legs, but she had no chance to get free. Maxine held her legs, and Leonard lit a candle, and brought it over to the bed.

Sarah wiggled and squirmed, but they put the lighted candle to her foot, and held it for a moment. The pain began, and went through her foot, and she moaned.

"She's sensitive," said Maxine, holding her down, sounding as cool as though she were at a church social. "She won't last long. Do it again to the other foot, Leonard."

He held the candle longer to the other foot. The pain

shot through her, a fierce pain that made her feel faint. She arched up, bucking on the bed, hurting so much she wanted to scream, but she could not.

The shot startled them all.

Bang! And the door burst open.

Joel and Hugo burst through the open door, and jumped them. Hugo got Leonard, and fought him down to the floor, punching him hard. Joel got hold of Maxine, and when she struggled, he hit her over the head, and knocked her out. Sarah stared at him, unable to believe it, stared until her eyes were so full of tears he was a beautiful blur in her eyes.

Clarence followed them into the room, slowly, glancing about as though he could not quite believe it. Billy Dexter hobbled after him, holding his shotgun lightly, effectively on Leonard.

"Got them, I reckon," said Billy Dexter thoughtfully. "Never could have believed it if I hadn't seen it with my own eyes." Maxine was lying across the bed, knocked out. Sarah shuddered away from the contact as Maxine's arm half fell across her.

Joel was untying her, unfastening the gag. His face was hard, taut, twisted. "Oh, my God, Sarah, my God—" He was whispering it over and over as he released her.

He lifted her up in his arms, hugged her tightly. Tears were rolling down her cheeks, from the pain, the terror, the relief. She held him with her arms, weakly, never wanting to let go.

Maxine stirred, slowly sat up. She stared around at them, her face settling into mad sullen lines.

She glared at Clarence Gibson. "You told, Dad, you told!" she said accusingly.

His shoulders were drooping. "Yes, I had to," he said, simply. "I knew, I had a feeling, that you had killed Old Adam. I sort of felt he deserved it, though he was my friend, he was ornery, and he had sent Tim to war. But old Roscoe—he never hurt you."

"He tried to betray us!" she shrilled.

"And Sarah—Sarah is a good girl, nice. She would never have hurt you," he said, gently, as though explaining to a child. "You should not have tried to kill her, Maxine. That was wrong!"

She glared at him. "She is like Old Adam. She would have hurt us!" she said. "She would have done something. And I hate her, because she *is* like Old Adam!"

"Did they tell you?" asked Joel, speaking to Sarah. "Did they confess? They really did kill Old Adam and Roscoe?"

She nodded weakly, her head so comfortably on his shoulder she never wanted to move it away. "Yes. They confessed. Maxine trained the horse to shy—with snakes, and cutting the horse. Leonard fixed the accident. When—Old Adam was in the ditch, Maxine said he didn't have the nerve to go on. So she got in the ditch—and hit him—and hit him—until he—died."

"My good God," said Hugo, coldly shocked. He stared at the sullen wild face of Maxine, the beautiful creamy face, and the lovely violet eyes. "She—murdered—with her own hands?" He looked down at the hands which had tenderly bandaged his own hands, and shuddered with revulsion.

"Yes, and she—slit Roscoe's throat. She said—Leonard couldn't kill him—with his hands—so she—cut his throat," said Sarah, the nausea coming up in her throat as she thought of the thick pools of blood under the old man's body, as he lay on the carpet in his room.

She felt Joel shuddering also. He had been friends of these people since his childhood. What did he think? What was he feeling now?

"We'll take care of them two," said Billy Dexter, waving his huge shotgun casually at Leonard and Maxine. "You take little Sarah back to her rooms, and get those feet tended to. Look kind of burned."

"They were torturing—me—to make me tell where

the gold—was," said Sarah, faintly. "But they—were going—to kill me—anyway, when I told—so I didn't tell—"

"Just like Old Adam," said Billy Dexter, delightedly. "Chip off the old block. Right, Maxine? She's just like Old Adam, and she outsmarted you, right enough!"

Maxine screamed at him, incoherently, and flew at him. He caught her easily with his good arm, the shotgun dropping. Hugo took over the shotgun, evidently preferring to hold the shotgun on her than try to touch her.

"Let's get out," said Joel, shortly. He carried Sarah out the door, and down the hall to the front stairs. "You crazy, crazy girl, I'll never let you out of my sight again! I thought you would be safe, I was right in the kitchen waiting. Never figured on Maxine, never thought she would come through the inn to you. Damn fool I was." He was hugging her closely as he carried her.

"I can walk—Joel—really—I'm heavy—"

"About as heavy as a peck of feathers," he said, not letting go of her.

He carried her out of the store, quickly across the rainy patch, to the inn veranda, and up the stairs inside. He was panting and out of breath when they came to her rooms, but he did not let her down until they reached her bed. He laid her down, then, and bent over and kissed her mouth.

The kiss was angry, hard, full of relief and fury mingled.

"And don't you ever—dass—scare me like that again! Don't you dass!"

She wound her arms around his neck, comfortable and happy in spite of her burning feet and her wrenched arms from the ropes. In spite of the prick of the knife stings in her throat, and the cold fear and shaking.

"Oh, Joel, don't you ever leave me again," she whispered, shamelessly, and pulled him closer.

Chapter 18

〰〰〰〰〰〰〰〰〰〰〰〰〰〰〰〰〰〰〰〰〰〰〰〰〰〰〰

Sarah would have been content to stay there forever, Joel's arms hard about her, feeling his hard half-angry kisses on her mouth. But they were interrupted. She sighed as she heard Justina's scolding, and finally drew herself part-way from Joel's wonderful grip.

"What's going on here? What happened to my Miss Sarah? Whyfore you don't tell me what's going? Miss Sarah, what they do to you? Oh, yore pore feet! My lands, God have mercy, what been going on?"

Joel got up very reluctantly. His face was flushed, and the laugh lines were back. "Damn it all, no peace at all," he growled.

Justina glared at him, affectionately. "Mr. Hugo, he said to bring the ointment. Now, you tell me what happened!"

Joel told her, briefly, while he and Justina washed and anointed Sarah's burned feet. Joel wound the bandages around tenderly and carefully, while Justina clucked and exclaimed over the whole story.

"And it was pretty Miss Maxine, and that Mr. Leonard, after all! And she being so friendly and all. Always making over Old Adam, and then over Miss Sarah! You just can't tell!"

"I knew about it," said a small timid voice. They all

looked around to where Pearl stood, a small shadow, near the open door. Her small frail hands twisted and twisted in her apron, there were tears of relief in her dark eyes.

"You, Pearl?" asked Sarah, quietly, not to startle her. "You knew something. That was why you were afraid. What did you see? You started to tell me."

"They—they did get that Miss Maxine?" she whispered, anxiously, her big eyes lifting up to her mother's.

Justina said, half-fiercely, "Pearl, honey, you-all tell me what you saw! You mean, you knew about Miss Maxine?"

Pearl nodded. "I—saw," she whispered. "That night—when Miss Sarah came—I heard things. I heard steps. I went to the door, out into the kitchen. I was afraid. I went up the stairs, and I saw them—I saw Miss Maxine with her knife, and she stabbed, and stabbed—at dear ol' Roscoe, and he lying there dying on the rug—" She choked, and began to cry.

Billy Dexter had come into the room behind her. He was staring down at little Pearl. He shook his head in amazement. "She knew, all the time. Damn me! And I never even guessed! That sweet pretty girl—crazy as a loon, and a killer!"

"Yes, I think she had gone crazy," said Joel, quietly. "She adored Tim, but that was not all. She was restless here, she wanted him to take her away East, to big cities, to have fun. He refused to go. I think—he saw the mistake of their marriage. He jumped at the chance to go to war, to prove himself, to think things out. She must have suspected that he had become disillusioned about her—"

They were quiet, then, thinking about the beautiful mad girl, the girl who had had everything, and let it slip from her grasp like water.

Billy Dexter finally said, "Mr. Forrester and me, we been talking about it. When the folks here find out what she done, they'll be right crazy. I think we better get her and Leonard away, take them by boat down to Cincinnati, to the jail there. Only safe thing to do. No telling when the bridges can get fixed."

Joel said, "That sounds like a good idea. I'll go with you."

"No, not you, Joel!" Sarah reached out anxiously to touch his hand. He looked down at her, and his face softened wondrously.

Billy Dexter's kind eyes studied them both. "No, reckon not, Joel. Me and Hugo can handle them two."

Justina said that Zeke could go with them. The rains had let up again, as suddenly as they had started. Hugo and Billy Dexter started out the next morning.

But first, Hugo took the statements of Pearl and of Sarah. He thought they would later have to go to Cincinnati to give evidence at the trial, if Maxine and Leonard decided to fight the case. Otherwise, the statements attested to would be sufficient.

Zeke went along to help with the boat. Billy Dexter took his immense shotgun, and Hugo had a rifle and pistol. Even so, Sarah thought she would worry about them until they had returned safely.

Hugo had paused to say a few words to her before they left.

"I realize now that you and Joel—" he paused, awkwardly, not so fluent in his words as usual.

"Yes, we—we love each other," she said, simply, flushing.

"I hope you will both be very happy, Sarah. I am sure that you will. He is a fine man, and he will always protect you. Of course—" he grimaced a little, with some humor. "I am sorry for myself! I thought I had found the perfect girl for myself! And I had, you know."

"I am sure that—someday—you will find the right girl for you, Hugo. I know she will be proud and happy to have such a wonderful husband as you will be."

He smiled, with a regretful light in his eyes, that warned her he would not find forgetting her very easy.

But he was a gentleman, she thought. He would never again speak of his love for her. It warmed her heart that he had been so kind to her, so careful of her. When a man like Hugo Forrester loved a girl, she thought, that girl ought to be warmed the rest of her life, knowing she had been found worthy of such a man.

But for her—Joel was the only one. And she felt a glowing color when she thought of him—so happy, so light-hearted and thrilled that she waited for his every footstep. His voice could make her jolt upright in bed, eagerly waiting for him to come in.

They made her rest in bed the next couple of days, after the shock and the torture. Her feet were quite painful, and she was glad to keep them up on soft cushions.

After seeing Hugo and Billy and their passengers off in a boat, Joel came back to her. He sat down in the rocker and looked at her. Then he grinned.

"Well, Sarah, what next? Have you any more plots and schemes in that pretty head?"

"Just one," she sighed. "That blasted gold. I guess I ought to get it to the bank."

"Darn. Forgot it. You really did find it then?"

"Yes, Joel. The gold is melted down and formed again into the golden goose and her egg. You know, the inn sign."

He stared at her, his jaw loose. "Aw—no," he groaned. "Aw—no! That devil, Old Adam! Aw—of all the places. Oh, darn, Sarah, you know what I was going to do?"

He sounded so rueful, so aghast, that she opened her eyes wide at him. "What, Joel?"

"Blast it! I saw the sign was all tarnished, I even went up and looked it over. I got some gilding from Clarence, and I was going to repaint it for a surprise— as soon as the rain let up!"

She stared at him. He stared at her. They burst out laughing—laughing until the tears ran down their cheeks. If Joel had repainted that golden goose and her egg, it might have been years before they had discovered the gold.

Justina heard them laughing hilariously, and came upstairs with a tray of her cure-all, tea and biscuits. "What's so funny, here, now?" she inquired, beaming fondly at them. "I hear you laughing all the way outdoors."

Sarah told her, though she waited until the tea-tray was safely down on a table before she began. Justina went limp, and sank down onto the small sofa near the bed.

"No—no! God have mercy on us—the Lawd does hear—that gold—in the golden goose—aw, no! And Mr. Joel was going to repaint it, and you might never find—aw, Miss Sarah, that ain't funny, no-how!"

But she finally chuckled weakly with them, wiping her eyes on her ample apron. She called little Pearl, who came scampering up the steps to hear about the funny story of the golden goose and her egg. How the child's eyes widened and widened at the story that must have seemed like a story out of a dim past, a fairy story, a story of elves and goblins.

Joel got the banker and a couple of men, and they carefully took down the grinning goose and its egg, and transported them to the bank vault. Their path went necessarily through the main streets of the town, and within a few minutes everybody knew the whole story. There were signs of admiration for Old Adam's cleverness, and Miss Sarah's smartness in finding the gold, and awe at the size of the golden hoard.

The banker, Mr. George Crawford, was more excited than any of them over the gold. He fussed and fumed over how to write the receipt for it, before putting it in the vault. Joel reported to Sarah gleefully.

"He couldn't write it out. He didn't know how much it was worth, he said. Finally I told him, forget how much it is. Just weigh it out, and give us a receipt for the weight. But he didn't have the scales for that kind, just for little bits of pieces of gold. So I went over to the butcher's, and got his scales, and of course, the butcher, he got to come back with me, and see the gold weighed in, and promise it was true weight—"

And Joel laughed in such a happy rollicking fashion that Sarah and Justina and even little solemn Pearl had to laugh with him.

"That Old Adam, he was a smart one," said Justina, with a happy sigh, as the story reached its good conclusion. "All said and done, he was a good man. He lived a good life, and I bet he be in heaven, smiling down on us, and on his granddaughter, who's ever bit as smart and kind as he be. Come on, Pearl, we got dinner to fix, and we going to celebrate," she ended, with such emphasis that Sarah knew she could expect a veritable feast of joy expressed in cooking.

There was a little awkward silence, as Sarah and Joel were finally left alone for a time. The door to the suite was wide open and the shadows had departed from the inn. And now it rung with laughter, and the voices in it were joyous. Sarah thought, this is the way my inn ought to be. Old Adam's inn which he left to me—full of happiness and laughter.

And Joel would make it that way. He could make her laugh, had always been able to right from the first. No matter what the horrors each had seen, Joel could make her laugh and be happy, and forget the nightmares.

"Are you tired, Sarah?" he asked, gently, now, from the rocking chair. His dark gray eyes were thoughtful.

"No, Joel. I slept fine last night, about the first night since I came. No—no bad dreams."

He smiled at her. "That's good, Sarah. You've had a bad time of it, but you came through great. Just like Old Adam—"

She was a little tired of that. "Well, in case you had not noticed," she said, rather tartly, "I am not like Old Adam in one thing!"

"What's that?" he asked, innocently, a laughter crease in each cheek.

"I'm a woman!" she said, flushing hotly. She wondered with sudden alarm if she had mistaken Joel. Perhaps he was only feeling kindly to her, that he was not really in love with her.

"I've noticed that," he said, solemnly, a wicked twinkle in his eyes. "And prettier than Old Adam ever was, if you don't mind my saying so."

She moved restlessly in bed. "I don't mind," she said, but sounded more sullen than sultry, she thought. She glared at him anxiously. Didn't he love her? What would she do if he didn't love her? Suddenly, life which had seemed so full and happy started to feel quite empty and foolish.

He got up from the chair, and came over to sit on the bed beside her, facing her. "Sarah, we have some business to discuss," he said, seriously.

She peeped at him dubiously. Not with that sparkle in his eyes, he didn't have business to discuss! She took some hope from his look.

"Business? What business, Joel?" And now her voice was soft and feminine and more sultry.

"I've been thinking. Before Old Adam—went—we had been discussing joining the inn and the stagecoach offices. He was getting older, and I was helping him more and more in the inn. He told me we might join the two, and both work on it. What do you think about that, Sarah?"

He was so close, his face so near hers, that she couldn't think much at all. She said, rather faintly, "Oh, wouldn't that—be difficult, Joel? I mean, keeping the—accounts—separate? And I—I don't know much about running the inn, much less the stagecoach office. You would—have to do—lots of the work. Would that—be fair?"

"Oh, we could work it out," he said, his mouth coming even closer to hers. "You know accounts, and I could take care of registering, and you would supervise the servants, and I would look after repairs, and—"

His mouth was very close. She was looking at it instead of listening to his words.

"Oh—Joel," she said, faintly.

"Hell," he said, so strongly that she jerked in bed. "I can't keep my mind on what I'm saying! Hell, Sarah, you have to marry me! You're driving me right out of my mind!"

And his mouth came down on hers, and she wound her arms around his neck, and held him tight, as their lips met tenderly—expressing their love for each other.

When his lips managed to leave hers for a moment, they went roaming over her soft neck and chin, her cheeks and over to her ears. She felt half-faint with the wildness of his embrace, as he held her tightly to him.

"Sarah, Sarah," he whispered, and his mouth explored hers again.

"Oh, Joel—honey," she whispered, and took his head between her hands as their lips met long and sweetly.

"Mr. Joel, ain't you got no shame? Courting in full daylight, with the door wide open!" It was Justina's rich voice, much too close.

Sarah reluctantly turned her head sufficiently to see Justina's broad smile over Joel's shoulder. "Oh, Justina, we're going to get married," she said.

"And hell, go away, Justina!" added Joel. "I've had enough of interruptions in my courting! Can't a feller go kissing his own girl without people standing over him?" And his face came down against Sarah's neck and he nuzzled and kissed at her.

"There's just one thing, Mr. Joel," said Justina's voice, severely. "You got to cut out that cussing. When you got babies around, learning how to talk, why they pick up those cuss words of yores so fast, it make you 'shamed! You got to quit cussing right now, 'cause I figure you gonna have those babies pretty soon!"

And she laughed out loud. As she went away, down the stairs to her own domain of the kitchen, they heard her chuckling and chuckling at her own wit.

Sarah was blushing and hot at Justina's words, but even more so because Joel was holding her so tightly.

His hands were stroking her, softly, possessively, as he kissed her lips.

"Joel?" she asked, finally. "Did you—really—start loving me—right away?"

He pulled up enough to look down into her face and answer her. "Right away. Before the first night I saw you. I started loving you when I saw your picture. Why do you think I took that miniature to war with me, honey?"

She thought he was teasing, until she saw his eyes, and knew he was not. A thrill of pleasure went through her. "Oh—Joel—really?" she said, softly.

"Then—you came, and I saw your face, so weary, with all the sparkle gone from your eyes. And I thought to myself, I won't rest easy until I got her happy again, with the shine to her all back again. Seems like everything was against me, though, with old Roscoe getting murdered, and all the mystery and attacks going on. I about went crazy, thinking I couldn't even protect you," he added, simply.

"You did, though. I felt you protecting me all the time, and it was a comfort, Joel. And it gave me the courage to go on and do what I had to do," she told him, and pressed her hands gently over his cheeks, and thrust her finger into one of the laugh lines.

He turned her hand, so his lips could kiss the palm, and she drew a deep happy breath. She was so warm and comfortable, and so secure, and Joel was such a dear good man—

He would never hurt her or harm her, he was so good—

"All I got to say about that," he said, with steel in his voice. "If you ever—ever—dare pull such a trick again, I'll beat your backside until you can't lie down for a week! I mean it! You won't ever pull such a trick again, and go doing things without telling me. You hear me, woman?"

She opened her eyes wide at him. He wouldn't, he couldn't beat her—

"And don't look at me with your big blue eyes like that! You think I can't smack you when I'm mad? You bet I can! You don't ever pull such a trick again—hear me, my Sarah?"

He bent down, and put his warm mouth to her throat. She put her arms about him, a little dazed. He did mean it! Like a good obedient fiancee, about to be a wife, she answered,

"Yes, Joel. I hear you."